WARBRINGER

Descendants of the Fall Book I

AARON HODGES

Edited by Genevieve Lerner
Proofread by Sara Houston
Illustration by Eva Urbanikova
Map by Michael Hodges

ABOUT THE AUTHOR

Aaron Hodges was born in 1989 in the small town of Whakatane, New Zealand. He studied for five years at the University of Auckland, completing a Bachelors of Science in Biology and Geography, and a Masters of Environmental Engineering. After working as an environmental consultant for two years, he grew tired of office work and decided to quit his job in 2014 and see the world. One year later, he published his first novel - Stormwielder.

FOLLOW AARON HODGES...

And receive TWO FREE novels and a short story!
www.aaronhodges.co.nz/newsletter-signup/

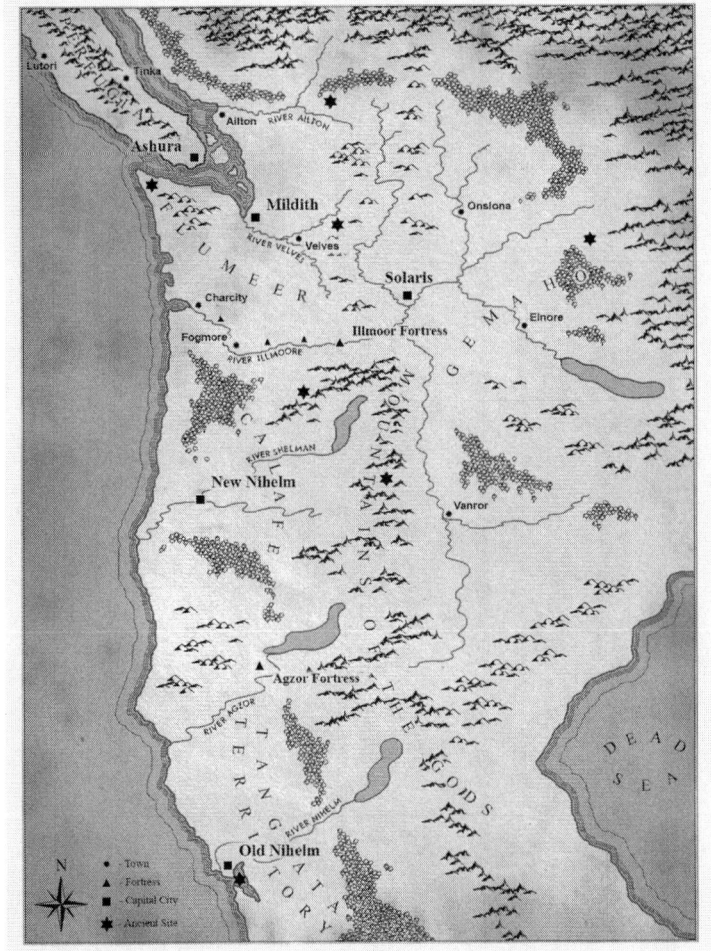

PROLOGUE
THE WARRIOR

R omaine shivered as a breeze shook the treetops and somehow found its way through a gap in his clothing. He pulled the cloak tighter around his shoulders, eager to keep the winter cold at bay. The soft *thump* of falling snow came from nearby and he chuckled as two of his companions flinched. Settling himself more comfortably in the saddle, he flicked the lieutenant a glance.

"Want me to check it out?" Romaine asked, voice serious but the hint of a smile betraying his mirth.

The lieutenant scowled, though Romaine noticed the man loosened his sword in its scabbard before urging his mount onwards. Shaking his head, he let the lieutenant take the lead. The four other scouts fell in behind Romaine, nervous eyes on the dense forest to either side of the deer trail.

They were right to be nervous. Ten miles south of the Illmoor River, they were deep in no man's land, far from the paved roads and walled cities of the northern nations. This was Calafe, a land of seemingly endless forest and great plateaus of tussock, of rugged hills and racing streams, with only the occasional settlement to prove the existence of humanity. This was *his* country, *his* home.

Or at least, it had been, until the Tangata.

Another tremor slid down his spine, though this time it had nothing to do with the cold. For ten years he'd fought to halt the Tangatan advance, ten long, brutal years of war. He'd been a simple woodsman once, but everything had changed with the destruction of their southern fortress, the Castle of Agzor. For a century it had barred the Tangata from the kingdoms of man, but with its battlements broken, its citadel cast down...nothing could halt the enemy advance.

And so those ten years of battle had proven futile. Just a few short months past, the last of Calafe's territory had been lost. The allied armies had fought for every patch of earth, but in the end it had not been enough. The tide of the Tangata could not be stopped.

It had pained Romaine to leave behind his nation. Most of the Calafe army had already fallen by then, and yet more of his fellows had chosen to remain with the rearguard. They had been overwhelmed before the ships could return for them. Injured aboard one of the vessels, Romaine had been forced to watch as his comrades perished.

Thankfully, the enemy had not yet sought to strike across the Illmoor river. Some said they would remain in the south, but Romaine knew it was only a matter of time before they came. After all, people had once said the same of the Agzor Fortress, that it would stand forever against the beasts.

Romaine's horse was struggling now, the snowdrifts growing deeper as they tracked their way eastward into the foothills of the Mountains of the Gods. Ahead, the lieutenant started to curse. Grimacing, Romaine edged his gelding alongside his superior.

"We'd best turn back," he grunted. He didn't bother with any honorifics—he rode with the Flumeerens, but he was not one of them. "If we press hard through the afternoon, we might make the crossing before nightfall."

The lieutenant flicked Romaine an irritated glance. He was a young man, still in his mid-twenties, the son of some minor noble. Romaine could almost see the gears turning behind his eyes. Reaching the river before dark meant shelter over their heads and a hot meal for the night. But if they abandoned their path and missed some enemy movement…

"A little further," the lieutenant replied finally. "We'll turn around if the way becomes impassable."

Romaine responded with a grunt. Pressing his horse forward, he continued along the trail, eyes on the way ahead. The storm had come upon them unexpectedly in the night, howling through the fir trees like a beast unleashed and burying the world in white.

They should have turned back then, but the lieutenant was new, still earning his stripes. Their orders had been to spend three days scouting for signs of the enemy. This being only their second, Romaine should have guessed the lieutenant would be hesitant to return. No doubt he feared the failure would be a black mark against his name.

It was an infuriating thought—evidence that the Flumeeren did not truly understand what came for them. They and the dregs of Perfugia might have fought alongside Calafe this last decade, but it had never been their land at risk, never their families, their very way of life.

That was about to change.

For if they could not stop the enemy at the Illmoor,

Flumeer would be the next to fall.

Returning his thoughts to the present, Romaine scanned the path ahead. The snow had thinned again and the horses were making better progress. At least the fresh snow made Romaine's task easier; not even the Tangata could move in these conditions without leaving tracks—

Romaine pulled sharply on his reins, bringing his horse to a stop. Beside him, the lieutenant cursed, but Romaine didn't spare the man a glance. His eyes were on the trees, scanning the upper branches, the shadows beneath the broad trunks, seeking sign, however small, of an ambush. The wind had fallen off now, and he saw no movement. He let out a sigh as the others began to murmur. Breath fogged before his face as he returned his gaze to the trail.

Two sets of bootprints led away from them in the snow.

"What is it?" the lieutenant asked sharply as he got his horse under control. He had not noticed the tracks.

"Tangata," Romaine replied.

The word cut through the whispers like a knife. Silence fell like a blanket over the six riders. The men looked to Romaine, faces as white as the snow all around them. Romaine might have laughed, if not for the racing of his own heart. Unlike the others though, it was not from fear.

This land had been abandoned months ago. There was no one left, not of his people, at least. It meant the general's fears were true. The Tangata were moving north.

Kicking his horse forward, he followed the prints for several yards. In places the strides were separated by as much as six feet—no doubt now, their owners were Tangata.

"We should bring word to the general," the lieutenant's voice carried from back down the trail. He and the other scouts had not followed Romaine.

A smile touched the Calafe warrior's cheeks. "Word of what? A single scouting pair?"

"Our orders were to return if we found sign of the enemy."

"Sign of an enemy *army*," Romaine corrected. "Do you really want to be known as the lieutenant who turned tail and ran at the first sight of the enemy?"

"There are *two* of them," the lieutenant hissed. He edged his horse forward, hands fiddling nervously with his reins. "What do you propose we do?"

Romaine stifled a sigh. The man was right to be afraid —if they'd been on foot, two Tangata would be more than their match. But mounted and with the element of surprise, there was a better than even chance of victory.

"We're downwind of them," Romaine replied finally. "If there's only two, they're no threat to the frontier. But if they're part of a larger force…General Curtis needs to know."

The lieutenant stared at Romaine for a long moment, the muscles of his jaw stretched taut as he contemplated the suggestion. Like before, Romaine could see he was weighing his options. But Romaine's last words about the general were too tempting to resist. The officer who brought such vital information would not soon be forgotten.

"Very well," the lieutenant said, nodding quickly. "Take the lead, Calafe."

Romaine grimaced at the man's cowardice, but held his tongue. He had what he wanted—a chance to follow the creatures, maybe even catch them. The thought of them loose in his land filled him with fury. No, unlike the green-horns riding behind him, Romaine did not fear the Tangata.

He *loathed* them.

"You should ready your lances," Romaine said, and gave a grim smile when the lieutenant's eyes widened. "Just in case."

It was almost too much for the man. His Adam's apple bobbed up and down as he swallowed, but to reverse his command now would be a show of cowardice.

"Cadet Flagers, ready the lances."

At the rear of the party, the Perfugian recruit dismounted clumsily and started unclipping the long package strapped to the packhorse. Safe on their island nation, the Sovereigns of Perfugia wasted little energy worrying over the Tangata. Unlike the treacherous King of Gemaho, they still honoured the ancient pact each kingdom had signed when the Tangata first appeared. Each month they sent their obligated hundred recruits to fight on the frontlines. Unfortunately, those they sent were generally…useless.

A sharp *clack* sounded as the skins holding the lances together suddenly came undone, sending the weapons tumbling to the ground. Muttered curses followed as Flagers dropped to his knees and tried to pick them back up.

"*Godsdamnit,*" the lieutenant swore as he swung from his saddle and strode to where the recruit crouched. "You trying to get us all killed, Flagers?"

"Sorry, sorry!" Arms clutched around the lances, Flagers stared up at the lieutenant with terror in his eyes.

He was barely a boy, really, untrained and unprepared for the horrors that waited out here. Pity touched Romaine, but he quickly pushed it aside. Against the Tangata, there was no room for weakness, no space for compassion. He'd learned that ten years ago, when the truce had first been broken. He would not repeat the same mistake now.

Instead, he watched in silence as the lieutenant snatched

the steel-tipped lances from the Perfugian's hands and handed them out amongst the scouts. Romaine only reached over his shoulder, lifting the giant twin-bladed axe from its sheath and settling it on the pommel of his saddle. Calafe warriors did not learn the lance.

As the men settled their weapons, Romaine cast a practiced glance over his companions. Despite their inexperience, they were well trained other than the Perfugian. They would not back down from a fight if it came to it. Turning to the lieutenant, he offered a nod, before starting off once more.

The bootprints had emerged from the surrounding trees, but even the Tangata apparently preferred a trail over the untamed forest in these parts, for they kept to the animal track for the next few miles. The sun grew higher as their party crossed frozen streams and occasional open meadows, all the while watching for the slightest hint of the enemy. Despite Romaine's earlier reservations, the snow cleared and they made good progress. With the trail beginning to loop northward, they might still make the Illmoor that night.

If they did not encounter the Tangata first.

Romaine kept his eyes on the trees as he rode. Despite what he'd said to the others, he wasn't altogether sure the Tangata did not know they were in the forest. They were inhuman creatures, capable of terrible violence. With so little known about them, it paid to be cautious whenever they were close. He glanced back at the bootprints, noticing how they'd grown close together. It suggested the creatures were travelling slowly...

...the prints changed again.

A curse slipped from Romaine's lips as he pulled his horse to a stop. Ahead, a third set of prints joined the trail.

Blood pounded in Romaine's ears as he tightened his fist around the hilt of his axe. Three Tangata was too many, even on horseback. Just one of the demonic creatures was a match for three men.

They had just become outnumbered.

Murmurs came from the men as Romaine edged his horse forward, examining the fresh bootprints. Then a frown touched his face. There was something unusual about the new set of tracks. He dismounted and knelt for a closer look. They had emerged from the forest to the east, the same as the others, but their owner was smaller by several boot sizes. And now that he was close…Romaine realised that the Tangata tracks overlaid the third pair.

The Tangata had not met with this new individual; they had come later.

His eyes travelled ahead and he saw the stride of the Tangata grow longer. They had started running, in pursuit. Could the third set of tracks belong to a Calafe, one of his own? It didn't seem possible that anyone could have survived out here, alone for months with naught but the Tangata. And yet…

Romaine stood suddenly and raced back to his horse. The lieutenant opened his mouth to ask a question, but Romaine was already swinging himself into the saddle. The tracks were recent, their edges still hard instead of crumbling. If they were quick, they might just reach them in time.

"Romaine…" the lieutenant began, but Romaine silenced the man with a glare.

"Whoever left the third pair of bootprints, they're no friend of the Tangata," he hissed.

Then Romaine kicked his horse into a gallop, leaving the lieutenant and his scouts with no choice but to follow.

THE WARRIOR

R omaine ducked as a snow-covered branch flashed for his face. A second later a muffled curse told him another of the scouts had not been so lucky. Without slowing, he glanced back and was reassured that five riders still followed.

Facing the trail once more, he studied the bootprints as they sped past. The snow was thinning now, the trail sloping back down towards the lowlands. Trees flickered past either side of him, but the forest was changing, the dense mountain firs giving way to cedar and maple. The trail split and re-joined around clumps of brush.

Romaine urged his gelding on, coaxing another ounce of speed from the beast. Without the prints to follow, they would struggle to track their quarry. He had to catch them before the last of the snow vanished. Behind, the cries of his comrades chased after him as they tried to keep pace, but this was not their land, not their fellow citizen standing alone against the Tangata, and they were losing ground.

Images flashed through Romaine's mind, of a woman

lying silent in the snow, of a boy's pale face, of lifeless eyes in the daylight. Blood pounded in his temples and his vision blurred, blinding him to the forest, the trail, until all that was left to him were the bootprints he followed.

A scream cut the air. At first, he barely registered the noise over the pounding of hooves. But it came again a cry of terror, of a woman alone, unmistakably human.

"Romaine!" His companion's voices called him back.

He slowed his horse, but only for a moment, to readjust his grip on the axe. Sunlight rippled across the twin blades, then he was surging forward once more, the gelding responding to his urging with a cry of its own. They were still downwind of the Tangata and the horses could smell them now, the unnatural scent of humanity mixed with something *else*, the madness of the enemy.

Suddenly the trees were falling away and Romaine found himself rushing across an open meadow. The pounding of hooves from behind told him his comrades still followed. For a second he was touched with guilt, that he had led them here so recklessly, but there was no time for second thoughts now. Ahead, two figures swung to face the newcomers. At first glance, they could have been mistaken as humans. Neither were larger than the average man— were smaller even than Romaine, in fact. Their clothes were of rough-spun cotton, faded and torn, but not far removed from that worn by a farmer or a woodsman—in summer. In this frozen forest, a human would have perished from exposure long ago.

But the Tangata did not feel the cold.

Each wore its hair in long, unkept braids—one jet-black, the other straw blond—and the finer features of one revealed it was female. Their scouts often hunted in pairs.

While little was known of their hierarchy, they were assumed to be mating couples.

Beyond the two, a woman in heavy winter furs staggered backwards, auburn hair flashing in the sunlight. Relief swept through Romaine—they were not too late.

His attention snapped back to the Tangata as growls came from across the clearing. He shivered as two pairs of slate-grey eyes fixed on him. More than anything, this feature marked the beasts as inhuman. Completely grey, the eyes of the Tangata held no empathy, no compassion, no emotion other than rage—and hatred. They were the eyes of the lost, their humanity washed away by the magic they had stolen from the long-departed Gods.

Watching the creatures now, Romaine's jaw clenched with a hatred of his own. These creatures had taken everything from him, consumed a decade of his life, stolen his nation. And still they came, still they sought more. The greed that had first driven them to betray the Divine lived still within them; they would not stop until the world was theirs.

Rage swept through Romaine like a wave, banishing fear and thought. Though the Flumeeren scouts had spread out behind him, in that moment there was only Romaine and the Tangata.

With a roar, he charged. Shouts came from behind Romaine as the gelding leapt forward. He trusted his comrades would follow. Howls met his battlecry as the Tangata sprang towards him, crossing half the clearing in a single bound.

Their speed was terrifying to behold, even on the snow-kissed ground. The creatures carried no weapons, but they hardly needed them. Ice slid down Romaine's spine as the male drew ahead and the slate-grey eyes locked with his.

Immediately the beast diverted its path, heading straight for the charging axeman.

A wicked grin split Romaine's face and he rose in the saddle, bellowing a challenge. Let it think him easy prey; this was not Romaine's first encounter with the beasts. He raised his axe as the distance closed, waiting for the moment…

Suddenly the Tangata was airborne, a bound of its powerful legs sending it soaring into the air—straight at Romaine. Beneath him, the gelding screamed and then it was rearing up, hooves lashing the air.

Only that saved Romaine. Instead of him, the full strength of the Tangata struck the horse. A sickening crunch followed as the two came together, iron-shod hooves striking flesh. Yet it was not the Tangata that fell. With almost a sigh, Romaine's mount toppled backwards, body limp.

Cursing, Romaine kicked free of his stirrups and fell sideways, narrowly avoiding being crushed. In one fluid movement, he rolled to his feet, boots crunching on the icy ground, axe still in hand. He had a second to glimpse the now lifeless corpse of the gelding, its head snapped where the creature's blow had struck—then the male was upon him.

It came as little more than a blur, teeth bared, arms raised to tear him apart. In a second it dissolved the space between them, and again it leapt, a scream shaking the snow from the branches of nearby trees.

This time, though, Romaine was ready. He swept his axe up, the twin points of its butterfly blades rising to meet his assailant. Mid-air, the creature could not adjust its attack, and with a soft *crunch*, its weight slammed down into the axe, driving the points deep into the creature's chest.

Triumph swept through Romaine—but a wild fist struck his shoulder. The axe was torn from his grasp as the blow sent him tumbling across the snowy earth. Stars flashed across his vision and he struggled to reclaim his senses, to regain his feet. Desperately he fumbled for the dagger on his belt; the beast could be on him any second. Finally he found the hilt and tore it loose. Swinging around, he gasped for breath, seeking his foe.

But the Tangata had not moved. Romaine's axe remained embedded in its flesh. Blood seeped from the wound, staining its tunic red. Slowly its head turned, and the grey eyes focused on Romaine. Fury flicked on the beast's face and it tried to take a step. The effort was too much, even for this creature. Its legs gave way and it tumbled forward.

Romaine flinched as the impact drove his axe deeper into the creature's chest. It moved no more.

He stood staring at his foe for a moment, but the satisfaction of its defeat was short lived. One more of the creatures was dead, but the death would not fill the emptiness...

A scream came from across the meadow, drawing Romaine's attention back to reality. His heart palpated as he recalled the second Tangata, then fell into the pit of his stomach as he saw the battle being fought across the clearing.

One of the scouts was already dead, eyes staring lifelessly up at the sky, while the Perfugian recruit, Flagers, lay nearby, hands clasping desperately at the silver cords spilling from his stomach. A moan came from his throat as the intestines slipped through his fingers, and his head swung around, eyes fixing on Romaine. He tried to cry out, but his words emerged as little more than a whisper.

Steeling his heart, Romaine forced his attention back to

the battle. He had seen such wounds before—Flagers was already dead. But the lieutenant and the two remaining scouts could still survive. They had managed to keep their horses, though only the lieutenant still held his lance. Another lance lay broken on the ground nearby, while the last had been driven through the thigh of the female Tangata.

Though terribly injured, the beast had managed to snap the lance in half. Its tip still jabbed through her thigh, dripping scarlet blood in the snow, but the other half she now flourished like a club, preventing the three horsemen from getting close enough to finish her.

Romaine staggered to his fallen foe and kicked the Tangata onto its back, then retrieved his axe. Silently, he started towards the female, eager to put an end to the creature before it harmed anyone else.

Before he could reach her, though, the female finally noticed its mate's death. A terrible scream echoed around the clearing as it spun towards Romaine, and he saw again the madness in its eyes, the desire to rend and tear and kill.

But for once the lieutenant acted without thinking. The only one left with a weapon, he urged his horse forward while the Tangata was distracted and drove the steel-tipped lance through the creature's back.

The awful howl was instantly cut short, and a *thud* followed as the beast crumpled to the snow. Silence returned to the clearing...only to be punctuated by the soft cries of Flagers.

For an instant, Romaine kept his eyes fixed on the Tangata. Blood pounded in his ears and he still felt the need for battle within him, that terrible rage demanding he charge forward, axe raised, battlecry on his lips.

But the fight was over, their enemies dead, and slowly the pounding subsided.

Despair rose to take its place, and silently Romaine turned to look again at the boy. Before he realized what he was doing, Romaine staggered forward and dropped to one knee beside the Perfugian. There was nothing he could do for the lad—not even a doctor could have saved him from such a wound.

"Romaine?" Flagers gasped, his voice trembling. "Romaine, it hurts…don't know what happened. I'm…sorry."

"It's okay, lad," Romaine murmured. As he spoke, he reached for the dagger on his belt. "It's going to be okay."

"It hurts, Romai…" The words trailed off as the boy's eyes slid closed. A few moments later, his breathing ceased as well.

Releasing the boy, Romaine sat back. His eyes were drawn to the blood pooling in the snow, still seeping from the wound he'd opened in the recruit's groin. A lump lodged in his throat and he felt the boy's lifeless eyes watching him, accusing. It had been a mercy, and yet…the face of another boy flickered into his mind. He lay not in snow but a bed of roses. Romaine scrunched his eyes closed, trying to banish the image.

"Is he…?"

A voice was calling from behind him. Shaking off his grief, Romaine stood and faced the lieutenant.

"Gone," he said shortly.

The lieutenant swallowed, his eyes drawn to the corpse. He held his sword in hand now, its tip trembling. It was probably the first time he had faced the Tangata in battle.

A flicker from across the clearing. The unfamiliar woman was standing beside the body of the male Tangata, staring at its gruesome remains. Her face was unusually pale for the Calafe and freckles dotted her cheeks, but the heavy fur coat and woollen leggings were familiar.

Romaine watched as she knelt beside the Tangata. She seemed more curious than afraid. The woman couldn't have more than twenty years to her name. What was she doing out here, all alone?

Casting one last glance at the dead boy, Romaine let out a sigh, then started towards the young woman. Her head whipped around at the sound of his footsteps, and amber eyes widened, fixing on the bloody axe he still carried in one hand. Seeing her fear, Romaine paused, then setting the weapon on the ground, he continued with empty hands.

"Easy now," he said.

"You killed him," the young woman murmured, rising to her feet and facing Romaine.

She spoke in a strange, singsong accent unfamiliar to Romaine—though that was not unusual in Calafe. His people were a nomadic sort, and there were many groups who would spend months or even years apart from civilisation. The isolation bred strange tones, though if this woman belonged to such a group, where were the others?

"Ay," Romaine replied to her question. "It's dead. You're safe now, lass."

A tremor shook the woman and she raised a hand, as though to keep him back. Her other hung limp at her side, and Romaine realised she had been injured. Well, she'd gotten lucky if all the Tangata had given her was a broken arm—they were said to do terrible things to those they captured.

"It's okay," Romaine said, trying again to comfort her. He reached out a hand. "We'll take you to safety."

"No!"

The woman's voice echoed from the nearby trees as she leapt away from him. But whether from the cold or some unknown injury, her legs failed to support her weight, and she crumpled into a snowdrift with a muffled cry—quickly silenced.

Romaine was at her side in an instant. Her broken arm lay at an awkward angle in the snow and her eyes were closed—she must have lost consciousness from the pain.

"Is she alright?" the lieutenant asked. He approached with sword still in hand, as though the woman might yet somehow prove to be an enemy.

Romaine placed a finger on the woman's throat. Her pulse was racing and erratic, but strong, and he nodded as the lieutenant drew to a stop alongside him.

"Her arm's broken. Passed out from the pain, or maybe shock. We'd better get her on one of the horses." There would be plenty spare, now.

"Poor lass," the lieutenant said as he looked at the woman. "What was she doing out here?"

"I'd like to know that myself," Romaine replied.

"I'll fetch Flagers's horse," the lieutenant murmured, then hesitated. "Shame, about the lad. I told him to hang back, but…" He shrugged and turned away.

Romaine said nothing. What more was there to say? The boy had never had any business being out here, untrained, unprepared. But then, he'd had little choice in the matter. Unlike the citizens of Flumeer or Calafe, Perfugians did not decide their own fates. That was a matter for their betters, a judgement passed down by their Sovereigns.

Rising, he lifted the woman in his arms and crossed to where one of the surviving scouts had gathered the horses. She was surprisingly heavy in her thick furs—or perhaps it was merely exhaustion finally catching him—but regardless, Romaine was relieved when he settled her in the saddle of Flagers's horse. Taking care with her arm, he bound the woman so she would not fall, and then looked for a mount of his own.

The dead scout's horse had emerged from the battle unscathed, and before long they were on the trail once more, riding north. The battle had cost them precious time and the light faded quickly. The sun plummeted towards the western treeline, setting the horizon alight.

It was still an hour from dark when the howling began in the forest behind them.

❧ 2 ❧

THE ARCHIVIST

Erika paused as she leaned backwards over the void, the darkness beckoning below. Only the corded rope looped around her waist held her in place. A shiver touched her, but now was not the time for second thoughts, and with a last look at her two assistants, she kicked off into the chasm. The rope slid through her fingers as she descended, the pitch-black reaching up to embrace her.

Soon the oil lantern clipped to her backpack became the only source of light, as the opening above shrank to nothing. The air grew colder, damp with the breath of the earth, and she shivered again, her eyes searching the absolute dark below for sign of the bottom. The lantern flickered and the black seemed to press closer, as though trying to repel her, to keep her from the secrets that had lain hidden from human eyes for centuries.

There were those who said these places were haunted, that they were the sacred sites of the Gods, or the birthplace of the Tangata. The details changed from story to story, but all agreed that entrance was forbidden, that to step foot in these hidden places was to call death down upon the human race.

As if that weren't already coming.

Erika ignored such superstitions. The small-minded who believed such fancy had held back humanity for long enough. They could no longer afford such ignorance. Flumeer needed every weapon it could find for the war to come.

Fortunately, the Flumeeren queen had finally come to see her point of view. Now Erika just had to discover something of use in these lost places, something that might change the tide of the war.

So far though, her search had proven fruitless. The other sites had been empty; whatever secrets they'd once contained long lost to the passage of time.

And the queen was not known for her patience. She had taken a gamble, supporting Erika in the face of resistance from nobles who preferred to leave the past buried. What would happen if Erika came back empty-handed a third time?

"This is the place," Erika whispered to herself, breath now fogging in the lanternlight. "This time I will find it."

The magic of the Gods.

Those had been the words that had convinced the queen. Erika had spent most of her life studying their long-lost deities, whose magic had once been shared freely with humanity. What wonders had her ancestors witnessed in those glorious times before The Fall? Before the traitors amongst their ranks had grown jealous of the Gods and stolen the forbidden powers?

Only legends told of that time now. The traitors had sought to use the stolen magics to reshape themselves, seeking to join the Divine. But when the Gods had discovered the violation, their rage had been terrible, and instead the thieves had been cursed to madness. They had become the Tangata.

If only the anger of the Gods could be so easily sated.

All humanity had been equal before their omniscient gaze, and so all humanity had been cast down.

A hundred years of darkness had followed.

Fools!

Just the thought of that ancient betrayal caused Erika to tighten her grip about the rope. The Tangata had ruined everything, sentenced humanity to crawl amidst the dirt like common beasts for their avarice. Even when the light had finally returned, humanity had found the Gods gone, returned to their citadels amidst the clouds.

But the Tangata had remained.

Surely there was a design in that, some divine plan. Erika was convinced it was a test, a trial to see whether humanity could put right the mistakes of their ancestors. The Gods would not have left them alone to face the beasts, not unless there was a reason, a chance for victory.

And so she searched in these ancient places, searching for what had been forgotten by the mind of men, for a power left to them by the Gods to defeat the Tangata.

She had dedicated her entire life to it.

Thunk.

Erika stumbled as her feet struck solid earth. She would have fallen, but instinctively she had stopped letting out rope and now it brought her up short. Getting her feet back under her, she straightened.

Overhead, the entrance was little more than a pinprick now. Unclipping the lantern from her pack, she held it high to make sure she was truly at the bottom. On three sides the shaft was hard rock, but on the fourth a tunnel led into the darkness. She swore at the sight of water dripping from the walls. That was as the other sites had been, their contents rotted away long ago.

Not this time, please, Gods, not this time.

Her lantern illuminated walls of white limestone. Stalactites had begun to form in the ceiling, young yet, while water and the relentless passage of time had carved grooves in the stone beneath her feet. Silver threads criss-crossed the air, reflecting light from her lantern, but she saw no sign of the arachnids that had spun them.

Satisfied she had reached the bottom of the shaft, Erika set the lantern on the ground beside her and unclipped herself from the rope. Three tugs signalled to her assistants it was safe to descend. It would not pay to venture too far into this place alone.

She looked again at the walls. So much had been lost to the passage of time, but Erika knew for herself that some powers had remained from the time of the Gods. Her mother had…become a scavenger, digging in the dirt for scraps of metal that she could sell to the local blacksmith.

Their poverty in her later childhood stung Erika even now, though at least her mother's occupation had given birth to her fascination with the Gods. The woman had collected trinkets found during her digging—pieces of glass and strange, bendable materials that were of no worth to the local tradesmen. Most had been inert, remnants of a time long lost.

But one had been different.

Erika had found it amongst her mother's collection—a smooth, round piece of glass. It had seemed no different from the others, but for an impurity at its centre. Some mistake in its crafting, her younger self had thought.

Until she'd squeezed it between her fingers, and a brilliant light had burst forth.

She'd dropped it, so great had been her shock. The artefact had struck a rock and cracked in half, its light dying with a final flash. Half-blinded, Erika had scrambled to put it back together, before she'd smelt the burning.

Only as her vision cleared did she see the tiny drop of moisture that had been expelled from the glass. Solid stone had dissolved at its touch, leaving a smoking hole in the rock. Frozen in terror at what she might have unleashed, her younger self had sat frozen as the house filled with a terrible, molten stench. The stone had burnt for an hour before whatever magic had been hidden within the glass finally consumed itself. It had left a hole almost the size of Erika's fist in the unadorned floor.

Erika had not soon forgotten the beating she'd received for the incident, though today it was the loss of the object she regretted. Who knew what power it might have possessed? She'd found other objects over the years, but none had retained their magic.

The scuffing of boots on stone announced the arrival of her first assistant. A plump Flumeeren man by the name of Ibran, he had been one of the first to record the known locations of these sites. He'd been reluctant to join the expedition, concerned as he was by the wrath of the Gods, but his academic's mind had finally proven stronger than his superstition. Unclipping himself from the rope, Ibran took up another lantern and stepped aside for her second assistant to make his descent.

Sythe was Ibran's opposite in every way, more fighter than academic. The queen had offered his services to ensure their safety on the journey. So far, they had not had to test his skills as a warrior, though his strength had been a welcome addition. He came into view now, descending rapidly, a massive pack looped over his shoulders. A pickaxe was clipped to the side and within were their supplies—rope and food for several days, water, even a blasting cap, in case they had to break through a collapse in the cave network.

She might have travelled with a larger party, but Erika was not the only one interested in the world before The Fall. She'd heard whispers of Archivists in Gemaho who sought the same secrets as herself. With the fall of Calafe, the world was growing desperate for an answer to the Tangata.

When Sythe had landed and unclipped, Erika nodded for him to take the lead. "Slowly," she murmured, "if anything remains, I don't want to disturb it."

"Yes, Archivist," Sythe said with a nod. He was not a man of many words.

Ibran took up position behind Erika as they started off into the caves. He too carried a pack, though like hers, it only held his food and water for the day, along with a few scrolls to help with translating the language of the Gods. Though breathing in the moisture-laden air, Erika felt they might be getting ahead of themselves.

The ancient sites seemed to follow a similar pattern to one another, though the rock that surrounded them was smooth, unbroken by a single joint. Had the Gods carved them from the bedrock itself? The thought of such power sent a shudder down Erika's spine. Surely even a fraction would be enough to destroy the Tangata.

Using sketches of the last site they'd visited as a map, the three wound their way deeper into the darkness. The tunnel branched at regular intervals, creating a maze far beneath the surface. Smaller openings appeared in the walls, revealing all manner of chambers.

The moisture seemed to lessen as they pressed on,

though as the hours stretched out, they still saw no sign of relics. Doubt touched Erika. What had she been thinking, pinning her future on a wild goose chase? She should have known nothing would remain of the time before The Fall, not even in these secret places. If only they had been sealed away, protected from the elements. Instead they had remained opened to the world, their contents rotted away, or perhaps even stolen by early explorers.

Steeling herself, Erika forced her chin higher. They had barely started. It would take days to explore the entire network. Plenty of time yet for a discovery.

There would be a chamber somewhere here, something that had been protected, that still held its secrets. She continued on, counting steps, checking each chamber she came too, then continuing. Always they were spaced the same number of steps apart---

Erika frowned, pausing midstride. There should have been another opening ahead, but instead she found only smooth, untouched stone. Still in the lead, Sythe continued on, unaware of the break in pattern, but she stopped.

"Something wrong, Archivist?" Ibran asked.

Shaking her head, Erika did not reply. Had she lost track of her footsteps? No, she had long grown used to keeping the count while other thoughts occupied her mind. Following the pattern of the other sites, there should be a chamber here.

But there was nothing but solid stone.

Erika's heart hammered in her chest as she held the lantern closer to the limestone wall. Not a single crack showed in the silvery stone, nothing to indicate a cave-in had closed off the chamber. Had the Gods changed their pattern in this place? But no, the rest of the site had been a mirror image of the others.

"An irregularity," she murmured, more to herself than her companions.

It didn't make sense. Why change the pattern here? She leaned in closer, inspecting the pale rock. Light from her lantern shimmered as it caught in the thin trails of water trickling down the wall. She frowned as an idea came to her. Wasn't it odd, that these places had been carved from the bedrock—then left unadorned? With the power at their fingertips, why would the Gods choose to leave their sacred places so…plain?

Unless the limestone was not, in fact, the original stone.

"The pickaxe," she said, turning to Sythe.

Sythe raised an eyebrow, but he was a former soldier and accustomed to obeying orders without question. Shrugging the pack from his back, he unclipped the pickaxe and handed it over.

Carefully she stepped up to the wall. The white stone seemed to glow in the lantern light, as though the rock had somehow absorbed the great magics that had once been worked here. Erika cared little for its beauty—only for what might lie beneath. Using the razor-sharp point of the pickaxe, she scraped at the rock, gently at first, then with greater pressure as the limestone crumbled.

She kept at her task until, with a sharp grating noise, the pick struck something unyielding beneath the white rock. The breath caught in her throat and she withdrew the pick, revealing darkness beneath. For a moment, Erika thought it was stone—then Ibran moved his lantern, and light reflected from the black.

"Metal," she whispered.

"Truly?" Ibran leaned in closer, trying to get a better look. "That's…impossible. It would have corroded, rusted away long ago."

"And yet it remains," Erika murmured. That was a question for another day, though. Turning to Sythe, she handed the pickaxe back to him. "Let's see how far it extends."

The warrior nodded. He worked with more care than Erika would have expected from one untrained in the Archivists arts. The queen had apparently chosen her people well. Chunks of stone fell away and slowly a great panel of reflective metal was revealed. Dust covered its surface, but it remained unmarked by the pickaxe. Whatever the Gods had used in its creation, it was apparently harder than steel.

Blood pounded in Erika's ears as Sythe finally stepped back, revealing the full extent of his work. He had removed the limestone a foot to either side of the panel, though here his administrations had only revealed another type of rock. It confirmed Erika's suspicions. The limestone had not been there during the time of the Gods—it had formed later, deposited as a thin layer by the calcite laden waters.

She turned her attention back to the metal sheet. Its surface was unadorned, giving no indication of its purpose. But Erika knew, had guessed it the second she'd uncovered the reflective surface. This panel was the reason for the missing chamber.

"It's a door," she murmured.

"But how to open it?" Ibran replied.

He had a point. There was no handle that might have released the door from its frame. In fact, the steel joined so tightly with the rock on either side that it formed a perfect seal. Erika's hands began to shake. If this door had kept out the moisture, its contents might have been protected from the relentless passage of time.

This was what she'd been searching for!

"Can you knock it down?" she asked, excitement washing away her usual caution.

Sythe flicked her a glance, then stepping back from the door, he lurched forward and slammed a boot into the metal. The panel did not so much as budge. He tried again, and a final time, but it was clear the metal would take more than human strength to move.

Erika swallowed. Dare she risk the explosive charges? They could bring the roof down on them, or destroy whatever lay on the other side. But what other choice did she have? The pickaxe had not even dented the strange metal.

"Sythe," she murmured. "The blasting cap."

"What?" Ibran hissed. "Archivist, you cannot be serious. The risk—"

"The risk is acceptable," Erika spoke over him. There was more than just her reputation at stake—the queen did not take kindly to failure. Especially if she learned they'd been so close and turned back. "Sythe, I trust you can open this door without bringing the ceiling down on top of us."

Sythe was already rummaging in his pack, but he paused long enough to nod. Ibran stuttered something incomprehensible and then started off back down the corridor. Ignoring him, Erika watched as Sythe set the charges. She had little experience with such things, and had to trust the man knew what he was doing. If they ended up destroying what lay within…

No, she could not doubt herself, not now. She needed to know what lay behind this door. Her fate, the fate of Flumeer, and perhaps even humanity itself, depended on it.

Finally, Sythe stepped back from the door. He had set two charges, one high, the other low, both on the left-hand side of the door. Taking the fuse from his pack, he attached it to the charges and then glanced at her.

"Ready."

Nodding, Erika led the way back down the tunnel. If the explosion did cause a cave-in, she didn't want to be anywhere near it. Sythe trailed the fuse out behind them as they went, until they reached the last chamber they'd passed. There they found a sulking Ibran. Erika joined him in the chamber's questionable shelter and then looked to Sythe.

He lit the fuse.

Erika held her breath as sparks leapt from the wire and vanished back into the main tunnel. Suddenly doubtful, she shared a glance with Ibran, but it was too late to change her mind now. Closing her eyes, she held her hands over her ears and waited.

Boom.

❧ 3 ❧

THE ARCHIVIST

L ight seared through Erika's eyelids as the explosion
shook the chamber. A shockwave followed and something struck her, driving her to the ground. Breath hissed
between her teeth as she dragged in a breath. Dust burned
in her nostrils and when she opened her eyes, Erika found
herself in absolute darkness.

For a second, she thought the worst had happened and
they'd all been buried. But then the weight shifted above her
and she heard a grunt as someone picked himself up. The
flare of a match illuminated Sythe's face, then the broken
lantern and the grumbling Ibran where he had fallen on the
other side of the cave. Sythe retrieved their spare lantern
from his backpack, though even with it lit, it was near
impossible to see with the dust and smoke still obscuring
the air.

Erika coughed as she dragged herself to her feet. "Did it
work?"

Without a word, Sythe moved to the doorway. The light

of his lantern drew them after him. Excitement pulsed in Erika's veins as she stepped back into the tunnel. An uncharacteristic grin split Sythe's face as he glanced back.

"Looks like it worked, Archivist."

She was at his side in an instant, her discomfort forgotten. Dust still danced in the lanternlight, but a gap in the steel panel was now evident. Beyond, darkness beckoned. Hardly able to contain her excitement, Erika staggered forward. The door had twisted in its frame, the blast blowing the bottom half of it inwards several inches, while the rest remained stubbornly fixed in place. Thankfully, the gap was large enough for even Ibran to fit.

She stepped towards it before a sense of self-preservation gave her pause. If this space had remained untouched since The Fall, the magic of the Gods might still prevail—along with any traps they might have set for intruders. She considered sending Sythe first...but no, if the unknown truly awaited, she wanted—needed—to be first.

Gathering herself, she ducked beneath the broken sheet of metal. Darkness swallowed her up as she left behind the lantern and set one foot, then another, on the unseen floor. Holding her breath, she straightened.

Clang.

A scream built in Erika's throat as something clicked overhead and she tried to throw herself back. But in the darkness, she misjudged the height of the hole in the door. Her shoulder collided with the heavy metal and threw her back, leaving her at the mercy of whatever trap she had triggered...

Light flooded the chamber.

Erika's scream turned to a gasp as she found herself face-to-face with the brilliance of the Gods. A magical glow now lit the chamber, stemming from great globes of glass fixed high on the walls—like giant versions of the artefact she had once held as a child. Mouth wide, she turned in a circle, eyes burning from the sudden brightness after the dark, but unable to turn away.

"Archivist?" Ibran's voice came from beyond the door. He sounded nervous. "Is…everything okay?

"See for yourself," she said, too engrossed with the magic to offer any explanation.

Scuffling came from beyond the door as her assistants followed, first Ibran, then Sythe bringing up the rear. Their eyes widened as they saw the source of the light. Erika shared their astonishment. What magic did the Gods possess, that their talismans retained power, even centuries after being abandoned?

"What sorcery is this?" Ibran murmured.

A grin came unbidden to Erika's face. "What we've been searching for."

"Perhaps the doubters were right," he croaked. She looked at him in surprise and saw his jowls quiver as he swallowed. "This…just being in this place, it feels like sacrilege."

The smile slipped from Erika's face. "Nonsense," she snapped, before returning her attention to the chamber.

There was no sign of water damage here—indeed, even after the explosion, there was barely any dust on this side of the door. Instead of limestone, the walls and floor were made of polished grey stone, their surfaces untouched by weakness or imperfections. Her breath caught as she saw a massive pane of black glass fixed to one wall. It would have been worth a fortune back in Mildeth—only the richest of nobles could afford windows of glass.

A table made from a similar metal to the door sat

pressed against the opposite wall. Blood pounded in Erika's ears as she stepped towards it. The metal surface was empty. Despite the magic lights, the shining glass and sealed door, there was…nothing.

No!

Erika darted forward as the light glinted from an object she'd almost missed—a glove, lying alone on the table. The way it reflected in the strange lights had camouflaged it. As she picked it up, she realised why. It had been woven from metal rather than wool. A gauntlet? What would the Gods have needed with such an object?

Instinctively, she lifted the gauntlet and slipped it onto her hand. Behind her, Ibran gasped, no doubt disturbed by her supposed sacrilege, but she ignored him. She had come to learn, to gain understanding of the Gods—not surrender to superstition. The time had come to throw caution to the winds.

The cold steel sent a shiver down her spine. She was surprised how well it fit—she had always imagined the Gods as giants. Though she supposed that was foolish, given how small these hidden tunnels were.

Holding the gauntlet up to the light, Erika wondered at how the steel fibres had been woven together. They rippled in the magical glow, seeming almost alive. What was the function of such an object? Her heart throbbed as an idea came to her. Could this be what she'd been looking for, some connection to the Gods and their magic?

"Erika…"

It was Ibran, but she was past listening to his cautions now. Standing there, illuminated by the magic of the Gods, surrounded by their riches, Erika *knew* what she had to do. Forgotten were the warnings, the legends of the Tangata and The Fall. She now held the magic that could destroy them in the palm of her hand, if only she had the strength to command it.

She closed her fist, reaching out with her mind for those ancient powers, seeking to wake them, to bring them forth for the first time in centuries. This was her purpose, the reason she had been drawn to these ancient places, to a lifetime dedicated to the study of the Gods…

Nothing happened.

Her heartbeat slowed and finally she opened her eyes, an exhaled breath whistling between her teeth. She turned her hand over, examining the gauntlet, but nothing had changed. Her elation subsided, the thrill of just moments before fading away. It was no more than an ordinary glove. Perhaps this had been the height of fashion for those who had lived alongside the Gods. A revelation of great interest to scholars like Ibran, no doubt, but for her…

Erika's face warmed as she felt the eyes of her assistants upon her. Clenching her fists at her sides, she continued her inspection of the chamber, though she still sensed their mirth. She forced her mind back to that of a scholar. Magic or no, this was still a great discovery. Those crystals…how long would their light remain? Perhaps they could remove them from the walls, to show the queen that her expedition had not been entirely in vain.

Then her eyes alighted on a picture that had been plastered to the wall. She hadn't noticed it at first, so engrossed had she been in the crystal lights and the gauntlet. Something about the decoration caught her eye now. She took a step closer, frowning. It looked so familiar…

A gasp slipped from her throat as she realised what it was.

"It's a map," she murmured.

The map was so detailed and colourful, she hadn't

recognised it at first. Now its true nature practically leapt at her. There was the northern archipelago of Perfugia, and there the Mountains of the Gods, the southern coasts of Calafe. And so much more.

Reverently, Erika stretched out a hand and touched the map. She was surprised to find it was paper—how had such a delicate thing survived all this time? The steel door had truly sealed off this chamber from the world, from time itself, it seemed.

Her eyes continued to roam the lands depicted by the map, making connections. Dots labelled in the language of the ancients must have indicated cities. Erika was not surprised to see many corresponded with modern-day towns and cities—no doubt the benefits of their locations had not changed through the centuries. Several, though, were wastelands today, others the sites of mining extractions.

Footsteps sounded as her assistants approached, but Erika did not take her eyes from the precious paper. There was something else here, something important. Several locations had been marked with stars rather than dots and had not been labelled. They didn't seem to correspond with any modern cities, nor any significant feature that might have proven an advantage for a settlement…

The breath caught in her throat as the pattern clicked into place. Surely it couldn't be so simple? Quickly she tracked the distances, trying to judge the scale, to be sure. Yes, there was the site on the peninsula west of Mildeth. And there was the one in the foothills of the mountains…

"It shows the ancient sites," she whispered. "The hidden places of the Gods."

"Truly?" Ibran gasped, stepping up beside her. "That—"

Erika was barely listening to him, so engrossed was she

in the map. It didn't only show those sites they'd visited in Flumeer—it revealed *all* of them! They dotted the landscape, many matching sites already known to the Archivists, others that had yet been identified. Her heart throbbed, sending blood rushing to her temples.

If those sites had remained undiscovered all this time, if they were sealed as this chamber had been…who knew what treasures they might have preserved?

Then a frown touched her lips as she noticed an absence. Of the dozen or so stars on the map, only three were located in Flumeer. The three they had already visited…

Thump.

Erika jumped as something heavy struck the ground. She swung on Ibran, ready to reprimand him for his carelessness, but the words died on her lips. Her assistant lay facedown on the floor, blood oozing from an awful wound in his neck. A scream built in her throat, her sluggish mind trying to put the pieces together, to understand how he had come to be there…

…her eyes fell on the bloody dagger clutched in Sythe's hand.

"What did you do?" she hissed.

"Step 'way from the map," the man said calmly.

Ice spread through Erika's veins. His voice had changed, losing the western tang of the Flumeeren people. He sounded almost…

"I said, *step away*," Sythe repeated, voice deepening to a growl. He took a step towards her, dagger poised to strike.

Instinctively, Erika tried to back away, but the table brought her up short. It took a moment for his words to register. They sent a shudder down her spine. Step away from the most important finding of her career, a map to all the secret places of the Gods? Even if there were no other sites in Flumeer, the discovery was a priceless treasure.

Scanning her surroundings, Erika searched for a way to fight back. The chamber was only ten by ten feet and Sythe was a big man, easily twice her size, and the knife in his hand was almost two foot long. Any plan that resulted in physical conflict would not go her way. But that didn't mean she would surrender her prize without resistance.

"Stay back!" she hissed.

Her eyes flickered to the ruined door, but even if she could grab the map and make it past Sythe, she would never make it through the gap before he caught her.

A smile touched Sythe's face, as though he could read her thoughts. "Hey," he murmured, lowering the point of his knife half an inch. "No need for ya to join 'im, ay?" He gestured to Ibran. A pool of blood was already beginning to form beneath the man.

Erika shook her head, adopting the manner of a terrified youth. It didn't take much to be convincing—the blood dripping from Sythe's knife was enough to drive her to the edge of panic. *This couldn't be happening.*

"Why are you doing this?" she whispered.

Sythe's lips drew back, revealing yellowed teeth. "The King pays well for secrets."

"The king?" Erika said, momentarily confused, before the man's accent clicked into place. "Gemaho!" she gasped.

She hadn't heard the accent often as a child, when visitors had dined with her father. But that had been before the war, before she'd fled with her mother; she hadn't heard the accent in years now. Gemaho had broken the war pact when the allied expedition south of the Agzor Fortress had failed. Afterwards, they had retreated within their borders and barred entrance to all foreigners. Sythe—if that was even his true name—only laughed in confirmation of her suspicions.

"What interest does the King of the West have in my work?" she asked, trying to regain the initiative. Maybe if she could negotiate…

Sythe laughed. "New age is approaching, Archivist," he rasped, accents mixing. "Kingdoms are doomed, without'a new weapon. Or an old one. Whichever kingdom uncovers the magic of the Gods, will rule the world."

"That's insanity!" Erika gasped. "The kingdoms stand united—"

"Ha!" Sythe interrupted. "'ought you were smart. Wars comin', one the king ain't intending to lose."

"But—"

"Enough," Sythe barked. He swung the dagger in a lazy arc.

"*No!*" Erika screamed, flinching against the table and thrusting out her gauntleted hand to fend off the blow.

The attack had only been a warning, but now Sythe's face darkened and he raised the blade high. Erika was sure she had only seconds left. Frustration burned in her soul. So much time, an entire life, wasted on the study of the Gods, and for what? To have someone else snatch away the prize at her moment of victory?

But as the blow swept towards her, Sythe stumbled, and the swing of his dagger fell short. A frown appeared on the assassin's unshaven cheeks and he shook his head, as though to dislodge something in his ears. It seemed to work, and he straightened—but only for a moment.

A scream tore from his throat as he staggered back, the dagger slipping from limp fingers. Hand still outstretched, Erika watched as the blade clattered harmlessly to the stone floor. Another cry came from Sythe as he crashed into the table, upending it on the floor. His screams turned to an awful gurgling as he slumped to his knees. Wild eyes, red with blood, swivelled in his skull, finding Erika standing frozen in place. He stretched out a hand, lips moving, trying to make sounds.

"Pleas—" he managed, as though the word had to be clawed from his throat.

Erika gaped as his face began to change. Blood seeped from his eyes and ears, leaving trails of red down his cheeks and neck. Another groan hissed from the man's throat as gore burst from his lips, splattering the stones between him and where Ibran lay dead.

Slowly Erika's horror turned to fascination. Her eyes moved from the Gemahan assassin to the gauntlet. This had to be its doing. Indeed, while unwatched, it had changed. Goosebumps tingled across her hand and she realised with a touch of fear that the fine wires had somehow become entwined with her flesh. Warmth spread through her hand and up her arm as a glow began in the unknown metal, like that of the crystals in the walls, but darker, more threatening.

Deadly.

Curious, Erika closed her fist. Immediately the light died. A sharp inhale from where Sythe had collapsed to the floor confirmed the traitor still lived, though he made no move to recover his dagger or feet. Soft sobs tore from the man's throat, and Erika wondered what style of agony could inspire such relief at its departure.

Heart pounding in her ears, Erika looked again at the gauntlet. She swallowed. *God magic.* She had hoped for this, prayed for it night and day since childhood. Now, though... she found herself wondering. What cost might this magic extract?

"Archivist?"

The faintest of whispers came from the assassin. He had not moved from where he lay, but now she saw his eyes moving, the bloody irises moving back and forth. Horror touched her and she forced herself to look away. She couldn't dwell on what her newfound power had done. There would be time for that later. For now, she needed to escape, in case others were working with the Gemahan.

The map!

It still hung from the wall, untouched in the conflict. Carefully she leaned across the table to recover it.

"Archivist," the call came again, though each word seemed to cause the man great pain. "Archivist...please... are you there?"

Icy cold slid down Erika's spine, but she ignored it. As she looked down at the map, she caught sight of another star. It lay beyond the borders of Flumeer, but not far, perhaps only two days ride south of the Illmoor. A secret site that no one had ever set eyes upon, that had never been opened. The treasures it might hold... surely they would make even the gauntlet look ordinary.

She rolled up the map and slid it into her satchel, then forced herself to look on Sythe. His eyes still flickered back and forth, but she saw now what the gauntlet had done. Its magic had shredded his corneas. He would never see again.

He tried to kill me!

Shaking off her pity, Erika slid along the table to the wall, avoiding where the assassin was still struggling to stand. Even blind, he might still prove a threat. Only when she reached the broken door did she pause to glance back. Sythe cried out again, crouched now beside Ibran.

"Archivist, *pleaaase!*"

Another cry drew her gaze back to Sythe. He crouched

on the floor, pitiful in his desperation, raw terror twisting his face.

Erika turned away. She would feel no compassion for the man. This was only justice. He had tried to kill her—worse, he had tried to steal her victory.

Let him rot down here in the darkness.

❦ 4 ❧

THE RECRUIT

Lukys's legs burned as he made his slow way up the slope. The weight of his pack and chainmail vest dragged him back but he kept on, teeth clenched, eyes fixed on the ground two yards ahead of his feet. Grunts came from the other Perfugian recruits walking around him, though little was said. After a week of hard marching, few could spare the breath for idle words.

On more than a few occasions, Lukys had wondered whether he could keep on. The way had been a brutal series of mountains, valleys and river crossings, with each night spent camped in the open, with only the canvas tents they carried on their backs for shelter. Exhaustion weighed on his shoulders; he had not enjoyed a good night's sleep since the voyage from Ashura. If only the ship had carried them further south, the march to the frontier could have been completed in a day.

Instead it had deposited them on the docks of Mildeth, the Flumeeren capital, leaving them to walk most of the way. Apparently, the galley was needed for more important tasks, such as ferrying the famous Flumeeren spices back to Ashura.

Many of the recruits felt affronted at the idea, but Lukys's childhood had been filled with hardships far worse than a cross-country march. His parents had been nobodies. That wasn't meant to matter in Perfugia. Children were taken from their families at eight and enrolled at the national academy, so that none would be privileged above others.

But even at the academy, the division had been clear. His dormitory had been old and crowded; the newest facilities given to the noble born. And so had passed his twelve years of study. He was glad to be rid of the place.

Now, at last, he would have a chance to prove himself.

It had come as a surprise when they'd named him. The Perfugian army was renown throughout the four kingdoms; it was a rare honour to serve in its ranks. Lukys's hopes had been for a position as a scribe or doctor, though he'd struggled with both in his final examinations.

But a soldier? He hadn't dared dream of such an assignment.

Noticing the slope lessening beneath his boots, Lukys finally glanced up. A sigh escaped him as he saw the top of the hill was close. Several recruits and the officers on their horses were already waiting there. His fellows were taking the opportunity to sit and rest their legs, while the officers talked softly amongst themselves.

Coming to a stop alongside the others, Lukys leaned against his spear with a groan, then drew out his waterskin and took a swig. The path up the hill had been dry and it felt good to wash the dust from his mouth. Laughter came from the nearby recruits as they looked in his direction.

"Finally made it, peasant?"

A scowl twisted Lukys's lips but he kept his mouth shut. The group were made up of some of the higher born from the academy, men and women who at various points over the last ten years had made his life difficult. He was used to their taunts, though he'd hoped they might have ceased now that they'd all been named professional soldiers.

"I hope we get to march into Calafe," one of them, Dale, was saying to the others. "Let's see how tough the Tangata are when they come up against Perfugian steel!"

The others cheered and clapped his back. The officers on their horses ignored the noise, though the recruits had been instructed to keep quiet as they neared the frontier. If the maps were to be believed, they were close now…

Putting away his waterskin, Lukys moved past the officers. The remaining recruits were still filing up the hillside. Several of the stragglers were at least ten minutes behind; he had time to look around.

The terrain ahead was greener than what they'd just climbed. Trees spotted the rolling hills, though they could not compare to the untouched forests of northern Perfugia. Then Lukys frowned as he noticed a blackened strip of land. Further down the hill, the forest had been burnt, leaving bare earth stretching all the way to the broad waters of a river.

A river…

The Illmoor!

His heart quickened as he scanned the banks of the famous river, searching, seeking, *there!*

Nestled in a bend of the Illmoor was a town—Fogmore. A grin stretched his cheeks as he looked upon the end of their long journey. It faded, however, as his eyes lingered on the town. The stockade walls were tiny, and many of the buildings he could see looked to be made of wood. In

Perfugia, even the poorest of villages were constructed of stone, built to last, to endure the wild storms that often bashed the island kingdom's coast. Wood was only ever used as decoration.

He supposed it was all a farming nation like Flumeer could afford on such a distant frontier. Even so, his stomach twisted at the thought of sleeping in such a matchbox— what would they do if a fire swept through the sprawling buildings?

And why had they burnt the forest?

Shouts came from behind, then the officers were trotting past. They didn't spare him a glance as they started down the winding path to the plains below. Lukys let out a sigh as he settled his pack more comfortably on his shoulders. Then he waited for Dale and his friends to go first—no doubt they would react unpleasantly to a mere peasant overtaking them.

The scraggly trees swallowed them up, sealing off the town from view for the time being. The weather had improved over the last day, but now Lukys noticed clumps of snow beneath the trees once more. The dry air of the valley they'd just traversed was replaced with a damp, cloying humidity, and by the time they reached the burnt section of land, clouds had gathered in the sky.

As they continued towards the distant town, Lukys looked on the ruined earth with sadness. Blackened tree stumps stood here and there, but the fire must have burnt hot—there was little remaining of the forest that covered the hillside further up. With the trees lost, the land already showed signs of erosion: deep rivulets carving through the ashy soil, exposed roots dotting the land, even a crumbling cliff that had collapsed across a section of the road.

Lukys couldn't begin to understand the destruction.

While they lived in cities of stone, every Perfugian regarded their forestland as sacred.

The aching had begun again in his legs and back, but the knowledge that every step brought him closer to a bed—however flammable its enclosure might be—gave Lukys strength. His eyes sought a fresh glimpse of the fortified town, but it hid behind the rolling hills now between the recruits and the river.

Only as the sun dipped towards the horizon did the land flatten out, bringing the town back into view. Less than a mile off now, Lukys glimpsed the flicker of movement as armoured soldiers shifted atop the palisade. They wore chainmail like himself and their half-helms matched the one hanging from Lukys's pack.

Pale faces turned to watch at the approaching column, though no trumpets sounded to announce their arrival. They had probably been spotted when they'd lingered on the mountaintop. No doubt word of the reinforcements had carried ahead, and Lukys straightened his shoulders in anticipation of their reception. They were not fully-fledged soldiers yet, just at the beginning of their training, but he wanted to at least look the part.

But there were no cheers to greet them, no welcoming applause. The gates facing the road north stood open and a small gathering of onlookers in plain clothing had gathered atop the stockade walls, but an unnatural silence hung over them, more like mourners at a funeral than a welcome party. Lukys let out a sigh: he shouldn't have expected any better from a city at war.

As the column approached the gates, the officers brought their horses to a stop and turned to face the recruits.

"Column, halt!"

A ripple went through the Perfugian ranks as fifty men and women came to a staggering stop. Lukys and the others glanced at one another, wondering why they'd stopped. They were just a few yards from the town now, surely whatever it was could wait…

"Column, form lines!"

Again the recruits looked at one another, but another shout from the officers had them scrambling. Chaos ensued as they bumped into one another, trying to arrange themselves into some semblance of order. Lukys's cheeks grew red as snickering carried down from overhead. The civilians were laughing at them!

He gripped his spear tight and focused on finding his place in line. Let them laugh; what did they know? They might be inexperienced, but they were Perfugian soldiers and they had won their right to be here! The citizens of Fogmore would be reminded of that soon enough, when the Tangata came.

Long minutes later the fifty recruits had organised themselves into rows of five wide, ten deep. Lukys stood with his spear held vertically at his side, eyes fixed straight ahead as he'd once seen the royal guards do when in the presence of the Sovereigns. To his embarrassment, he was one of the few to adopt an official pose—the others lounged in various states of boredom, apparently impatient to finally reach their destination and discard their packs.

"Column, advance!"

At the command, the recruits started forward. Their lines immediately disintegrated as those behind moved faster than the recruits in front, but the officers apparently no longer cared. Turning their horses, they started into the town without glancing back.

And so the Perfugian column entered Fogmore, somewhere between organised soldiers and disorganised mob. Lukys closed his ears to the howls coming from the ramparts —though as they entered, he realised the onlookers stood not so much on ramparts as an earthen mound built up against the wooden walls.

What is this place?

In Perfugia, towns and cities were guarded by great walls of granite and gneiss, topped by crenulations and watch towers. It was why in all their long history of war, no kingdom had ever managed to gain a foothold on the island nation.

Yet Fogmore, command centre for the war efforts against the Tangata, looked to be little more sophisticated than the hilltribes that had once occupied Perfugia's mountain forests. The buildings were indeed made of wood—and looked little better than temporary shacks propped up by nails. Fresh snow was just beginning to fall and Lukys couldn't imagine the shabby walls doing anything to keep in the warmth—or keep out the snow, for that matter.

Lukys exhaled hard, his anger turning to disdain. These people dared to mock them, when not a building in this town could compare to even his parents' modest cottage? The streets weren't even paved—and the passage of men and women had long since made them slick with mud. Back home, not even the most insignificant of towns would have suffered such an indignity. The entire place had a temporary feel to it, as though the Flumeerens had thrown it up overnight.

The column made its slow way through the town, struggling on through the thick mud. The fresh snow only made matters worse, and those at the rear began to lag, though their grumbles did not reach the officers on their tall horses.

It was a relief when the buildings finally gave way to a

broad central plaza—though it hardly deserved such a title. The churned earth continued without so much as a street sign, except where several boulders the size of small wagons dotted the ground. For a moment, Lukys thought they might have been placed as ornaments and was impressed. Then he noticed that the rocks were smooth, untouched by so much as a chisel, and realised they probably predated the town. Too large to be moved without great expense, Fogmore had simply been built around the boulders.

No, the square was little more than a muddy paddock. Snow had been piled up in the corners beneath the eaves of the surrounding buildings, but that was the only sign of order present.

Doubt touched Lukys as the column came to a halt, and he found himself looking at the officers. What were they doing in a place like this? Surely they weren't expected to live—and fight—alongside such savages?

"Column, form lines!"

The command came again. This time the chaos was worse, as the recruits became entangled in the thick mud. Several ended up face-first in the muck. Lukys couldn't imagine how anyone could live in these conditions. Did the Flumeerens hold themselves in such low regard?

"*Enough!*"

The word cracked like a whip over the head of the recruits. Lukys flinched at the unfamiliar voice, freezing in place. Movement flickered in the corner of his eye, and he watched as a man in plain clothing stalked to the front of the assembly. A frown wrinkled Lukys's face at the sight of a civilian giving orders to soldiers. Who did this man think he was?

The thump of boots striking earth followed as the Perfugian officers dismounted. Lukys expected them to reprimand the newcomer for interrupting, but instead the three snapped to attention, backs straight, eyes fixed ahead as the civilian approached. Shocked, Lukys turned his eyes back to the newcomer.

The man stood some five feet and nine inches, little taller than Lukys, though his frame carried far more muscle. Greying hair had been cropped short in the style of the military, but his barber had apparently ignored the strands sprouting from his ears. He wore long silver furs across his shoulders and a heavy cape draped down his back, while beneath he sported a tunic of rough spun wool. Fresh stubble shaded his jaw and frown lines streaked his face, suggesting a man who rarely smiled. Despite his obviously advancing years, his eyes were sharp as they swept the square, inspecting the recent arrivals.

It was clear from his scowl that he was not impressed.

"General Curtis, sir!" one of the Perfugian officers announced. "Your fresh batch of recruits, as scheduled."

Lukys's jaw almost struck the ground. Surely this couldn't be *the* General Curtis. The man was a legend, his career stretching back decades. He had been one of the few who'd warned against a resurgence of Tangata, before their surprise incursion into Calafe ten years prior.

Those had been innocent times, when the kingdoms had thought the beasts contained south of the Agzor Fortress. The attack had proven them all wrong, and hundreds had died before the creatures were hunted down. All because men like General Curtis had been ignored.

At least the general had commanded the allied retaliation. Disastrous as it had ended, the outcome might have been worse yet without his presence. An army of ten thousand had marched south of the Agzor Fortress, intent on crushing the Tangata once and for all. That had been the last time soldiers from all four kingdoms fought together, a noble sight for any who watched them depart, no doubt.

Two months later, General Curtis and the warrior queen of Flumeer had led the routed forces back through the gates of the Agzor Fortress. The enemy had taken them by surprise, surrounding and almost destroying them before the Flumeeren forces had broken free. The Calafe King had fallen in the battle, and barely two thousand soldiers had escaped, but at least some had survived.

Unfortunately, the Tangata had soon followed. The unbreakable Agzor Fortress had fallen in days, and the war for Calafe had begun.

Ten years and thousands of lives later, Calafe was lost, and still the Tangata came.

Lukys shivered, looking at the man with fresh eyes. If ever a soldier had earned the right to repudiate his uniform, it was this one. Where would the four kingdoms have been without his brilliance?

It did not bear considering.

"So these are the best the Perfugian Sovereigns have to offer," the general muttered.

He almost seemed to be speaking to himself, but Lukys drew himself up at the man's words, chest swelling, spear clutched tightly at his side.

"A more wretched bunch I've not seen since your last batch." Shaking his head, the general turned back to the officers. "I suppose you've filled their heads with the usual nonsense of glory and Perfugian superiority?" He snorted. "You're short fifty men."

The officers shared a glance while Lukys and the other recruits stood gaping. What had the general said?

Clearing his throat, the head officer of their column

stepped forward. "There were not sufficient candidates of quality this year—"

"Ha!" the general laughed. "You mean these fools were the only ones to fail your preposterous examinations."

Fail... Lukys opened his mouth and closed it. He had failed? Murmurs came from around him as his comrades glanced at one another, but Lukys couldn't tear his eyes off their superiors. *I failed?*

The officers shifted nervously on their feet, but they did not refute the general's claims. What was going on? There was anger in the general's eyes as he looked at the Perfugian officers, but finally he gave them a dismissing nod and turned back to the recruits.

"My name is General Curtis," he barked. "Though while you live, you will address me as 'sir.' I do not expect that to be long."

The whispers started again at his words.

"*Silence!*"

The shout rang from the walls, so loud that Lukys actually leapt backwards. The movement sent him crashing into the recruit behind him. The mud slipped beneath their boots and before either could recover, they both went tumbling to the ground. Shocked, the other recruits stepped back as though they were contagious.

Grunting, Lukys pushed himself to his knees. The mud clung to his clothes and he raised his hands. "Sorry!"

The recruit he'd knocked down looked as surprised as Lukys, but at the apology he only nodded and flashed a grin. "No worries."

Lukys let out a breath as the recruit offered him a hand, but before he could take it, a shadow fell across the two of them.

"What is your name, recruit?"

Crouched in the dirt, Lukys found himself staring into the ferocious eyes of the general. His heart dropped into his stomach and he would have thrown himself backwards again, had terror not frozen him in place. His mouth opened and closed, but the words took several tries to come out.

"Lu…Lukys…sir!"

"Do you make a habit of sitting in the presence of your commanders, recruit?"

"N…no, no sir!"

"Then get on your Godsdamn feet!"

Lukys practically flew off the ground as the scream rattled in his ears. Somehow the recruit he'd knocked down was already up, back straight, eyes fixed straight ahead as though he'd never fallen. Only the streak of mud on his trousers betrayed him. Lukys thought he might have been another of the noble born, but did not know his name.

The general flashed Lukys one last look of contempt, then spun on his heel and marched back to the centre of the square. His voice rang from the walls of the nearby buildings as he addressed the column.

"Welcome to the frontier, ladies and gentlemen," he shouted, "though I daresay such titles are above you." Clenching his hands behind his back, he turned to face them once more. "I would say we are pleased for the reinforcements, but it's been a long time since the soldiers of Perfugia were worth more than tits on a bull. I daresay you lot will fare no better."

Lukys's insides twisted. Surely it couldn't be true. The Perfugian military were renown amongst the kingdoms…he had been chosen, honoured…

…yet wasn't this the man who had saved the civilised world? Who was Lukys to question him, to doubt the cruel words he spoke? His eyes fell to the ground and his shoulders slumped, the spear hanging loose in his grip. Could it be true?

"I have no interest in dealing with the discards of your privileged kingdom. We have no resources to waste training failures, so you will be assigned to hard labour. Your beloved Sovereigns saw no more use for you than death, but perhaps you might yet make this dump a little more bearable. At least until the Tangata come." His eyes shone as he appraised them.

"Make no mistake though," he continued, "when the beasts *do* come, it is the duty of every soul in this city to take up arms against them. You *will* fight with us on the frontline."

The man's words turned Lukys's innards to ice. Not even Dale's boastfulness could ignore the fact they were woefully unprepared to face the frightful creatures. They would be slaughtered!

"Perhaps you'll be lucky, and the Tangata will be long in their arrival." He grinned. "I wouldn't suggest holding out hope though."

"We don't even know how to use a spear!" another recruit called out. "How can we fight without training?"

The general did not denounce the interruption, but a cold smile appeared on his lips. He seemed to take a grim amusement from their predicament—but what had they ever done to deserve such cruelty?

"Perhaps you'll get lucky, and distract the beasts long enough for the real soldiers to do their job," he replied. "Regardless, try not to die too quickly. I shudder to think what your beloved Sovereigns would send to replace *you*."

With that, he turned and marched from the square. The Perfugian recruits stared after him, shocked to silence by his words. A pall of terror had fallen over the square, and Lukys found himself shaking his head. Surely this couldn't be real, must be some cruel joke played on new arrivals. The general would return in a moment and reveal the truth, surely…

Whoorl.

The song of a horn cut through the silence.

❧ 5 ❧

THE WARRIOR

Romaine stood at the stern of the ship, watching as the shores of Calafe retreated into the mist. It had been close for a time, racing through the fading light, seeking the ever-elusive waters of the Illmoor as the howls of the Tangata grew closer. Just their luck that more of the creatures had been in the area.

In the end, the river had come upon them suddenly, the twisted trees giving way to an open field that stretched along the riverbanks. Even then, it had been a nervous wait once they'd signalled the other side, listening to the Tangata coming ever closer.

Now as the mist rose around the ship, Romaine listened with satisfaction as the howls of the hunt fell silent. The creatures had reached the shore and discovered their quarry escaped. Turning from the bow, he shared a nod with the lieutenant. The last hours had rattled the man, but there was open relief on his face now.

The other scouts sat in silence around the galley, eyes distant, as though reliving some waking nightmare. They did not seem to notice the sailors moving about them. Romaine knew that look well, had seen it on the faces of half-a-hundred soldiers over the past decade. It was the look of the guilty, of a man who knew he had survived while others had fallen. But these men were strong; they would rise above their despair, and be better for it. More prepared to face the Tangata when next they came.

Long oars propelled the galley through the rushing waters, towards the unseen shores of Flumeer. The Illmoor stretched almost a mile wide in these parts. They'd emerged from the forest close to their rendezvous point, but even then, they'd been lucky the ship captain kept his crew alert. The torch the scouts lit for signalling was bright, but in the heavy mist it could have easily been missed by a less attentive captain.

Ignoring the crew, Romaine wandered towards the bow where the horses had been stowed in makeshift stalls. He had sequestered the woman in a nook behind, where the captain stored extra sailcloth and rope. There she was safely out from under the feet of the sailors as they went about their work. Boards creaked beneath his boots as he approached, and Romaine glimpsed movement in the shadows.

Moonlight caught on the amber eyes as she appeared from the darkness, almost feral with fear. Romaine raised his hands to show he was unarmed—he'd left his axe with the horses. He took another step closer and his shadow shifted, allowing a nearby torch to illuminate the woman's face. This time she did not flinch away, though she cradled her injured arm to her chest. Romaine had placed it in a makeshift splint while they waited for the galley, but it would need the attention of a doctor when they reached safety.

"Who are you?" she whispered in that singsong voice of hers.

"Romaine," he replied. "Of Calafe."

Pursing her lips, the woman nodded. She lowered herself down onto one of the benches running along the side of the ship, but otherwise she did not respond.

Romaine raised an eyebrow. "It's customary to offer a name in return."

The woman stared at him for a long moment, and it seemed to Romaine she was weighing him up. Again, he wondered where she had come from, what she had been through to find herself alone in Tangata territory.

"Cara," she said at last.

Romaine offered his best smile, though on his bearded face and in the flickering light, it might have been mistaken for a sneer. When Cara said nothing, he gestured to the bench attached to the other side of the ship.

"May I?"

Again the long stare, but finally she nodded, and Romaine sat with a groan. "Long ride," he explained, then nodded to her splint. "How's the arm? I'm sorry about before, about startling you."

As though his words had reminded her of the injury, Cara cradled the arm to her chest once more. "I fell..." she said, and for a moment her eyes took on a haunted look. "I've never fallen before." Then she shook her head, her expression turning blank as she looked at him. "Where are we?"

"Crossing the Illmoor River, into Flumeer."

"Flumeer!"

Instantly, the woman was on her feet, head whipping around, eyes wide with fright. But in her haste, the injured arm slammed against the side of the galley and whatever she might have said next turned into a moan. Romaine rose quickly as she staggered, ready to catch her if she lost consciousness again. The colour had drained from her face and she swayed on her feet, but eventually she slumped back to the bench.

"I can't go to Flumeer," she whispered, rocking on her haunches. "There's…people there."

"We must," Romaine said softly. "It's not safe where we found you, not anymore. Did your…people not receive the news? New Nihelm has fallen. Calafe belongs to the Tangata now."

"*New* Nihelm?" Cara's eyes were wide. She turned to face the mist. "Gone?"

"I'm sorry." He paused, watching as the wind tugged her hair. He shivered, but in her bulky furs, Cara did not seem to notice the chill. "Your people…" He trailed off, then added, "You were alone when we found you."

Cara nodded, facing him again. "I was lost…"

"Then your family, they're still in the forest, still alive?"

Cara shook her head, and Romaine's stomach twisted as his own grief called out its sympathy. He reached out a hand to pat her shoulder, but at the last moment she glimpsed the movement.

"*Don't touch me!*"

Screaming, she flinched away, coming to her feet again in a rush. This time she tripped over a loose coil of rope and instead of fleeing, she went crashing to the ground. Another cry tore from her throat as she fell and she tried to roll away. Rope and cloth went with her and in a panic she thrashed, tangling them around her.

Romaine had come to his feet, but he dared not try to help her, lest he spur another outburst. Finally her terror seemed to subside. She slumped against the deck, gasping as though she had just climbed a mountain. A tremor followed, seeming to sweep her from head to toe, until her entire body was shaking.

"Are you…I'm sorry, are you okay?" he whispered, hardly daring to make a move towards her.

Cara's eyes slid closed and she drew in a great breath. The tremors slowed, then ceased. Exhaling, she pushed herself up with her good hand. She gulped in another breath, as though fighting against some terrible pain, and slowly unravelled the rope and sail that had wrapped around her. Finally she managed to stand and sink back to her bench. There she pulled her knees up to her chest and closed her eyes, a single tear streaking her cheek.

"I…I don't like to be touched," she croaked when she finally looked at him again.

Romaine nodded, though silently he wondered again what horrors the woman had endured alone in the wilds of Calafe.

"You killed them." A frown crossed the woman's brow as she looked at him. "The Tangata. How?"

"How?" he repeated, then shrugged, recalling the battle, the pounding in his ears, the rush of adrenaline. "It was not the first time."

"You were so fast," Cara murmured. "Almost as quick as them."

"Not quite," Romaine replied. He rubbed his chest where the male had struck him and winced. "But I knew what it was going to do."

She nodded, as though what he'd said made perfect sense to her. Silence fell between them, and Romaine sat back, listening to the soft moaning of the ship, the lapping of water against the hull, the cursing of sailors at the oars. He tried to imagine himself back in the silent winter forests of his homeland, but instead he saw Flagers, lying dead in the blood-red snow.

His eyes snapped open and he rose. To his surprise, the mist had lifted and now the waters around the ship were clear. Ahead, burning torches lit the night and he sighed. That would be Fogmore, where he and the other scouts were barracked. It had been a sleepy town on the banks of the Illmoor once—until the war had come. Now it hosted the command post for the Flumeeren army.

They were closer than he'd thought, and inwardly Romaine suppressed a sigh. Seeing the stockade city only served to remind Romaine of his own loss. With Calafe fallen, he was now a man without a kingdom, forced to rely on the generosity of others for a place to stand, to sleep.

"Where are the trees?"

Romaine glanced sideways as Cara joined him on her feet. Her eyes were on the distant lights and it took him a moment to realise what she was talking about. In the darkness, it was difficult to see the barren hills around the city.

"Some were cut down to form the palisade, others for the new buildings needed to host the army. The rest…" He trailed off, thinking of the infernos that had lit the shores of the Illmoor from ocean to mountains. "They were burnt."

"Why?"

"To keep the Tangata from slipping past our scouts," Romaine replied.

"That's horrible," Cara murmured.

"Can you walk?"

She nodded, and turning, Romaine led her past the horse stalls. As they reached the main deck, the ship shuddered and the sound of wood crunching against gravel carried to their ears. He didn't need to look over the side to know they'd reached the shore, though he noticed the wide-eyed look on Cara's face as she spun around. Unbidden, a smile touched his lips.

"We've arrived," he grunted.

The announcement finally seemed to shake his comrades from their stupor, and rising, they moved to free the horses from their stalls. Romaine made no move to help —the busy work would be good for them. He turned as footsteps announced the lieutenant's approach, and he offered the man a nod, but his attention was focused on Romaine's new ward.

"Awake at last, I see!" the lieutenant said in what he must have thought was a friendly tone. He offered a friendly bow. "Lieutenant Marco, at your service."

Cara only stared at the man, lips clenched tight. The lieutenant turned to Romaine with a frown.

"Does she speak?" he asked.

Chuckling, Romaine clapped the man on the shoulder. "Not to you, apparently," he said with a grin. Nearby, the sailors were raising the gangplank from where it had been sequestered beside the railing. The current had turned the ship side-on to the riverbank, and with a groan of steel hinges, the plank slammed down into muddy shore. "Come," Romaine added. "We'd best get out of the way of these men. No doubt they'd like to return to the safety of the river before the night grows too old."

Ignoring the lieutenant, he led Cara down the gang-plank to the shore, then raised an eyebrow at the woman. The faintest hint of a smile touched her lips, but it faded as she looked ahead. Romaine could hardly blame her. Fogmore was anything but welcoming. The wooden palisade waited some two hundred yards from the river, though the ground sloped upwards from where they stood, so that the city seemed to loom above them.

Torches had been lit at regular intervals along the palisade, and the flickers of shadows revealed the guards on watch. Nothing could be seen of the city beyond, though the gates were already swinging open in preparation to admit the new arrivals. Once a gravel path had wound its way up the slope to the gates, but the constant passage of marching boots had turned it to a muddy, rutted mess.

"Welcome to…" Romaine sighed. "To my new home."

Wrinkling her nose, Cara flashed him a glance. "You sure you wouldn't rather the Tangata?"

Romaine blinked, then let out a snort. "They might yet convince me."

Movement came from the gangplank as the lieutenant started down. Gesturing to the path, Romaine started off before the man could reach them. The thump of boots on wood picked up pace as the lieutenant sped up, and Romaine let out a sigh. The man caught them before they'd gone ten yards, puffing softly. It was difficult to move quickly on the muddy path. To Romaine's relief, the lieutenant said nothing and they plodded on.

The other scouts overtook them when they were half-way. They waved from the backs of their horses and continued ahead, broad grins on their faces. Now that they had reached the safety of home, the guilt and fear had receded, replaced by joy at their own survival. Romaine clenched his jaw as he felt himself longing for the men's innocence, for their hope and optimism. His had died long ago.

"Are you okay, lass?" the lieutenant asked as the last of the horses overtook them. "Sure you wouldn't like a ride?"

Cara was managing better than either of them in the mud, though she must have been in pain from her arm. Romaine cursed inwardly that he had not made the offer sooner, but Cara only raised her eyebrows. The lieutenant shared a glance with Romaine, but he only shrugged. Shaking his head, the man returned his attention to the path.

Despite his sorrow at leaving his homeland once again, Romaine still felt a touch of relief at the sight of the city. Packed and chaotic as it was, he would at least be extended a hot meal and a bed. These days, he didn't want for much more than that.

When they were still some fifty yards from the gates, Cara suddenly slowed. Romaine pulled alongside her as she glanced back, the fine features of her face twisting in a frown. For a moment, he thought she was having second thoughts about entering the city. Then her entire body went taut, and she opened her mouth to cry out.

Whooorl.

Romaine's heart lurched as horns sounded from atop the palisade walls, drowning out Cara's scream. Atop the walls, soldiers pointed down at them. No, past them—down at the distant river. Romaine followed their gestures, gaze travelling back to where their galley had landed.

The ship should have been pushing back from the shore by now, but it remained where they'd left it, sailors racing back and forth across the deck...

...No, not sailors.

Another howl sounded in the night, but this time it was not the Flumeeren trumpets.

Tangata!

Dozens of the creatures were swarming over the ship. Their clothes were soaked from the river waters and Romaine could hardly believe what he was seeing.

They had swum!

The sailors didn't even have a chance to scream before

the Tangata overtook them. In a matter of moments, their bodies lay scattered across the decks. A *whoosh* carried up the slope as a lantern was smashed against a railing, scattering flames across the wooden boards.

"*Run!*" Romaine bellowed.

Cold grey eyes turned after them as Romaine spun. Forgetting Cara's affliction, he grabbed her by the shoulder and dragged her up the path. A cry came from the woman and she tore herself loose, but whatever panic she felt, she channelled into movement. The lieutenant had already seen the danger and had taken off without a second thought for those behind.

Whooorl.

The horns sounded again, followed by the soft creak of hinges. Romaine's eyes snapped to the gates, just thirty yards away now. Slowly, they began to swing closed.

Fear touched Romaine and he bellowed for them to wait. If the guards heard, they took no notice. The other scouts had already reached the safety of the town. Only the three of them remained outside.

Light burst from atop the palisade walls as bales of straw were set aflame and pushed over the side. Their glow swept down the slope, illuminating the way ahead. And what came behind.

Glancing over his shoulder, Romaine glimpsed shadows streaking up the hill towards them. Moving with incredible speed, the Tangata had already covered half the distance to the town. Another minute and they would be upon them. He set his eyes on the closing gates and pounded on.

A bowstring twanged overhead. Angry shouts followed —a superior reprimanding the archer for releasing his arrow early. The Tangata were still too far away. Even in his desperate state, Romaine appreciated the officer's discipline in the face of the attack.

A dozen Tangata…where had they come from? Why now?

Moments later, a chorus of *twangs* lifted from the ramparts, and fifty arrows flashed past overhead. Romaine didn't need to look back now to know how close the beasts were. Convention dictated a crossbow volley be fired at sixty yards. Ahead, the gates continued to close, the squeal of their hinges sounding their doom.

"Wait!" There was open terror in the lieutenant's voice, but he should have saved the effort.

At least a dozen Tangata came behind them. If even one were to enter the city, the havoc it would wreak amongst the civilians would be terrible. The officer in charge of the watch could not take the risk—not solely for the lives of two men and an unknown woman.

Romaine cursed. He didn't even have his axe. They were just ten yards away now, so close. But they weren't going to make it.

Suddenly the gates stopped moving. A figure appeared in the gap—Romaine recognised one of their fellow scouts, waving frantically for them to hurry.

Then they were through, the gates slamming closed behind them. A *thud* followed just as the locking bar dropped into place, shaking the wooden boards. Howls chased after them, then the twang of arrows came from overhead as the archers fired again.

All sound from outside ceased.

Then the screaming began.

Panting, Romaine straightened to take stock of the situation. His fear deepened as he witnessed the chaos that had taken hold of the city. Men and women raced in all directions, some towards the ramparts, others in seemingly mind-less circles.

Terror was spreading.

And the Tangata were at the walls.

"Someone get me my axe," Romaine growled.

THE RECRUIT

Lukys stood frozen as the trumpets sounded again. Not even the officers moved from where they stood, but all turned their faces to look southward. Darkness had fallen almost unnoticed; the torches lit around the square casting their orange light across the snow. A third call sounded from the direction of the river.

"To arms!"

Lukys never saw who gave the call, but with those two words, the peace was broken. Chaos descended on the square as others picked up the cry. The general's words were proven true as men and women went racing from the nearby buildings, some dressed in chainmail and carrying swords or spears, others in the plain clothes of civilians. Many of these carried hatchets or long knives, a few had construction hammers, one a pitchfork.

Standing in the centre of the square, armed with their spears and protected by heavy chainmail, not one of the Perfugian recruits moved. It was as though a spell had been cast over them. All Lukys could hear in his mind were the general's words.

Death, death, death.

It was like a prophecy, a chant rattling around his skull, demanding deliverance.

The Perfugian officers swung into their saddles, but they said nothing to their charges. Instead, they put heels to flesh and galloped from the square—heading north, not south. Lukys watched them go, mouth wide, his last trickle of hope fading to nothing. Their commanders had fled, had left them here to die.

Death, death, death.

Lukys's heart pounded in his chest as he looked at the spear in his hands. He had carried it all this way, had worn the chainmail, but he had never *used* them. He stared at the spear now, willing himself to lift it, to shout a war cry and race to aid his fellows.

He couldn't.

A moan came from his throat as he looked around, seeking help from someone, anyone. Dale stood nearby, but his face was pale, forehead beaded in sweat. His eyes were fixed to the ground and as Lukys watched, a shudder went through the man, as though he were on the verge of tears. Gone was the bravado of just a few hours earlier.

The Tangata had come, and they didn't care whether your blood was noble or poor. They would kill you all the same.

Death, death, death.

A tremor shook Lukys as the first scream sounded over the blowing of horns. His eyes fixed in the direction of the river. The palisade was hidden by the nearby rooftops, yet it couldn't be far, not if they could hear sounds of battle, of the dying…

Lukys's gaze caught movement in the windows of the nearby houses. Faces peered out at them, an older woman with two young children, their eyes wide with terror. He swallowed, seeing others now, the old and young, the injured and the infirm. They stayed in their homes, unable to fight, only to wait and see who would prevail.

Lukys's stomach twisted in a knot as he looked from them to the Perfugian recruits.

Cowards.

How could he and his comrades stand here, frozen in terror, while others bled for their freedom? What did it matter whether they were failures or heroes, when there were those here who fought with pitchforks? At least they had spears, at least they had *armour.*

A soft *thud* whispered across the square as Lukys dropped his pack. Almost unconsciously, he reached down and tore the half-helm from its strap and placed it on his head. Then he was stepping forward, mud splashing beneath his boots. The spear came up, its tip dropping in what Lukys approximated to be the correct position. Hairs rose on the back of his neck as he sensed the eyes of the other recruits on him, but Lukys ignored them.

Eyes fixed straight ahead, he walked through the ranks of his fellow Perfugians, towards the distant screams of battle.

Thud, thud, thud.

Lukys glanced around as the sound of objects striking earth came from behind him. Other recruits were moving forward now, spears held at the ready, determined. He glimpsed the man he'd knocked down earlier amongst them, and offered a nod. A woman stepped up alongside Lukys and they shared a glance. He saw a steely resolve in the hazel depths of her eyes, a determination to do her kingdom proud—whatever the bastard general might have said of them.

Movement came from all around now as the spell shattered. Like a wave breaking against the shore, the fifty recruits surged forward with a cry, racing to reinforce their fellows in the battle for humanity's freedom.

Running down the muddy streets, Lukys's heart soared. There was no time to think about what was to come, about strategy or logistics, only to charge, spear raised towards the enemy. The palisade came into view, the sloped earth leading up to makeshift ramparts packed with soldiers.

Lukys's fear came rushing back.

The Tangata did not appear to be attacking this section of wall, but somehow that only made the fear worse. His guts turned to liquid as he listened to the sharp *twang* of bowstrings. Somewhere, men and women were screaming, but ahead a strange peace hung over the soldiers, the calm before the storm.

Lukys's stride faltered and he slowed his pace, allowing several recruits to overtake him. But he didn't allow himself to stop. If he stopped, he'd never be able to start moving again.

Soon the ground was rising beneath his feet. Lukys clenched his teeth and clutched his spear tighter as they approached the waiting soldiers. Unbidden, the recruits spread out along the wall, seeking areas where there was space for them to stand. Screams came from away to their right and Lukys craned his head. Even in his terror, he longed for a glimpse of the villainous Tangata.

Then he was standing atop the fortifications, the spiked palisade stretching up to his waist, a twenty-foot drop beyond. A barrel was burning nearby, casting light out across the ramparts, while below great bales of hay turned the river flats to red.

Ghosts moved amongst the flames.

Death, death, death.

The hairs on Lukys's neck stood on end as he tried to track the creatures below. They were effervescent in the darkness: a flash of their eyes catching the light here, a flicker of shadows there, always moving. Bowstrings twanged along the wall, but Lukys sensed few would find their mark—not in this darkness, not with these creatures.

Taking a two-handed grip of his spear, he looked left and right. Soldiers wearing the red embroidered uniforms of Flumeer made up the bulk of the front ranks—few of the blue-clad Perfugians had been so bold as to step right to the edge.

Thwack.

Lukys gaped as just a few feet from where he stood, a man crumpled to the ground, head caved in from some unseen projectile. The helmet had done nothing to protect him. Other defenders cried out as the *crack* of rocks striking wood came from the palisade—then they were throwing themselves down. Lukys mimicked their actions, though his eyes were still fixed on the dead man. A rock the size of a fist lay on the ground beside him.

What The Fall am I doing here?

Standing amongst the soldiers of Flumeer, Lukys realised in that moment he had no business being on that wall, in that city, on the frontline. He had no idea what he was doing, no clue about how to fight, what to do when the Tangata came.

The pounding of rocks ceased as quickly as it had begun. Maybe the Tangata had run out of projectiles—or perhaps they were only waiting for fresh targets to present themselves. The Flumeerens must have thought the same, for they were slow to regain their feet.

Eventually, some of the bolder archers began to fire into the darkness again. Still crouched, spear clutched at his side, Lukys watched a woman draw back a bowstring, eyes fixed on some point down below…

Lukys blinked. The woman had vanished…no, not vanished—her body lay a yard from where she'd stood, neck snapped in two, eyes still staring at some distant point.

Something else took her place.

Lukys didn't move, didn't dare even breathe as finally he laid eyes upon the monster that haunted the dreams of every Perfugian child. It could have been human; indeed, there was no outward difference in its appearance. There was no disfiguration, no sharpened teeth or talons, as some of the legends claimed. Nothing other than eyes as grey as stones.

Those eyes swept the ranks of defenders surrounding it, and as one they drew back. The Tangata smiled.

Death, death, death.

The chant had become a cacophony in Lukys's mind now, booming along to the racing of his heart. Fear lodged in his throat, suffocating him, robbing him of strength. The tip of his spear shook; he almost dropped it.

A howl shook the night.

And the soldiers of Flumeer charged.

Sword raised, a man leapt at the beast, steel point aimed for its throat. The Tangata wore no armour, carried no weapon that Lukys could see, but it moved far faster than its foe. It spun, and the soldier's sword found only empty air. A hand flashed out and caught the soldier by the throat. Though he wore an iron bevor, the steel offered little protection against the strength of the

73

Tangata. The creature wrenched its wrist, and then the man was dead.

Lukys's stomach churned as blood sprayed across the mud, but the loss did not slow the man's comrades. Screaming their rage, they struck at the creature, though it was already moving, evading their attempts to trap it, to drive their blades home. Lukys watched on from his knees, unable to find the courage to stand.

He had never understood until now. Sure, he had heard the tales, knew the stories, the legends of these creatures who had dared defy the Gods.

But no one in Perfugia truly understood.

He knew that now. If they did, all the might of their island nation would already be here, battling on to hold the line, to push back against the inhuman hordes.

The Tangata were no ordinary enemy, no human kingdom you could surrender to. The creature before him was mad, possessed by the magic its ancestors had stolen, utterly corrupted.

If the Tangata could not be stopped...

They were all going to die.

Lukys climbed to his feet, spear held out before him. A second Flumeeren soldier had already fallen. The creature swept up the man's sword before others could converge on it, and a third man fell, head separated from his shoulders in a single swing. Growling, it continued forward.

Screams rent the air as Lukys watched the creature come, unable to move, to run, to do anything but wait for death to find him. It stalked across the rampart, dealing death with each step, and Lukys raised his spear, preparing for a final stand. But the soldiers of Flumeer were not finished yet.

A woman stepped between Lukys and the creature, bow

in hand with arrow nocked. Before the creature could spot the danger, she loosed. A howl sounded in the night as her red-plumed arrow sprouted from the Tangata's chest. It stumbled back, grey eyes showing a moment's surprise. But the wound was not mortal, and with a roar, the beast drew back an arm and hurled the stolen sword.

There was a sickening *thwack* as the blade slammed into the woman's chest. Thought fled Lukys's mind as he dropped his spear and stepped forward to catch her. She sagged into his arms, the strength gone from her legs. The chainmail vest she wore had done nothing to save her, and staggering, Lukys lowered her carefully to the earthen ramparts.

Blood bubbled from her lips as she struggled to breathe. Desperately, Lukys tried to recall the teachings of the master doctor. But the sword embedded in the woman's ribs was beyond anything he'd learnt in the academy. With a last sigh, her eyes slid closed and the harsh rattling of her breath faded to nothing.

Lukys sat back on his haunches. Around him, the world was on fire. Winds blew from across the river, catching in the hay below the walls and sending flaming strands swirling through the air. Acrid smoke stung his nostrils as he inhaled, and his throat burned. Terror robbed him of strength.

He drew on what final dredges of courage remained to him. Clasping at his fallen spear, he forced himself up—and found himself staring into the stony eyes of the beast.

It stood just a yard away, close enough that it could have reached out and snapped his neck at any moment. It didn't. Wrinkles creased its forehead as it watched him. The spear shook in Lukys's hand as he realised this was his chance.

But even as he tightened his grip on the weapon, the

Tangata tensed, its features closing over. A smile twisted its lips, revealing yellowed teeth.

Death, death, death.

Laughter sounded in Lukys's ears and the beast raised a hand, gesturing him forward.

Screaming, Lukys leapt, spear held at the ready. He knew he could not win, that this was the end, but in that moment he didn't care. All that mattered was the spear in his hands and the beast.

The tip of his spear flashed out, aimed clumsily for the creature's stomach. The Tangata was quicker, its hand swiping down, catching his weapon by the haft and snapping it in two with a quick wrench. Lukys staggered back, half of his now useless weapon still clutched to his chest. The tip of Lukys's spear clasped in one hand, the Tangata advanced.

A cry escaped Lukys as his boots failed to find purchase in the mud. He crashed to the ground, broken spear tumbling from his fingers. Mouth wide in terror, he looked up, expecting to see death descending upon him.

A warrior stood between Lukys and the Tangata, twin-bladed axe extended towards the beast. The weapon rippled in the firelight as it swept out. The Tangata leapt away, twisting from the path of the blade, but even with its superhuman speed, it could not avoid the blow completely.

A shriek rent the air as the axe sliced the creature's thigh. Blood pulsed from the wound as it staggered. Lukys was surprised to see it bled red. Despite their distinctly human appearance, surely the monsters could not be the same within?

Pain contorted the Tangata's face as it faced the axeman. Then a change seemed to come over the creature, a wave of pure rage sweeping away its agony. Its eyes flashed and it rushed forward—now in total silence.

The axeman did not retreat from its fury. He charged with a shout, words lost in the chaos, massive shoulders sending the axe flashing for the Tangata. Somehow, the creature seemed sluggish by comparison. Perhaps the wound had slowed it. Regardless, it realised its mistake too late, and with a sickening *thud*, the axe slammed into its shoulder, slicing through bone and sinew to bury itself in the beast's chest.

An awful gurgling came from the Tangata as it struggled to step forward, to reach the enemy that had slain it. But not even these creatures could survive such a blow, and with a sharp whistle of departing air, it slumped to its knees and fell alongside Lukys.

The warrior towered over the beast. His shoulders heaved as blue eyes scanned the ramparts, seeking out signs of fresh danger. Another Tangata lay nearby, its body peppered with arrows and impaled by several spears. In the distance, the sounds of battle were fading, an eerie stillness coming over the night.

The battle was won.

Looking up at the massive axeman, Lukys could hardly believe he was alive. If not for the ferocious warrior, he wouldn't be. Only now did he notice the man did not wear the familiar red of Flumeer, nor the blue of Perfugia. Instead, his chainmail had been woven through with the deepest green, remnant of the forest.

Calafe.

He hadn't realised there were any Calafe warriors left. They had passed the refugee camps outside Mildeth, but it was said that the last of their soldiers had refused to leave their land, and had died on the shores of the Illmoor. What did this man fight for now, with his kingdom overcome?

"Need some help?"

Lukys started as the man spoke, dragging him from his thoughts. Seeing the hand the warrior was extending, he took it. His slender fingers were ingulfed by the warrior's giant mitts and he was yanked to his feet. Lukys stumbled before righting himself, his gaze catching on the body of the Tangata once more. The blood had stopped flowing from the awful wound the man's axe had left.

It almost killed me.

Before he could stop himself, Lukys was bent in two and retching in the mud.

Gentle laughter came from beside him. "First battle?"

Gasping, Lukys managed a nod.

"You'll get used to it," the warrior grunted.

With that, he took a hold of his axe. Placing a boot on the Tangata's chest, he yanked the weapon free with a sickening *squelch*, then turned and walked away along the ramparts.

Lukys watched him go, a reply on his lips, though he couldn't bring himself to say it. The warrior was wrong. He would never get used to this. He would never get the chance.

He'd be dead long before then.

৯্ঠ 7 ২ঠ

THE ARCHIVIST

Erika was sagging in the saddle by the time the walls of Mildeth finally came into view. The short winter days had made the journey hard, forcing her to wake in the darkness and ride until long after the sun had shrunk beneath the horizon. Blessedly, it was still high now; her five day journey would be at an end by nightfall.

Now her excitement began to rise as she contemplated what awaited her in Mildeth. They had all been expecting her to fail, every noble in the blasted court. Only the queen had shown faith, and even she had warned Erika that there would be no more expeditions should she return empty handed.

But this time, Erika had succeeded.

This time there would be no reprisals.

This time she would offer Queen Amina the true magic of the Gods.

She had spent the long journey intermittently dreaming of what might lie hidden in northern Calafe, and practicing with the power she now literally held in the palm of her hand. Not long after leaving the caverns, she had discovered the metal fibres had indeed fused to her flesh. It should have frightened her, but instead she found herself relieved the magic could not be taken away.

Each night she had practiced with it, trying to discover its secrets. She had experimented first with its ability to summon light. In her rush to escape the caverns, Erika hadn't realised she'd forgotten the lantern until halfway to the exit. It was only then she'd noticed the magical glow that had followed her, seeping from her hand. Now she could summon not only light, but warmth at will by clenching her fist, though she found if she practiced too long, she grew fatigued.

She'd had less success replicating its more deadly nature. The magic seemed to have no impact on inanimate objects; the trees she'd practiced on hadn't so much as shaken before her power. Erika hadn't dared test it on anything living yet; she would have to trust it would work when needed.

The rolling hills fell behind Erika and the last of the snow with them, while the walls of Mildeth grew larger. Built of red sandstone, they rose from the land like a bloody scar, standing defiant against the wild green of the surrounding farmland. Joining the Queen's Highway, Erika began to overtake wagons. Many were loaded with food goods, broad beans and cabbage and onions, late crops, the last to be harvested before the snows had started. Others were escorted by armed men, their contents hidden by heavy tarps. These would be from the mines, filled with gold or silver or other precious metals. Maybe even marble, cut from high in the mountains and conveyed to distant Mildeth to grow the ever-expanding citadel in the city's centre.

Erika's heart raced at the thought that one of those new apartments might soon be hers. Finally she would be granted the position in court she deserved. But her excitement was short-lived, as ascending the final hill before the city, she looked down at the plains surrounding Mildeth.

A mass of humanity crowded the earth beneath the walls. Here was the fate of the failed, all that remained of the ruin that was Calafe. Flumeeren guards stood at the gates, inspecting each wagon and barring entrance to those who lacked the proper papers. There were simply too many for the city to hold; already Mildeth was bursting at the seams.

And so they gathered without, women and children, the old and crippled and infirm, all waiting upon the queen's mercy. Some had raised worn canvas tents, while others had gathered enough garbage and detritus to create lean-tos or makeshift buildings—though that was perhaps too strong a word for the pitiful structures they had erected.

The Calafe had never been builders. Though many spoke of the beauty of New Nihelm and Fort Agzor before they had fallen, most of its people were said to be nomads, surviving upon the fruits of the forests.

Only there were few forests in Flumeer. Those had given way long ago to farmland, a necessity to feed not only the growing population, but the ever-expanding army.

Raising her hood, Erika drew the cloak tighter around herself and rode on. After the assassination attempt in the caverns, she was wary of being recognised. Though she would be forced to show her papers to the guards, there was no need to shout her arrival to every watcher in the city.

She kept her gaze fixed straight ahead as she entered the crowds, eager to avoid contact. A long line of wagons clogged the road ahead, waiting to be processed and checked, but alone on her horse, Erika was able to press forward unopposed. Even so, she felt the refugees pressing in, their desperate eyes upon her back. Clenching her fist, she summoned warmth to her gauntlet, drawing strength from the magic's presence.

However, it could not keep the stench from her nostrils. Closer to the city, the refugees grew denser, bunching up against the walls in their desperation for shelter. Erika wrinkled her nose as she caught a whiff of another unpleasant smell. She didn't need to ask what happened to their waste in such tight conditions.

Approaching the gates, she could no longer avoid setting eyes upon her poverty-stricken neighbours. They were everywhere, crowding onto the Queen's Highway, pressing at the guards, the wagons. Images flashed before Erika's eyes, of a pale-skinned, dark-haired woman wearing a thread-worn dress. Even the memory made her cheeks grow warm. Her past was like an anchor, ever seeking to drag her back to the poverty she and her mother had experienced when they'd first arrived in Flumeer…

The last wagon in line was being searched as Erika rode past. She didn't spare the contents a glance. Ahead, the gates were open, though a company of soldiers stood at the ready should any of the human debris camped outside attempt to gain passage. They closed ranks at her approach and Erika pulled her horse to a stop before them.

She dismounted as one of the soldiers wearing the badge of a lieutenant pinned to his chest stepped towards her. "Papers, ma'am?"

"Erika, the Queen's Archivist" she replied, reaching into her coat for the documents. As she did, her hand brushed the ancient map and a thrill of excitement touched her. Shaking it off, she offered her papers to the man. "I trust everything is in order," she added, adopting an elevated tone.

The lieutenant cast a cursory glance over the papers, then back at her. He raised an eyebrow. "Long journey, ma'am?"

Erika's cheeks warmed as she saw the judgement in his eyes. She'd hardly had time to find food on the long journey south, let alone bathe or purchase new clothes appropriate for her rank. In truth, she looked little better than the Calafe refugees. But the news she brought could not wait.

"We are at war, Lieutenant," she answered curtly, anger washing away her embarrassment. "I come with urgent news for the queen."

"Yes, I'm sure ancient history is *littered* with urgent news," the man replied drolly. Erika balled her gauntleted hand into a fist, but after a moment he handed back the papers and stepped aside. "Go, though I suggest you bathe before entering the presence of Her Esteemed Majesty."

Snatching back her papers, Erika flashed him a scowl, but the lieutenant was already returning to his men. Stepping back into the saddle, she directed her mare into the gate tunnel. Snickers came from the guards as they watched her go but she ignored them. Their insolence would not be forgotten. Soon she would be one of the elites, a noble of Flumeer. Then the lieutenant and his men would learn the error of their ways.

The shadows of the walls enclosed her as she entered the tunnel. She shivered in the sudden darkness, feeling the weight of stone looming overhead. The passage narrowed as she edged her horse around a corner designed to slow intruders, and in the black she felt herself losing control. Suddenly, she was back in the tunnels beneath the earth, in the realm of the Gods, and Sythe was creeping towards her, knife extended...

She exhaled hard, fighting for control. Ahead, the

tunnel twisted again, a shimmer of light promising an exit. She pressed her heels to the mare and with a snort it broke into a trot.

A moment later she returned to the light. The nightmare banished, Erika pulled her mount to a stop and dragged in great lungfuls of air. Lifting her hand, she clenched and unclenched her gauntleted fist. Light danced upon the metal, though in full daylight it was difficult to pick the source. She knew, though…

Nightmares banished, Erika lowered her hand and continued her journey. There were still several more hours of daylight remaining, but the city was large and she intended to call upon the queen before the court retired for the day.

Beyond the gate tunnel, she found herself in a broad plaza with a dozen roads leading off from it. The buildings here were of the same red sandstone as the outer fortifications. They were squat and ugly things, reflecting the average Flumeeren's mind for practicality over beauty.

Erika directed her horse down the central avenue, settling her hood back in place. The walls protected the streets of Mildeth from the worst of winter's winds, but she was still wary of being recognised. Sythe might have died with her secrets, but returning without her assistants would be suspicious. And who knew where else the Gemahan king might have watchers?

Stones clicked beneath steel hooves as she made her way through the city. The streets were peaceful compared to the chaos beyond the city gates, the pavements clear of waste and detritus. Guards stood watch at intersections and citizens made their way through the grid-like streets with smiles on their faces. The occasional wagon rumbled by on the way to and from the docks.

The order restored calm to Erika's soul, banishing the stress of the past week. This was where she belonged, standing shoulder to shoulder amidst the elite of society. Memories of her past were naught but a passing shadow on a sunny day.

It took her an hour to reach the citadel. She made only one stop on the way, a brief detour through a perfumery in which she was able to clean her face and augment the scent of a week spent on the road. This time she would approach the guards with more confidence, to avoid any further delays by men inflated by their own sense of power.

Yet when she turned the final corner to the citadel, she couldn't help a fluttering in her stomach. The sight that greeted her would have intimidated anyone. Soldiers in gold-embossed breastplates and full-faced helms lined the street. Each was armed with shield and spear, with swords strapped to their waists for good measure. To the ignorant, they might have appeared as statues, decorations to bid guests welcome to the towering citadel beyond.

But Erika was anything but ignorant. Behind each of those impenetrable helmets was a veteran of a dozen battles. Soldiers did not earn a place amongst the warrior queen's guard without proving their worth.

Wind whistled between the rooftops as Erika made her way between the silent men. Goosebumps lifted on her neck as she sensed the unseen eyes watching her, but not one of them moved. Silence hung over the street like a blanket, heavy, suffocating, until she wanted nothing more than to scream. She continued, her horse plodding slowly towards the palace gates.

Only there did movement finally come. As she stopped to dismount, she saw suddenly that soldiers had moved behind her, barring the path back down the street. For men in full-plate armour, they moved quickly, and with frightening silence.

"Archivist."

One foot still in the stirrups, Erika spun towards the citadel, and almost ended up face-first in the dust. Thankfully she managed to get a hand on her saddle to steady herself before disaster struck, but too late to entirely save her dignity. Agitated, she finished dismounting and looked to the speaker.

"Your return was not expected for another week," the man continued before Erika could get a word in. Wearing a silken doublet of Flumeeren scarlet, he stood with arms clasped behind his back and a look of carefully crafted indifference on his face. "The queen trusts you have not returned empty-handed…again."

Erika's mouth opened and then closed, her veins turning cold. His words cast her back to that last failure, when she had stood before the queen and her court and begged for one final chance. Most had called for her dismissal—or worse. The queen had been moved by her words, but she had implied another failure would require recourse.

I did not fail!

Clenching her gauntleted fist, Erika straightened and looked the queen's emissary in the eye.

"Take me to Her Majesty, steward," she commanded. "I bring news that will change the future of the war."

THE WARRIOR

Romaine sat in silence as the sun clawed its way over the eastern mountains, casting back the dark. Exhaustion hung across his shoulders like a cloak, but he had not slept. Through the long night he had waited, axe in hand, to see whether the Tangata would return. Now as he watched the light reclaim the world, he felt the weight of disappointment on his soul.

It wasn't that he wished to die. Only that…he was so tired of the pain. Every morning when he woke, there was a short moment when he did not remember, the briefest of seconds when his heart was free.

Then the memories would return, and with them the agony of loss.

Exhaling, Romaine looked across the earthen rampart to where Lieutenant Marco lay in the mud. Romaine hadn't seen the man's death, though it must have happened in the first hour of the attack. One of the beasts had torn out his throat. At least it had been quick.

The irony of the man's death was not missed on

Romaine. Marco had survived the Tangata in the forest and the crossing, made it all the way back to Fogmore—only for death to find him on the town walls.

Below, the mudflats were silent, the enemy long dead. He should have slept, should have retired to his bed after the long journey. But he could never sleep after a battle. And so he had sat here in the darkness, waiting, remembering.

The light around the mountains grew brighter as the sun reached for open skies, and soon movement began below. Soldiers emerged from the river gates and walked amongst the dead, claiming armour and weapons to be inherited by a new generation of recruits. Slowly the dead were gathered into piles, one for the human fallen, another for the Tangata. The bodies cloaked in red and blue must have outnumbered the beasts five to one.

Romaine was still sitting atop the ramparts when the first of the pyres was lit. By then a soft snow was falling. The ice flakes glistened in the dawn light as they drifted down, settling on the barren earth. Come noon the combination of ice and marching boots would churn the ground to mud. Fogmore truly was a Godsforsaken place.

Only when Romaine's breath began to fog on the frozen air did he finally lift his axe and rise to turn away…

…only to find a pair of amber eyes watching him.

He had forgotten the strange Calafe woman, and the sight of her sitting on a nearby barrel gave him pause. He'd assumed someone had seen her to safety, but in the chaos, he supposed no one had thought to take responsibility for her safety. It was a miracle she had survived.

"What are you doing here, lass?"

Cara shrugged, her eyes lingering on the lieutenant's body. Though she had not known the man, Romaine glimpsed sadness in those amber depths. He remembered having such compassion once. He had lost it long ago, somewhere between the endless battles and death. There had been no choice—caring, loving, it offered nothing but pain in this war. Against the Tangata, death was inevitable. It was just a matter of when.

"I wanted to see," Cara replied, her gaze turning to the burning pyres, and the blackened ruins of the ship that had carried them clear of her homeland.

Romaine frowned. "I would have thought you saw enough last night."

A shudder shook the woman. "So much evil." Her eyes did not leave the flickering fire. "So much death."

"They kill everything that crosses their path," Romaine murmured, pain wrapping its thorny tendrils around his heart.

Finally Cara broke off her watch over the fires. "You have suffered from them?"

Romaine couldn't help but shiver as their eyes met. There was something about the woman's gaze, some ageless quality, as though she had seen far more than her youthful appearance implied. What had happened to her out there in those woods? How long had she wandered, without her family?

After a moment, he realised he hadn't answered her question. He shook his head and forced a grim smile. There was no point reliving that pain; it was enough that he still lived, and that his axe had sent another of the beasts into the abyss.

"We should do something about your arm," he said instead, nodding to his makeshift cast. "You might have other injuries too. The camp doctor should really check you over…"

"*No!*" Cara hissed, taking a step back from him, eyes wide with fright.

Romaine raised his hands, his heart inexplicably racing. "Okay, okay," he murmured, "but we still need to do something about that arm. I'm no doctor, and that splint I made is already half falling off. You don't want the bone to mend crooked."

Lips pursed, Cara looked from Romaine to her injured arm. As if to test his words, she stretched out her hand, and flinched. Pain tightened her face and she sank back to her barrel—though to her credit, she did not cry out.

"I…I might be able to help."

Quick as a viper, Cara was back on her feet, arms raised as she swung on the newcomer. Beyond her, a young man in Perfugian colours yelped and leapt backwards. His feet slipped in the mud before he could flee and sent him crashing to the ground. Landing face-first in the mud atop the ramparts, he thrashed, and would have probably gone tumbling down the slope back to the city had Romaine not strode across and plucked him from the muck.

"Hey…what…get off!" the man cried.

Chuckling, Romaine set the man carefully on his feet. Behind him, Cara mirrored his mirth, her laughter peeling from the ramparts. The man's blue uniform, along with his face, was now stained top to bottom with mud. Pink tinged his pale cheeks as he stood there, head bowed, brown eyes locked to the ground as though it had been cast by some great artist.

"So, what were you saying, lad?" Romaine asked when the laughter finally died away.

The man's eyes flashed as he glanced at Cara, but she only responded with an innocent smile. Whatever the

Perfugian had been expecting, it had not been that. Shaking his head, he looked back at Romaine.

"You saved my life," he said softly.

Romaine raised his eyebrows. It was a moment before his memories clicked into place and he recognised where he'd seen the young man before. This was the recruit who had crouched at the feet of the Tangata Romaine had killed earlier.

"It was nothing, lad," he grunted. "I've made a habit of gutting the bastards." A grin split his bearded cheeks. "Though you might want to consider keeping on your feet next time." He glanced at the Perfugian's mud-stained clothing. "Falling over is not a habit I would recommend around these parts."

The pink in the Perfugian's cheeks darkened to red but Romaine only clapped him on the shoulder. From the crispness of the man's uniform, he guessed this was one of the fresh recruits from Perfugia. Word amongst the Flumeeren soldiers was that the column had arrived just before the battle, and had actually participated. It was more than could be said for most of the recruits out of Perfugia, though from the number of blue uniforms amidst the pyres, it seemed their bravery had come at a hefty cost.

"So what's the name, lad?" he asked when the recruit did not respond to his goad.

The recruit started, his head jerking up, as though surprised to be asked the question. "Lu...Lukys," he stammered.

"Romaine." He held out a hand, and after a moment Lukys took it in his. "Now," Romaine continued, "what were you saying about helping young Cara here?"

Lukys blinked, looking at the still smiling woman, then back to Romaine. "What...oh, yes right, her arm."

"Her arm," Romaine agreed.

"It's broken?"

The axe man sighed, already regretting entertaining the young man. "Well, we'd need a doctor to say for sure…"

"Yes," Cara interrupted. She stepped up beside them, arm cradled to her chest. "I fell, out there," she said, indicating the land beyond the river. "I'm sorry for laughing," she added. "I am not used to…people."

Silence answered her words. Romaine glanced at Lukys and saw the youth's mouth had fallen open. His eyes were on the river, and he realised the recruit probably knew nothing about Calafe and his people.

"You…were…you came…from Calafe?" the young man finally managed to stammer.

Laughter danced in Cara's eyes as she shared a glance with Romaine, but this time she was wise enough not to voice it. Instead she nodded to her forearm. "Do you think you can help?"

Lukys glanced from the river to Cara. "I…" He swallowed, then drew in a great breath. It must have helped him gather his wits, for when he spoke next, his tone was almost calm. "I…yes, I think so. They taught us all sorts of things at the academy, to prepare us, you see, may I?"

It took a moment for Romaine to pick the meaning from the man's jumbled words. It took Cara longer still, but after a pause she finally offered her arm. She stood with her back arched, jaw clenched as Lukys gently took her arm in his hands.

"You're a medic?" Romaine asked, attempting to distract the woman from her phobia.

"What?" Lukys murmured, then shook his head. "No, I wanted to be, but I…failed, apparently," he answered before Romaine could repeat the question. He didn't seem to notice the tension in his patient as he carefully removed the makeshift splint Romaine had made. "We...all did, I suppose, all of us here." His eyes flickered and Romaine glimpsed the shame that hid there. "But then, you already knew that."

"We're all failures at something, lad."

Lukys snorted, but this time he did not reply. The last bandage came loose, revealing the purple bruises that marked Cara's pale skin. They spread almost the length of her forearm. It must have been quite the fall, to leave such a bad break.

"Fortunately, I do remember how to treat a fracture," Lukys added finally. He shot Cara a smile, as though to reassure her.

Cara did not reply. All colour had drained from her face and she looked like she might explode from her coat of heavy furs at any moment. The recruit's eyebrows lifted in surprise and he glanced at Romaine in question.

"Will you heal her with your hands, lad?" Romaine asked in response.

"I..." He trailed off, looking around, as though checking for listeners. "I have some supplies in my pack. I left it in the plaza, but I can get them." Carefully he lowered Cara's arm to her side and released her, then turned and hurried down the slope into the town.

In his absence, Romaine turned back to Cara. "You okay, lass?"

Cara nodded, though she had grown pale enough to be mistaken for a ghost. "Are...all the people of Perfugia so strange?" she asked.

Romaine grinned and took a seat on another of the water barrels that stood nearby. "Hard to say," he replied. "We only get the misfits down here. Lad's heart seems in the right place. You sure you don't want a real doctor though? They've got stuff that'll help with the pain."

Cara's face darkened. "No," she said shortly.

After that, they waited in silence for the young man to return. He appeared a few minutes later, large pack strapped to his back. A spear hung from one side, a helmet the other. With a sleeping roll atop, he looked more tortoise than man as he rattled his way up the slope. Romaine watched his approach with amusement, too fatigued to go down and help.

"You carried all that from Perfugia?" he asked when the young man finally reached them.

Lukys was puffing so hard he only managed a nod by way of answer. Uncaring for the mud, he threw the pack down near Cara and started rummaging around inside. When he rose again, he held several rods of copper and a handful of dried herbs. He handed them to Romaine before pulling out a pack of bandages.

Cara flinched as he turned towards her, and he paused, glancing uncertainly at Romaine.

"Only the arm," Cara whispered, drawing the recruit's attention back to her. She lifted the offending limb, as though it were an offering for some sacrifice.

Lukys still hesitated, his eyes on Romaine. The axeman shrugged. "She doesn't like to be touched."

Understanding blossomed in the recruit's eyes. "I'll try to be careful," he murmured.

He gestured for Cara to seat herself on the barrel, then waited until she was comfortable before moving alongside her. Taking the dried herbs from Romaine, he plucked a flower from the tip of one and offered it to Cara.

"For the pain," he explained. "Chew, but don't swallow, or you won't be able to taste food for a week."

"No," the young woman replied, shaking her head.

Lukys raised an eyebrow. "This…is going to hurt. I need to check whether the bone is set right."

"Thank you," Cara said shortly, "but I can handle the pain."

The lad hesitated a moment longer than was wise, but when Cara still made no move to accept his offering, he finally relinquished. Romaine sat back on his barrel as Lukys took Cara's arm in his hands once more.

Her face immediately lost the last of its colour, though this time Romaine wasn't sure whether it was from pain or fear.

With meticulous care, Lukys peeled back the sleeves of her coat once more. "Is this okay?" he asked, placing a finger on the injury.

Cara flinched, and her lips drew back in a snarl. Romaine expected the young Perfugian to retreat in fear, but curiously he stood his ground, brown eyes fixed on his patient. Cara's breath came in short gasps and Romaine feared she was working herself into a panic, but finally she gave a short nod.

Permission granted, Lukys moved his hands softly over the purpled flesh, fingers prodding gently at the bone beneath. Pain flickered on the young woman's face and her jaw remained clenched, though she did not let out even a squeak to show her pain.

"Okay, it's only broken in one place," Lukys said finally, straightening to look her in the eye. "You were lucky."

Cara's face was still pale, but she offered a fleeting smile. "I'll remind you of that next time you break something."

"That's fair," Lukys chuckled.

With his hands at work, he seemed more relaxed than

earlier. Taking the copper rods from Romaine, he lined them up with her arm.

"Could you hold these here for me?" he asked, flashing his patient a smile.

The grimace had returned to Cara's face with his touch, but she did as he bid. Lukys placed his fingers back on her arm, and then hesitated.

"Are you sure you wouldn't like the—"

"Just do it," Cara practically snarled.

"Ahh, okay," Lukys said, and pressed his fingers to her wrist.

A shrill keen sounded from the back of Cara's throat as she arched atop the barrel. For a second, Romaine thought she would strike the young man. Veins bulging on her forehead, she clung to the copper rod.

Then it must have been done, for Lukys was removing his hands. Cara let out a short exhalation as the tension fled her body. Her shoulders rose and fell in rapid succession beneath the heavy cloak, her breathing short. Gently, Lukys took the rod from her hands and moved it back into alignment with her newly set arm. Taking up the bandages, he wrapped several layers around the rod before adding a second rod, then finally a third, until Cara's arm seemed twice the size as normal.

"There!" he exclaimed finally. "Done!"

Cara sat back with a sigh, though her face still showed her tension. "Thank you," she murmured. She sounded faint, and worried the woman might collapse, Romaine stepped closer. She waved him back, curious eyes turning on Lukys. "How did you learn to do something like that?"

Lukys only shrugged. "Like I said, the academy."

"An academy." She said the word as though tasting it.

"We all go," Lukys murmured, becoming self-conscious

again now that the job was done. He lowered his eyes. "But like I said, I failed."

"Oh…" Cara deflated. She clutched her arm to her chest for a moment, before her head came up again. "But you seem so good at this!"

Lukys scratched a spot of dried mud from his tunic, looking away. "I…well…" His cheeks grew red, standing in stark contrast to her paleness. "I throw up when I see vomit." The words came from his mouth in a rush.

Laughter burst from Romaine's lips before he could keep himself silent. The recruit's head snapped around, anger touching his brow. Rising from his barrel, Romaine clapped him on the shoulder.

"All got our weaknesses, lad."

"Some of us have a few more than others," Lukys replied, his eyes drifting out across the mudflats.

Pity welled in Romaine's stomach and he saw again the eyes of another young man, staring up at him from the snow, terror in their murky depths. Romaine quickly shoved the memory away. He couldn't afford such sentiment out here, not with the Tangata gathering. He wouldn't survive losing anybody else.

"Romaine." The young man's voice was taut as he spoke, his eyes still fixed in the distance.

Following his gaze, Romaine saw that the pyres had almost burned out, though there were still shapes amidst the embers…

"I don't want to die here."

That makes one of us.

Romaine said nothing. Faces flashed before his eyes, of those he'd lost, of those he hadn't been able to save, all the way back to that night ten years before…

"The general won't train us. He says we're not worth the

time. I…I won't last another battle against those things, not without help."

No, no, no!

"Please, I saw you fight. You're a warrior, a great one. Please, Romaine, will you train me?"

No.

It was a fool's request. Even had Romaine been inclined, General Curtis was right. He usually was. It took months to turn an untrained recruit into a soldier—and based on the night's assault, they might not even have a week before the true Tangatan army reached the frontier.

He let out a long sigh, readying himself to spurn the man's request, to crush this last hope before it could catch light. He faced the young recruit.

"Meet me here tomorrow, at first light." The words leapt unbidden from his mouth. "And we'll see whether there's hope for you yet."

❧ 9 ❧

THE RECRUIT

D*arkness.*
A full moon over silent peaks. Rock and snow and cold.
Light flashing, a shadow in the night, the hiss of an inhaled breath.

Pounding, the racing of a fleeing heart, the panting of pursuers.

Cold, *rushing water, fire and flames, shouts in the night.*

Loss, failure, death!

Lukys gasped as he snapped awake, sitting bolt upright in his cot—

Crack.

Cursing, he crumpled back into the tangle of blankets, head ringing from the blow he'd struck against the bunk above. Somewhere in the dark, the other recruits grumbled and muttered dire warnings against disturbing their slumber. Outside, a rooster crowed.

Holding a hand to his chest, Lukys tried to slow his racing heart. Already the dream was fading. The rooster crowed again. Beyond the heavy shutters, night still clung to the city. He needed to rise, to stumble out into the cold and meet with the bearded warrior of Calafe.

The thought did not fill him with excitement. By the faint glimmer of a shuttered lamp he could see his breath misting on the air above him. It would be worse outside the dormitory. Surely he could lie here a little longer.

But no, Romaine had said the hour before dawn.

Stifling another moan, he pushed himself up more carefully and swung out the bed. It was a drop of two feet to the ground. The bunks were three-tiered, and being one of the last to the barracks, he'd been left with one of the middle beds.

Unable to light a lamp, he fumbled in the dark for his clothes and quickly dressed himself in every layer he could find. The muttering began again but Lukys ignored it. There was little he could do about the noise. He continued collecting his gear and was just pulling on his chainmail vest when a rough hand grasped him by the shoulder and spun him around.

"What the Fall do you think you're doing, *peasant?*" Dale spat.

Eyes wide, Lukys found himself staring up at the larger man. Dale's lips were drawn back into a snarl and he looked ready to throw Lukys through the window. He quickly tore himself loose and raised his hands in a gesture of peace. Voices rose at the commotion and movement came from nearby beds as the other recruits woke.

"Sorry!" Lukys whispered, trying to get away from Dale.

Across the room, someone unshuttered the lantern, allowing a flicker of light to illuminate the scene. Dale's eyes narrowed at the sight of Lukys fully dressed, though he hadn't quite managed to get the chainmail into place.

"Where do you think you're going?" he snarled. He

gestured around the room, though most of the recruits looked like they'd rather be asleep. "Look, brothers, sisters, the peasant shows his true colours! The coward seeks to flee!"

Anger touched Lukys at the recruit's words, washing away his fatigue. He stepped up to confront the man, though Dale was several inches taller.

"Strange," Lukys said, keeping his voice soft. "I did not see you atop the wall, Dale. Where were you, when the Tangata came?"

A flicker passed across Dale's face and for a moment he did not seem able to reply. Lukys spoke into the silence:

"I'm no coward," he said softly, addressing the others in the room now. Thirty-seven of their number had survived the battle. "The rest of you can accept your fate, but not me. I won't let them throw away my life like yesterday's garbage."

"So you are a deserter," Dale snarled.

"No." Lukys flicked his eyes back to the recruit. "I'm going to train."

Dale sneered. "Who would train a runt like you?"

"A Calafe warrior," Lukys snapped.

With that he spun and strode to the door. A cold breeze swirled into the room as he yanked it open. He snatched a spear from the weapons closet beside the entrance, then stepped out into the darkness and slammed the door behind him.

There he paused, half thinking Dale would follow to continue the fight. But no one appeared, and after only a moment's stillness he found his teeth beginning to chatter. A faint glow lit the sky pink and he saw now that fresh snow had fallen during the night. It crunched beneath his boots as he started down the alleyway, making for the section of wall he had first met Cara and Romaine.

Romaine had said to meet there, and judging by the light in the sky, he was already late. He picked up the pace, but the cold had frozen the earth solid, making it precarious to go faster than a walk. Even then, he had added more than a few bruises to his already aching body by the time he found himself standing in the shadow of the palisade.

There was no one there.

Cursing, Lukys hugged his chest and shifted his weight from foot to foot. Where was the axeman? The dawn was still and the cold wind cut like knives through even his heavy coat. Had this all been some prank, some act at Lukys's expense?

His legs were just beginning to go numb when the crunch of footsteps came from overhead. The Calafe warrior appeared, jogging along the tops of the ramparts. He wore his full chainmail armour and the giant butterfly axe hung from a sheath on his back. The man lifted a hand in greeting.

"You're late, recruit," the axeman called down.

Lukys's face grew warm but when he opened his mouth to offer an excuse, Romaine only laughed.

"Relax, lad. Why don't you get on up here? View's better from the top."

Nodding, Lukys started up, but soon found the task more difficult than it appeared. With the earth frozen, the mound was now slick beneath his feet and he had to dig the toes of his boots into the earth with each step. Fortunately, he was able to use the butt of his spear for balance. He was puffing hard by the time he reached the top, but couldn't help but grin when he looked around at the Calafe warrior.

Romaine laughed, gesturing away to the side. "When it's frozen, we generally use the stairs."

Following the man's indication, Lukys groaned when he saw the makeshift steps that had been cut into the earthen rampart a few yards away. He looked into the distance and saw they repeated at regular intervals. How had he missed them earlier?

"Come," Romaine said, turning towards the wooden spikes that topped the wall, pointing towards the river.

Beyond, the sky had turned from pink to scarlet, the rising sun setting the distant mountains aflame. Looking upon those towering peaks, Lukys could almost imagine that time all those centuries ago, when the Gods had rained their fury down upon humanity. The conflagration had destroyed humanity's ancestors, reducing them to little more than animals, scavenging in the remnants of their former greatness. Only pockets of civilisation had survived—places such as the noble city of Ashura, guarded by the open seas.

Lukys glanced at Romaine, but the Calafe's eyes were not on the mountains. The warrior looked out across the river, and though a light mist clung to the waters, obscuring their view, Lukys sensed the man's mind was on the distant lands to the south.

"Do you miss it?" Lukys asked softly. "Your home, I mean?"

A rumble that might have been laughter came from the warrior. "I miss many things, lad," he said, then gestured to the river. "But time, like the Illmoor there, flows on whether we like it or not. Can't go back. If you fight the current, you die. So best just go along for the ride."

"Unless you have a ship," Lukys replied.

Romaine shot him a glare and Lukys's cheeks warmed with embarrassment.

"So," the warrior said, shaking his head. "What *did* they teach you in that academy of yours? About war and that spear of yours?"

"Not much," Lukys murmured. "I thought we would be trained when we arrived here, but…" He shrugged, not wanting to linger on the general's words.

"Good," Romaine grunted. Lukys gave him a sharp look and the Calafe grinned. "Means I shouldn't have to beat any bad habits out of you." His eyes flickered to the spear Lukys held awkwardly at his side. "Why don't you have a go at me with that thing?"

"*What?*" Lukys gasped, eyes widening. He glanced at the spear, its razor-sharp point shining in the sunlight, then back to Romaine. "I could *hurt* you."

Romaine chuckled. "I doubt that very much."

"You don't even have a weapon!"

A smile crossed the Calafe's face, and calmly he lifted the massive axe from his shoulders. Ice spread through Lukys's veins as the warrior shifted into a fighting stance. He clutched the spear in front of him, thinking of that axe flying at his face. The point of his spear began to shake.

Laughter boomed across the wall, and then Romaine was driving the head of his axe into the frozen earth.

"By the Gods, lad, you look like you might die of fright." He shook his head. "Was a joke. Come, most of the Tangata don't have weapons either. Let's see if you can hit me with that thing."

"I…"

Lukys stared at the man. Romaine's hands were empty now. Steel chainmail protected his chest and caked leather gauntlets his arms, but Lukys still couldn't help but fear he might harm the warrior. But he'd been given an order, and gripping the spear in two hands, he thrust out half-heartedly at the axeman.

Romaine moved calmly to the side and batted out with one arm, sending the spear careening into the earth. The shock of the weapon striking ground was almost enough to jar it from Lukys's hands. He opened his mouth to protest, but yelped instead as Romaine leapt and struck at him with an open palm.

Even through his chainmail and heavy furs, the blow to his chest sent Lukys staggering back. The breath hissed between his teeth and he doubled up around the spear. For once he managed to keep his footing, but as Lukys straightened he saw Romaine coming again, face dark, unreadable.

In terror, Lukys thrust out with his spear. A cry left his lips as he realised what he'd done, but it was too late. Romaine moved faster than thought, his arm flashing down to deflect the attack, and he narrowly avoided being skewered by the spearhead. Lukys flinched as the warrior straightened, but Romaine only chuckled and stepped away.

"Well, you're quick, I'll grant you that lad," he said, "but you're also right. You don't know much about spear work."

Lukys lowered his eyes and clutched the offending weapon to his chest. Despair touched him as he saw himself on the ground once more, the Tangata standing over him, that awful chant ringing in his mind.

Death, death, death.

He began to shake. That image had haunted him through the night. It was only a matter of time before the creatures returned. How could he ever hope to face such monsters?

"It's useless," he whispered, voice bitter. "It's too late. That general is right. I'll never learn. May as well just go back to my bed. Least it's *warm* there."

"Maybe you're right," Romaine rumbled. "Might be I'm wasting my time. After all, you're only a *Perfugian*."

Lukys's head snapped up, but the angry words died on his tongue as he saw the humour in Romaine's eyes. Grinning, the warrior crossed to one of the water barrels and sat, gesturing for Lukys to join him.

"You can quit if you like, lad," he said as Lukys lowered himself down. "The Gods know, you've drawn the short stick in this bloody frontier." He paused, steel-blue eyes flickering. "But don't quit because of what some old bugger told you. Even if that bugger *is* a legend. This is war, not bloody architecture. Anyone can learn to hold a spear, if he's determined, if he puts his heart into it."

"You don't really believe that," Lukys muttered.

"Oh?" Romaine rumbled. "You think I'm doing this out of the goodness of my heart then?"

Lukys hesitated. Why *was* Romaine doing this? He glanced at the grizzled warrior but found himself unable to ask the question. A sigh slipped from his lips and his gaze flickered in the direction of the hills. Two of the recruits had disappeared during the battle, but their bodies hadn't been found. Lukys was sure they'd taken advantage of the carnage to flee. If so, they wouldn't get far. The world was at war, and deserters were not treated kindly.

That only left one choice: Learn to fight.

"Okay, Romaine," he said, dragging his spirits from the chasm of despair. "I'll do my best."

The warrior grinned. "Don't look so glum, lad. This is going to be fun. Now, why don't you take a lap around the walls while I get a few things ready?"

"You want me to walk around the city?"

"I want you to *run*," Romaine corrected. "First rule of combat—be fitter than the other man."

"But the Tangata aren't…"

Lukys trailed off as he caught Romaine's blue eyes glaring at him. He hesitated, mouth still half-open, until Romaine reached down and plucked his axe from the mud.

Hefting his spear, Lukys ran.

❦ 10 ❦

THE ARCHIVIST

Striding through the scarlet halls of the royal citadel, Erika struggled to keep the apprehension from her face. The queen's steward walked ahead, while two of the royal guards trailed her on either side, as though they feared she would flee. Their presence made her nervous, with their shining swords and impenetrable helms, and it was with an effort of will that she forced herself to concentrate on her surroundings.

Like the rest of the city, the citadel had a certain practicality to its construction. The plain sandstone blocks did little to assuage the eye and the few windows were squat and high in the walls, allowing sunlight to enter while still keeping out the undesirable. Such designs stemmed from earlier ages, when Flumeer had been a collection of warring tribes rather than a united kingdom.

Even the layout of the corridors had been designed with defence in mind, winding inwards and upwards in a spiral pattern. An assailant would have to circumnavigate the building several times to reach the queen's quarters at the centre. In places, windows in the inner loops of the spiral looked down on the outer corridors, allowing defenders to fire down upon their attackers from a sheltered position.

They passed through several gates, each defended by another squadron of the royal guard, before sandstone walls gave way to marble. From there, they moved quickly through a series of courtyards, most empty on this cold winter afternoon, until finally they entered the inner palace.

Erika's heart began to race as she suddenly found herself before the golden doors of the royal court. They stood closed, their precious surface studded with gems and platinum decorations. Of all the passages they had passed, here alone had no thought been given to defence. Grand windows of stained glass turned the light in the corridor to red and green and blue, and not one guard had been left at the entrance to the court.

The queen's steward turned towards her. His face remained carefully schooled, though Erika could read the disdain in his eyes. He thought her a liar, that she had failed once again to claim the powers of the Gods and came now to beg for further clemency. A tingling came from her fingers, as though the gauntlet yearned to be used. She fought the temptation.

"I am ready, steward," she said to his unspoken question.

He spoke no further, only turned and pushed open the golden doors.

The buzz of voices ensued as she followed him into the chamber, though they died away as the queen's steward marched towards the throne. Row upon row of chairs stretched upward in tiers from the chamber floor, packed with the Flumeeren elite. Erika's legs turned to lead as she sensed their eyes upon her, but it was too late to turn back.

She heard her name called through the ringing in her ears. Turning, she saw the steward raising his arm.

"...Archivist to the queen, here with urgent news for the war," he finished, meeting her eyes from across the room. Erika could have sworn his neutral expression broke for half a second, revealing a mocking smile.

A hundred voices erupted from all around, echoing from the domed ceiling high above and ringing across the chamber, almost deafening. Erika felt her legs retreat a step and had to force herself to stand still, to endure. Behind her, the guards who had escorted her this far stood at attention beside the doors, barring her escape.

Steeling herself, Erika ignored the councillors and nobles that surrounded her and stepped up beside the steward. Across the floor of the chamber was a small dais. There were none of the decorations and grandeur of the palace here. The queen sat upon a simple wooden chair, legs crossed and fingers steepled, her emerald eyes on the crowd of nobles above.

Stranger, though, than the woman's plain surroundings, was the full suit of armour Queen Amina had donned. Plain steel covered the woman from her boots to her chest. Only the helm was missing, revealing shining auburn hair and a copper circlet upon her brow. The queen was only thirty-five, barely ten years her senior, but she carried herself with a poise Erika could only imagine. She wore a longsword at her side, and the crimson scar on her left cheek proved she knew how to use it. Indeed, she was not hailed as a warrior queen for nothing.

The sight of the queen in steel gave Erika pause. Amina only wore her armour during times of war. Had something changed on the frontier while she'd been away? Erika's heart quickened. If the Tangata had firmed their hold on northern Calafe, her plans to visit the ancient site were already doomed. But it was too late to change tactics now.

"Your Majesty," she said over the cacophony of voices in the chamber. "I bring a message of hope."

"My Archivist," the queen murmured. Eyes as hard as gemstones regarded Erika from across the room. "Pray, tell me you have brought more than just hopeful words."

"Of course!" Erika exclaimed, her voice rising to an undignified tone. She swallowed, regaining control of herself before going on. "I would not have returned so quickly had my quest not found success."

The queen seemed to consider her words. Then her eyes flickered, as though searching for someone else on the chamber floor. Her lips tightened to a frown. "Then where are the good assistants I sent with you?"

Erika hesitated. "I…" She bowed her head. "Alas, the noble Ibran fell," she replied. "And Sythe…was a traitor."

The room erupted at her words, the entire court of two hundred nobles leaping to their feet and shouting their disdain. Erika flinched at the discordance, but did not look away from the queen. The woman had not reacted to the news, though now she slowly came to her feet and raised a hand. Silence fell. Not even the nobles of Flumeer wanted to risk the queen's displeasure.

"A traitor?" she murmured.

"Yes, Your Majesty," Erika replied, bowing her head. "He killed Ibran, and tried to claim the treasure we discovered beneath the earth. For the King of Gemaho."

This time not one of the nobles said a word, though the revelation was even more scandalous than her earlier news. The queen was still on her feet.

"I see," the woman murmured, eyes fixed on Erika. "Yet you escaped?"

Erika swallowed, hearing the accusation in her voice, and drew herself up. "I did," she said. "I was determined to keep our discovery from the hands of the Gemahan."

"And what did you discover down there in the dark, Archivist?"

"A map, Your Majesty!" Erika replied, drawing the scroll from her pocket. The queen's brows lifted into her auburn locks. Swallowing, Erika quickly went on: "It compiles the ancient sites of the Gods, many yet undiscovered, untouched since the time before The Fall. It was discovered in a sealed room. I believe these other sites might be the same. If so, the treasures within, the magics…this is what the King of Gemaho wanted!" She finished in a rush, cheeks warm, heart racing in her excitement.

The queen did not move from where she stood. She regarded Erika in silence, one eyebrow still raised, iron arms folded across her chest.

"A map?" she said at last. Her voice did not share Erika's excitement. She lowered herself down into the wooden chair. "And where are these sites with their precious treasures?"

"Calafe!" Erika gasped. "In the northern region, there is a site just a few days south of the Illmoor. If we move quickly, I could recover its secrets with a single regiment. Just think, Your Majesty, the power that waits, enough to conquer nations, to destroy the Tangata for good!"

"I see," the queen murmured, tapping idly at the wooden arms of her chair. "Was that not what you promised before this latest venture?"

"I…" Erika trailed off, the words lodging in her throat.

"A venture which cost two persons of some prestige," the queen went on, her voice cold enough to send shivers down Erika's spine. "And now…now you ask for an entire *regiment?* Do you not realise, child, that the Tangata sit on our very *doorstep?*"

Murmurs spread around the hall, though this time the nobles did not seem angry. They could sense the blood in the water, the rage lurking beneath the queen's measured voice. So instead they watched, waiting for the kill.

"The map was not all I found!" Erika shrieked.

Why had she not mentioned the gauntlet first? Because...because it was *hers.* Her secret, her weapon, the only thing that had kept her alive down there in the darkness. She didn't *want* to share this discovery with the queen. Yet neither could she allow the murmuring around the chamber to continue, to allow herself to be condemned.

"Oh?" the queen asked. She made no effort to conceal the scepticism in her voice.

"Does Your Majesty still keep any of the Tangata captive here in the citadel?" Erika asked, struggling to hide the tremor in her voice.

Images flashed through her mind, of bronzed faces behind bars, of awful screams, of eyes dripping with hatred and rage.

"There is one that survives," Queen Amina replied.

"Bring it," Erika ordered, attempting to project confidence, before adding: "Should it please Your Majesty."

The queen regarded her for a long moment. Then the hint of a smile touched the queen's lips and she nodded. The two guards stationed at the doors turned and vanished into the corridor, presumably to retrieve the captive Tangata.

Sweat dripped down Erika's brow as she stood watching those golden doors, feeling the eyes of the entire court upon her. A lump lodged in her throat and she squeezed her fist tight.

What was she doing? Would the gauntlet even work on one of the Tangata? Could she even *make* it work? She still had not practiced with that ability…

Hinges squeaked as the doors swung open again, admitting the guards back onto the chamber floor. But they were no longer alone. A third figure stood between them, arms and legs chained, face streaked with filth, clothes in tatters.

Grey eyes staring.

Erika shivered as she looked into those eyes and saw… nothing. A frown touched her forehead. When she'd last been in the capital, the queen had paraded the creatures regularly before the court. Then, the rage that lurked within these creatures had been obvious, their hatred a raw, animalistic thing. But with this creature…its eyes showed only emptiness, only defeat.

"Well, Archivist?"

Erika swallowed, glancing back at the queen. Drawing in a lungful of air, she raised her gauntleted fist. "I found this in the ruins of the Gods," she said softly.

"A glove?" the queen murmured archly.

"No," Erika said shortly. She turned her back on the queen and faced the wretched Tangata. "My Queen, let me show you the power of the Gods."

She didn't wait for permission. Stepping up before the beast, she lifted the gauntlet. The Tangata's head bobbed at the movement, its eyes slowly coming into focus, fixing on her. It made no move to attack, though the guards held its chains tight all the same. Erika hesitated, sensing the beast's despair.

Whispers spread around the room as the moment stretched out. Erika could sense her audience's impatience. She had promised them magic; if she failed now…

Erika opened her fist and pointed her palm at the Tangata.

The screams began.

The beast took long minutes to die. By the time it fell silent, not a soul in the throne room moved. A terrible silence hung over the chamber as Erika stood over the Tangata, looking down at its tormented face. Blood stained its cheeks and turned its eyes red. It had died in agony.

It was a monster. It would have killed you if it could have.

Releasing a breath she hadn't realised she'd been holding, she turned to face the queen. Steel rattled as the royal guards moved between them. They were wary of her now, frightened by the power she had revealed, but the queen waved them back. Rising, she stepped from the dais and moved to stand before Erika.

"You have done well, Archivist," the queen said. Then she held out her hand. "Give it to me."

Erika swallowed, but met the woman's eyes. "Alas, My Queen, I cannot. The gauntlet has fused to my flesh. Its power is a part of me now. But…grant me my request, and I will find you more objects of power, perhaps even greater than this one."

The queen stared at her for a long while, but finally she nodded, and a smile touched her lips. "Very well," she murmured. "You have done well, Archivist. You will have your regiment."

Erika's heart was thundering in her ears and she hardly heard the queen's words. She felt suddenly drained, as though she had just sprinted the length of the city. Was that the gauntlet, or simply the rush of the moment? Hardly knowing how to react, she bowed her head in acceptance.

"You will leave with the dawn," the queen continued. With that she turned and returned to the dais. Only when she reached her throne did she hesitate. Slowly, the woman turned to face Erika once more. "And Archivist?"

"Yes, Your Majesty?" Erika asked, her head jerking up.

"This will be your last expedition," the queen said. Her eyes narrowed. "Do not fail me, or one way or another, I will have that magic."

The ice in her words left Erika in no doubt as to how she would claim it.

THE WARRIOR

Romaine's breath puffed in the cold morning air as he jogged along the earthen rampart, chainmail jingling with each tread of his heavy boots. An ache had taken hold in the small of his back, and at times it seemed his knees were one bad day away from giving in. He didn't know exactly what day his age had caught him. It was like an assassin, creeping up slowly, until suddenly it stood before him with knife in hand.

Gritting his teeth, Romaine pressed on. Weakness meant death out here, and he refused to surrender to its call. Finally he found himself back where he had started and drew to a stop, panting softly in the dawn light.

"Why do you run?"

He spun at the voice and cursed. Cara sat on a nearby water barrel, those strange amber eyes watching him through the morning mists. The general had provided her with lodging on Romaine's request. He'd seen enough of his people homeless without adding another to their number. But what was she doing atop the palisade?

"Sorry?" he asked, straightening and forcing his breathing to slow.

A smile touched the woman's lips as she came smoothly to her feet. Her broken arm hung from a sling, but otherwise she seemed fully recovered from the trauma of a few days past. Hugging the heavy furs tight around herself, she wandered over to where he stood.

"The running," she said. "It hurts you."

Romaine stared at the woman for a long moment, then shrugged. "The Tangata do not care about my pain. I cannot afford to be slow. So I run."

Cara nodded as though he had confirmed some secret suspicion of hers. Her eyes flickered out over the rooftops of the city. The streets remained silent, though soon soldiers would rise to begin their days.

The thump of jogging boots approached and Romaine turned to watch Lukys stagger to a stop beside the water barrel. Gasping, he bent in two, and Romaine chuckled. Truthfully, he was impressed the young man had managed to keep pace as long as he had. The overland march from Mildeth had at least put a little muscle on the Perfugian recruit.

"Cara!" Lukys suddenly burst out, finally noticing the woman. He straightened immediately. "What are you doing here?"

"What, afraid of practicing the spear with an audience, lad?"

"An audience…" Lukys murmured, thick eyebrows knitting together in a frown. "Wait, we're going to practice the spear today?"

The day before Romaine had only taken Lukys through exercises to help build his strength and stamina. But such exercises did little to dislodge the despair in Lukys's eyes. He needed something to restore his confidence, or training the man was a lost cause.

Grinning, Romaine nodded to where two practice staves leaned against the stockade crenulations. "The spear is not my weapon of choice, but it's better than most when facing the Tangata."

"It's…awkward," Lukys said, picking up one of the staves and holding it before him. "Like it's too long for my arms."

"You'll be thankful for that reach when next you encounter the Tangata," Romaine replied, claiming the second stave.

He faced Lukys across the earthen rampart and adopted the basic fighting stance for the spear. Meanwhile, Cara sat herself on the water barrel and pulled her knees up to her chest to watch. A brilliant orange light shone from the horizon and the mist was beginning to lift. They were alone atop the wall but for a few guards, and they mostly kept to their own sections. Voices carried up from the streets of Fogmore as the first citizens rose to greet the day. The faint scent of burning wood carried on the air.

"So," Romaine said, "show me your best strike, lad."

Raising his stave, Lukys bit his lip. His eyes looked Romaine up and down and the warrior smiled. The lad was right to be cautious, but hesitation could prove costly against the Tangata. So with a roar, Romaine took the initiative, his practice spear thrusting out for the recruit's chest. Lukys's eyes widened and he stumbled on the slick mud, unable to move fast enough to avoid the blow. A soft *thump* followed as the wooden stave struck him in the chest, followed by a crash as Lukys tumbled to the ground.

"Stop hesitating," Romaine said, setting the butt of his

stave to the earth and offering the recruit a hand. "The Tangata won't wait for you to make up your mind."

"Sorry," Lukys muttered, accepting Romaine's assistance.

He gathered his stave with a groan, lifting it slowly, as though in great pain. Romaine sighed and was about to offer a break when Lukys lunged forward with his weapon. Taken off-guard, Romaine struggled to get his own practice spear into position. Wood clacked upon wood, but he failed to completely deflect the strike. The stave connected with his shoulder, forcing a grunt from the axeman.

Stepping back, he brought his weapon around, prepared to fend off another strike from the recruit. But Lukys did not follow up. Instead, he stood staring at his weapon, as though surprised by what he'd done. Romaine grinned.

"Well done, lad," he laughed. "We might just make a soldier of you yet!"

Lukys looked up from the spear. "I…sorry! I thought you would stop it!"

Romaine only shook his head, still grinning, until laughter came from nearby. Glancing around, he saw Cara's eyes dancing with mirth.

"You're getting slow," she said. "I am not sure the running is working."

The grin slipped from Romaine's lips. "Even the greatest of warriors can be taken by surprise," he said, scowling. "Now, are you going to let us practice?"

Cara nodded quickly, moving her finger across her lips in a strange gesture. Shaking his head, Romaine faced Lukys once more.

"That was good," he said again, ignoring the eyes on his back, "but you almost overbalanced on the strike."

"What do you mean?" Lukys asked, running his fingers over the stave.

Romaine gestured him forward. "Try that again, I'll show you."

Lukys nodded—then thrust out with the makeshift spear. This time Romaine was ready for the strike and he twisted easily from the path of the blow. Then he swung out with his spare hand, snatching at the wooden staff and dragging it forward. Lukys cried out. His attack had thrown his centre of balance forward, and now Romaine dragged him beyond the tipping point. He struck the ground with a *thump*.

"*That* is what I meant," Romaine said.

Grumbling, Lukys picked himself up off the ground. Brushing the mud from his clothing, he flashed a glare at Cara, though the woman remained silent this time. She only raised her eyebrows at Lukys. Scowling, he turned back to Romaine.

"What am I doing wrong?" he gasped, his frustration clear.

"Patience, lad," Romaine responded, stepping forward and patting the man's shoulder. "It's only a matter of balance."

"Oh yes, *only*," Lukys replied with a scowl.

Romaine chuckled. "You seem upset."

The recruit shook his head. "If you hadn't noticed, I tend to fall down occasionally."

A snicker of laughter came from behind them and Lukys's cheeks reddened.

"You think balance is a talent you lack?" Romaine asked, pointedly ignoring Cara.

"Isn't it?"

"For some it comes naturally," Romaine admitted. He

shifted so he was standing up straight, feet directly beneath him. "But not everyone is so lucky. Here, try to push me over."

Lukys looked him up and down, obviously expecting some trick. Tossing the stave aside, Romaine spread his arms, indicating he was defenceless. Even so, Lukys approached cautiously. Romaine could hardly blame the lad —he had some fifty pounds on the young recruit.

Suddenly Lukys darted forward, palms connecting hard into Romaine's chest. With his legs directly beneath him, Romaine was unable to brace for the blow. He toppled backwards, feet staggering in search of purchase but unable to find it, and went down like a sack of bricks.

Stumbling to a stop, Lukys gaped down at him, open horror on his face. "I'm so sorry," he gasped.

Grunting, Romaine picked himself up off the ground. Sensing the nervousness in the young man, he took a moment to calmly brush the mud from his clothes. Then he darted at Lukys in a sudden rush.

"Argh!" Lukys shrieked, leaping back, arms raised, face going white with terror.

Romaine threw back his head and laughed, bellowing his mirth out across the town. He would never admit it, but he hadn't had this much fun in a long time. Fighting, slaying Tangata, marching through the open wilderness, practicing with the blade, that was one thing. But by the Gods, he'd missed this, the camaraderie of the army. Why had he avoided others for so long…

A pale face, blue eyes, staring up from a bed of white.

The laughter left him. Letting out a sigh, he nodded to Lukys, who still looked like he half-expected Romaine to throttle him.

"Sorry, lad," he said, adopting a serious tone. "A joke.

But you see now? Even a big man like me can be knocked down by a smaller foe if he adopts the wrong stance." As he spoke, he moved his legs so that they were shoulder width apart, left foot slightly ahead, right slightly behind. "Now," he murmured, "try again."

Lukys narrowed his eyes. The laughter had angered him, but he was cautious now of a trap. His chest swelled as he drew in a breath, then he leapt. Romaine did nothing to defend himself, but this time as Lukys connected, he was able to brace. With a grunt the recruit stumbled back, eyes widening as he saw Romaine had barely budged.

"Again," Romaine rumbled.

Hesitation showed in the recruit's eyes, but he obeyed, coming at Romaine in a rush. This time the axeman softened his stance, so that when Lukys struck the blow pushed him back. But with his feet correctly aligned, he simply stepped his left foot back, maintaining balance.

Lukys, meanwhile, had thrown too much of himself into the blow. With Romaine's sudden withdrawal, he found himself overbalancing once more. His arms windmilled and he tumbled forward—

Romaine caught him by the shoulder and set him back upright. "Easy now," he said with a smile. "I can only stand to watch you plant your face in the mud so many times in one day."

Shrugging off Romaine's hand, Lukys shook his head. "What am I doing wrong?" he croaked. He quickly lowered his head, though not before Romaine saw the glint of tears in the young man's eyes. Then he swung around, locking sights on Cara. "I'd like to see you do any better!"

Shocked by the outburst, Romaine took a step back. Across the palisade, a stunned look showed on Cara's face, her eyebrows lifting into her fringe of copper hair. Her mouth opened, as though to shout something back, but after a moment she closed it again. She rose from the barrel and stalked off without another world.

"Well that wasn't very gracious of you," Romaine commented.

Lukys sighed. "Sorry," he murmured, eyes to the ground. "I just...I'm no good at this, Romaine!"

"Lad, you gotta walk before you can run," Romaine replied. "Or in this case, you need to know *why* you fall, before you can figure out how to stay standing up."

"And that means?"

Romaine sighed. "I see this is going to be a long lesson." He gestured to the ground. "Look, a warrior's strength, his balance, his mobility, it all comes from his feet." As he spoke, he shifted so that his legs were rigid and directly beneath him. "A man who stands like this balances all his weight on a narrow base. He cannot move quickly, and is easily toppled." He moved his feet to the basic fighting stance. "But stand like this, and suddenly you're able to brace against an attack, or move easily from offence to defence." He leaned forward then backwards in demonstration, always keeping his feet in the same position.

Frown lines creased Lukys's forehead as he watched. When Romaine finished, he did his best to adopt the same stance. Romaine shifted his feet a little, placing them closer to shoulder width, and then stepped back with a nod.

"This is what we call a forward stance," he said to Lukys's questioning look. "It's how you avoid ending up on your ass in battle."

This time, Lukys didn't seem to notice the gibe. His eyes were on his feet and concentration was etched across his face. Romaine smiled.

"Now, step forward with your right foot. Keep this

stance in mind as you move, so when you place your foot down, you remain in the position." Romaine mimicked the instructions as he spoke, his right boot becoming the forward foot. He waited for Lukys to copy and corrected his stance again before continuing. "Now left foot forward."

They continued in that fashion, advancing and retreating across the palisade to the amused glances of the soldiers on watch. But Romaine did not see Cara's face among them, and he made a mental note to remind Lukys to apologise later. No point in letting animosity grow between those forced to live inside the walls of Fogmore.

"Are you sure this isn't another of your jokes?" Lukys asked suddenly after half an hour of marching up and down in forward stance.

Romaine raised an eyebrow. "Let's see, shall we?"

They were back where they'd left the staves. Romaine swept one into his hands and leapt at the recruit. A yelp tore from Lukys and he jumped back as the wooden tip lanced for his face. The makeshift spear missed him by an inch.

Gasping, Lukys lowered his hands. "What The Fall was that?" he shouted at Romaine.

Romaine grinned. "You didn't fall."

"What?"

He gestured with the baton at Lukys's feet. "You kept your feet in the forward stance."

"I…" Lukys trailed off, looking from the stave to his feet. Realisation dawned in his eyes and a grin split his face. "I did!"

"Good work," Romaine said. Then he tossed his stave to Lukys and swept up the second. "Now, guard up!"

Lukys was still staring at the makeshift spear in his hands when Romaine attacked. This time he didn't move with the same speed, his mind obviously tangled between using the spear and moving his feet, and a muffled *thud* followed as Romaine's stave struck the recruit on the shoulder.

A grunt came from Lukys as he stepped back, losing his stance. Romaine advanced, stave flashing out to prod him in the chest. With a cry, Lukys's feet went out from under him, and he slammed into the packed earth.

Romaine towered over the young man.

"What?" he said, a grin on his lips. "You didn't think you'd become a warrior in just one day, did you?"

❧ 12 ❧

THE ARCHIVIST

Erika's spirits lifted as her horse topped the hill and started down the other side, cutting off her view of Mildeth and its host of refugees. She had spent the night in luxury, bathing in the royal saunas, sleeping in private apartments reserved for the most important of foreign dignitaries. But despite the extravagance and her aspirations to make such an existence her reality, Erika had felt stifled, trapped by the towering walls.

She felt almost excited to be on the road again, setting off towards distant horizons. There was a freedom to this life, especially now that she rode alone. The queen had offered another assistant to help with her work, but after her experience down in the darkness, Erika had declined the offer. There was no telling who she could trust now; better she ride alone and have faith that the magic would defend her.

There was one drawback to this journey—every mile she rode carried her deeper into the frozen south, back towards Calafe and a past she had thought left long behind.

A shiver ran down her spine and Erika forced her mind to her surroundings. The road ran straight from Mildeth along a valley that cut through the rolling hills of lowland Flumeer. The terrain would provide for easy riding the first day, and regular waystations along the Queen's Highway meant she should not need the canvas tent stuffed into her saddlebags.

Which was just as well, for it had always been Sythe who'd set their camp each night.

That would change once she crossed the Illmoor, but then she would have a full regiment of soldiers to perform such menial tasks. The queen had provided her documents to sequester the force from one of the border cities. By Erika's calculations, the journey would require a total of five days in Calafe land—two to reach the site, one to explore the ruins, and another two back. Surely they would encounter no problems with the Tangata in such a short time. Not in the wide, untouched wilderness of Calafe, at least.

In the meantime, riding through the snow-sprinkled farmland of lowland Flumeer was a far sight more pleasant than her prior excursions.

She rode hard through that first day, stopping only occasionally to eat or walk her horse. The road was well-used and well-kept, and she encountered plenty of other travellers along the way. Some were farmers with wagons loaded up with wares, others merchants from further afield, though these were fewer now that Calafe had fallen.

Many more, though, were refugees—not from Calafe now, but people of Flumeer. They were obvious from the carts they brought with them, loaded up not with wares for sale, but ordinary goods—tables and chairs and kitchenware, the items of worth they had been able to carry away with them. These were the wealthy of the south, those with the power and resources to leave behind their former lives and set out in search of safer pastures. They were leaving now, before the Tangata came. Those who were left behind would not be so fortunate.

Erika nodded politely to those travellers who offered greetings, but her mind remained in the darkness beneath the earth. Now her discovery was known, there would be those who sought to take it from her. She imagined in each of the strangers the eyes of a killer, waiting to slay her on behalf of a foreign king. Whenever they came close, she would raise her gauntlet, ready to defend herself if necessary.

Only when the sun dropped towards the distant horizon did she start looking for a place to sleep. The road had begun to wind between the hills now, cutting off sight of the way ahead and behind. She continued on, eyes alert for an inn, but unconcerned by the empty land around her. The queen's steward had assured her that inns were in plentiful supply on these southern passages.

A half hour later the first traces of worry began to form in Erika's mind. There were no travellers on the road now and she realised she hadn't seen even a farmhouse for quite some time. The sun was already disappearing beneath the horizon, its glow fading by the minute. Without its heat, the temperature plummeted. Pulling the coat tighter around herself, she kicked her horse into a canter.

It was almost dark when she found herself beside a stream. Alone on the road, she cursed winter and its short days. It seemed there would be no feathered bed for her tonight. Out of options, she dismounted and led the mare from the road. At least the creek would provide fresh water.

Directing her horse upstream, she walked a hundred

yards through a neighbouring field, until the curve of a hill hid her from the road. If she was going to camp alone in the open, she didn't want her presence known to every rogue and bandit in the area.

She found an old willow tree overhanging a section of riverbank, its twisted limbs stretched far out over the river. Tying her horse's reins to one of its branches, she then rummaged round in her saddlebags and pulled out the canvas tent. Above, the sky was clear, the first twinkling of the northern star just beginning to shine. She hoped that meant it wouldn't snow that night.

The tent was so heavy Erika almost dropped it when she finally dragged it from the saddlebags. Cursing, she stumbled away from the horse to an empty patch of grass and tossed it to the ground. Then she stood staring at the bundle, and for the first time, began to regret not bringing at least a porter. She was unaccustomed to the day-to-day tasks of preparing a camp, and while she'd occasionally watched Sythe...she hadn't really been paying much attention.

"How hard can it be?" she muttered to herself.

An hour and several ropes jerry-rigged to the willow tree later, she finally admitted to herself that pitching a tent was perhaps slightly more difficult than she'd thought. Nearby, her horse snickered and she rolled her eyes. The tent looked like a strong breeze might knock it down, but with only the light of a half-moon for guidance, it was as good as it was going to get. She would have to pray the night remained clear.

Returning to her horse, she struggled to remove its saddle then threw a blanket over its back. By the time she was done her teeth were chattering and her fingers so numb it hurt to move them. Clenching her fist, she sighed as warmth ignited in the gauntlet.

Only then did she recall Sythe had usually lit the fire *before* it grew dark.

Swearing, she fumbled at the saddlebags for tinder and flint. Thankfully there were plenty of fallen branches beneath the willow, and with little rain the last few days, they were mostly dry. She knelt and gathered the twigs into a pile, the tinder at the centre. Then she took up the flint and struck it towards the wood…

…and cursed as she struck her hand instead. The stone tumbled from her fingers as she leapt to her feet, cursing loud enough to wake the ancients. The cold only seemed to make the pain worse, and she balled her uninjured hand into a fist, wishing in that moment for an enemy she could take her anger out upon—

"Looks like you could use a hand."

Erika's heart twisted in her chest as a woman's voice spoke from the darkness. Pain forgotten, she lurched to her feet and swung around, gauntlet raised as she searched for the speaker. But whoever it was, they stood just out of line of sight—which wasn't far, admittedly, with only the half-moon for light.

"Who's there?" she hissed. "Show yourself!"

"Easy, Archivist," came the response. "I mean you no harm."

The breath caught in Erika's throat. Whoever the woman was, she knew who Erika was. That meant…

A soft glow emerged from the gauntlet, not enough to illuminate her foe, but it gave her reassurance.

"I said, *show yourself*," she hissed.

The woman laughed in response. "Of course," she said, "just as soon as you promise I will come to no harm."

Erika swung her arm backward and forward, but if the gauntlet was working, its range must be limited. There was no choice. She lowered her hand—it would still be a simple thing to strike the woman down should she prove dangerous.

"Thank you, Archivist." Shadows shifted in the night as a woman stepped forward, hands raised. "I left my weapons near the road," she said quietly, "as I said, I mean no harm."

"That has yet to be seen," Erika replied, eyes narrowed.

Swathed in a black cloak and heavy winter clothes, little could be seen of the speaker but her face. Erika lifted her fist higher, and the glow of her gauntlet illuminated wide, circular eyes and a narrow jaw. The woman's lips pursed and Erika didn't miss how her gaze lingered on the magic. She allowed herself a smile.

"Why are you here?" she asked again. "How do you know who I am?"

"All in good time," the stranger said, lowering her hands before nodding to Erika's stack of wood. "I find winter nights to be more comfortable with a fire. May I?"

Erika hesitated, wondering whether this was some elaborate trick to lower her guard. But if so, she could not see how it could be sprung, not with the gauntlet in her control. She gave a curt nod.

Smiling, the stranger crossed to the woodpile and began moving some of the branches around. Then she took up the flint and struck it twice into the kindling. The sparks caught with a tiny *whoosh*. Leaning close, she blew softly into the flames. Within minutes there was a small blaze burning.

The stranger paused, eyes lingering on something off to the side. Despite herself, Erika's cheeks grew warm as she realised the woman was looking at her tent. She raised an eyebrow, amusement showing on her twisted lips.

"Don't think I can help with that one," she chuckled.

"Enough," Erika snapped, using anger to cover her embarrassment. She pointed her gauntlet at the woman. Though her fist remained closed, the death magic dormant, she was pleased to see the self-assured smile leave the stranger's face.

"I asked you some questions," she said dangerously.

"So you did," the stranger said, straightening beside the fire. Erika flinched, but the woman only held her hands out to the flames. "What a creation, fire," she murmured. "Man's earliest, most important tool, the beginnings of all civilisation." She glanced at Erika. "And the end of many too."

Erika swallowed, looking from the woman to the flames, wondering if she was making a threat. But her visitor made no move towards her, and finally Erika shook her head.

"What nonsense are you spouting?"

"My master believes the secrets of the Gods could be the gateway to a new era," her mysterious visitor replied, "one without poverty or illness." She turned towards Erika, eyes aglow in the light of the fire. "But in the wrong hands…those secrets could destroy us."

"*This* magic deals only in death," Erika snarled. "If your master wants it, tell him to come and face me himself."

The stranger seemed amused at that. "My master is not interested in trinkets," she replied. "Your map, however, is of far greater interest."

Erika's heart beat faster and unconsciously she reached for the scroll in her inner pocket. No copies had been made —the risk was too great, after the attack beneath the earth.

She narrowed her eyes. "You were sent by the King of Gemaho."

"I was."

"He tried to kill me."

"An unfortunate misunderstanding," the stranger replied. "That was never his intention. He values the work of those rare souls who seek the truth. Your knowledge of the Gods and the ancients who once worked alongside them is irreplaceable. Your death would have been a terrible tragedy to his royal personage."

"I'm sure," Erika said shortly.

"Regardless of such miscommunications, I have been sent in peace, to heal the rift this unfortunate…accident, has opened between us."

"And why should I trust anything you say?" Erika hissed.

"Perhaps you should not," the woman said, extending her hands towards the flames. "It is up to us to prove our worth to you. That is why I was sent, to aid you in your journey."

"And rob me of my prize, should I succeed, no doubt."

"No," the stranger said, standing. "My king offers equal partnership."

Erika sneered. "I already have a partnership—with a monarch who has *not* tried to kill me."

"Not yet," her visitor replied softly, "though she came close, did she not?"

"I…" Erika trailed off, recalling that moment in court, the look in the queen's eyes. Doubt touched her, before anger swept it away. "Enough!" she snarled. "The queen is my ally, has granted me supplies and an army to ensure my success. I need no aid from the cowards of Gemaho."

"The world calls us cowards," the woman murmured, looking out into the dark, "but perhaps we are the only ones who have not been fooled." She shook herself, glancing back at Erika. "I will not fault you for your loyalty, Archivist, though it is misplaced."

"The queen has given me power, lifted me up to the highest of honours."

"Honours which can be easily taken away, should you fail." The woman's eyes bored into hers.

"*Enough*," Erika hissed, lifting her gauntlet. "I am tired of your lies. Tell your king to stay away. I want no part of your kingdom of traitors."

"Very well," the woman replied. She bowed her head, as though Erika's words had wounded her. Turning, she made to go, before glancing back. "But know this: our people are never far. Should the time come and you reconsider our offer, remember my words. In our king, you will always have a friend."

Then she was gone, disappearing into the night as though she had never been.

Erika stood standing beside the fire for a long time, staring at the place where the woman had stood. Her words rang in her ears. Now that she was gone, Erika could no longer deny their truth, could no longer hide from the doubt they had inspired. *Had* she given her loyalty to the wrong person?

No.

She could not trust a king whose assassin had tried to kill her just a week before. Shaking herself, she sat and added a log to the fire.

For the rest of the night though, she did not sleep, and when the sun rose it found her already on the road. For every night after that, she was sure to find an inn long before sunset.

❧ 13 ❧

THE RECRUIT

Light grew on the horizon as Lukys jogged his way around the earthen palisade. His shoulders ached, seeming to jar with each step, though at least he no longer carried the heavy pack. It had snowed again in the night, and while burning barrels atop the ramparts kept the snow from gathering there, the ground remained frozen beneath his boots.

He kept on despite the difficult conditions, eager today to beat the axeman at his own game. Lukys had slept the night in his clothing and risen early, leaving the barracks in silence to avoid further confrontation with Dale. Now he hoped to complete his loop of the city before Romaine arrived.

The run took him past several ranks of soldiers on guard. Each looked up at his approach, but upon seeing the blue colours of Perfugia, they quickly resumed whatever tasks he'd interrupted. The sight took some of the breath from Lukys. He would show them his worth eventually; for now, he could do little but accept their disdain.

Sunlight set the Mountains of the Gods aflame as he turned the final bend and approached his meeting point with Romaine. The Calafe warrior was only now striding up the steps, a bundle of practice spears carried over one shoulder. Lukys picked up his pace so that they both arrived at the same time.

Coming to a stop before the warrior, he sucked in a lungful of air and stood straight, doing his best to pretend the run had not tired him. Below, life began to stir in the town as its citizens stepped into the frosted streets.

"Early today?" Romaine asked, one eyebrow raised.

There was no sign of Cara. Lukys felt a twang in his chest. He shouldn't have driven her away, but there had been something uncomfortable about the way she watched him, and her laughter…her laughter had made him feel a fool.

Which he was.

Shaking his head, Lukys resolved to find her and apologise later. In the meantime, he offered Romaine a salute.

"Bright and early, sir." After his mortification at knocking Romaine to the ground the day before, he had decided to treat the warrior with the respect owed one of his professors back in the academy.

A scowl darkened the warrior's face. "Enough of that," he rumbled, tossing Lukys one of the practice spears. "I'm no blasted Flumeeren officer."

"I…" Lukys stammered, his cheeks going red. So much for showing respect. "Sorry…"

Romaine only grunted and hefted the spear. Before Lukys could ready himself, though, the sound of pounding hooves came from below. He turned back to the town and watched as mounted men in Flumeeren uniforms appeared, riding in the direction of the river. Each was garbed in full plate mail and carried shield and lance, armed for war.

Heart suddenly pounding in his chest, Lukys swung towards the river. The mist had melted away with the morning light and the waters were clear, the mudflats between the city and the banks empty of movement.

"Looks like the general's resuming the morning patrols. It's usually a half-regiment, different men each day. They'll cover twenty miles before returning," the warrior said in answer. "Dangerous after that attack. The creatures could be setting an ambush. But suppose it's necessary, to keep them from gaining a foothold our side of the river. And looks as though he's given them some reinforcement."

Lukys watched in silence as the wooden gates swung open and the riders spilled out onto the mudflats. There were at least fifty, a full regiment. More than enough to handle any stragglers that might still be in the area, even a Tangata pair, should they risk a crossing. Even so, Lukys did not envy them the task of facing down one of the creatures in the open.

Turning his back on the departing soldiers, Romaine hefted his spear. "Ready?"

"What? I—"

Romaine lunged before Lukys could finish. He leapt back, bringing up his spear in a rough estimate of the low block Romaine had shown him the day before. The wooden poles came together with sharp *clack*.

"Your stance," Romaine growled, continuing the attack.

Blocking again, Lukys forced himself to be mindful of his feet, of moving through the stances Romaine had demonstrated. He was surprised when he stayed upright, though he knew the Calafe warrior was taking things slow. It seemed the drills were working—he had practiced them during his free time after the last lesson, eager to prove to Romaine he was worth the time.

"You're getting better."

Lukys stumbled as Cara's voice came from behind him. He started to turn, only to receive a solid blow to the hip. Air hissed between his teeth as he staggered back, gasping curses.

"…wasn't ready!"

"In battle, a warrior cannot afford to be distracted," Romaine replied, though he wore a grin. Stepping past Lukys, he nodded to Cara. "Welcome back, lass."

Cara snorted as she walked past, amber eyes fixing on Lukys. He swallowed and dropped his gaze. "Sorry, about yesterday," he said quickly.

Sorry, sorry, sorry.

When she did not reply, Lukys lifted his head, expecting to find anger on her face. Instead, she smiled. "That's okay," she said slightly, gesturing with her bandaged arm. "I shouldn't have laughed; I don't know how to use a spear either."

"Really?" Romaine murmured. He seemed surprised. "Your…parents didn't teach you?"

Cara shrugged. "How to defend myself, sure. Just…not with weapons," she hesitated, looking up at Romaine from beneath her lashes. "Would you teach me as well?"

The question seemed to give Romaine pause. Lukys looked from one to the other, then blurted out the obvious: "But your arm!"

"My arm?" Cara glanced down at the offending limb, as though surprised to find it was still there. "Oh, right, well, I'm ambidextrous!"

"Ambi…what?" Romaine asked.

"It means she's comfortable using either hand," Lukys

explained, frowning. It seemed there was more to Cara than met the eye. He looked to the Calafe warrior. "But still…she can't—"

"Why not?" Cara interrupted. "Afraid of getting beat by a girl?"

Lukys's cheeks grew warm, though it wasn't that. Having the guards watch his ineptness was bad enough, he actually *liked* Cara. He didn't want to appear a fool in front of her, at least, any more than he already had. But unable to say as much, he only shook his head.

"No," he muttered, "but your broken bone, it needs rest to heal."

"Not to worry." A smile brightened Cara's face as she lifted the injured arm and waved it. "I had a good medic. Feels fine to me."

A long pause stretched out as Romaine and Lukys watched her, and finally she rolled her eyes. "I only need the one hand to wield a spear," she insisted. "The other is meant to be for a shield anyway."

"Fine," Romaine surrendered finally.

Lukys supressed a groan as the Calafe gestured for Cara to collect the spare stave. Pushing aside the emotion, he tried to focus on the bright side. At least he was no longer alone. And Cara said she hadn't practiced with weapons before. Perhaps she would be just as embarrassed as him—

"Lukys, *high block*," Romaine bellowed suddenly.

Flinching, Lukys tried to bring up his practice spear, but he'd been holding it awkwardly and the wooden stave caught between his legs as he retreated. Before he could stop himself, he was slamming into the ground. A groan slipped from his lips as he looked up from a puddle of mud.

"Did I at least get the stance right?"

Chuckling, Romaine offered his hand and pulled Lukys

back to his feet. "As you've already seen," he said, addressing Cara, "Lukys here still has a lot to learn. Why don't you two pair off."

Steeling himself, Lukys glanced at Cara, but for once she kept the smile from her face, though he still imagined he could hear her laughter, whispering in his ears. He shook his head, dismissing his embarrassment. Cara was just as much a beginner as he was…

Lukys narrowed his eyes, watching Cara as she approached. For the first time he noticed how smoothly she moved, her feet shifting naturally through the stances he had so struggled with the day before, body in constant balance. The breath caught in his throat as he saw the smile tugging at her lips.

"Again, Lukys, high block!" Romaine called, but Lukys hesitated.

"Romaine, I—"

The stave in Cara's left hand seemed to come alive, leaping for his face, and with a cry Lukys shoved his own spear upwards, barely deflecting the blow. He staggered back, struggling to recover his stance, but Cara still came on. The stave flicked out again and this time Lukys couldn't get his weapon up in time. A blow struck him in the shoulder, then chest, forcing him backwards.

Witch!

Though the blows stung, somehow Lukys managed to keep his feet. Enraged, he grabbed his stave in both hands and struck back, using the only attack Romaine had taught him. The practice spear thrust out, aimed at Cara's chest. At the last moment she twisted and the point of his stave slipped beneath her arm, missing its mark.

Faster than thought, Cara dropped her own weapon and grasped his. Lukys cried out as the stave was yanked from his grasp. The scream died on his lips as Cara spun his weapon, the tip flashing up…and coming to a stop just inches from his face.

A smile touched Cara's lips as she lowered the stave, and Romaine's laughter rumbled across the rampart. Lukys's cheeks grew warm and he swung away. A hand on his shoulder stopped him.

"Lukys," Cara called him back. "I'm sorry."

Cursing inwardly, Lukys drew in a breath and faced her. She still smiled, but he could see the apology in her eyes. He sighed and smiled despite himself.

"That's okay," he replied.

Stones crunched as Romaine approached. "Every child of Calafe learns to fight at a young age," he explained.

"I…" Cara started, before nodding. "Yeah."

"Though in this case, it seems young Cara wasn't entirely lying," Romaine added. "Those blows wouldn't have been much good with a spear."

Red creeped into Cara's pale cheeks at the warrior's words, and chuckling, Romaine went on. "Shall we see what I can teach the two of you then?"

So they continued for the rest of the morning, running through stances, spear thrusts, and blocks. The broken arm didn't seem to bother Cara much, and she needed no help with her balance, but using the stave like a spear seemed to give her more problems. Lukys, meanwhile, found himself growing increasingly frustrated about the repetition. Still, there was method to Romaine's madness, and as the morning progressed, Lukys found that the moves began to come more easily. Where before he had to think about each step, now the movements became instinctive, natural.

By the time Romaine dismissed them at noon, Lukys had collected a fresh assortment of bruises, but at least he was finally making progress. He wandered through the town, making for the northern gates. The Perfugian regiment had been assigned to the quarry just outside the city, breaking down shale rock into gravels that could be laid on the streets and ramparts of Fogmore to reduce the incessant mud that followed every rain and snowfall. While Lukys had been granted consent to train with Romaine in the mornings, he was meant to join them by noon.

The sound of steel slamming against rock carried down to Lukys and he belatedly picked up his pace, embarrassed that others were working while he was not. Perfugians did not skirt their duties, however much they might loathe their superiors.

As he drew close, Lukys saw the exposed stone was of a deep red. Pickaxes in hand, the other recruits were already working at the rockface. Or at least keeping up the pretence of work. A quick glance at their barrows showed little progress had been made in the hours they'd already been there.

Not that their overseers cared. The general certainly hadn't chosen his best to care for the Perfugian recruits. The three Flumeerens assigned to watch them had set a table in the shadow of the cliff and appeared to be busy playing cards. As Lukys watched, one even took a swig from a silver flask.

At least they didn't seem to notice his late arrival. Taking a pickaxe and barrow from the pile, he moved to join the others.

"Peasant!" Lukys flinched as a shout came from amongst the recruits on the other side of the quarry. He lowered his head and pulled back his axe to swing at the wall, but the voice came again. "Finally decided to join us, have you?"

Stones crunched as someone approached. Lukys's eyes flickered closed and he released the breath he'd been holding. It seemed there would be no avoiding this confrontation.

"Dale," he murmured, turning to face the recruit. "What do you want?"

"Who do you think you are, peasant?" Dale snarled as he came to a stop in front of Lukys. "Sneaking off, avoiding work. Think you're better than the rest of us, do you?"

"I—"

"You're trash, you hear me?" Dale spat, stepping closer and gesturing with his pickaxe. "You're nobody!"

Lukys reeled back, raising his hands in front of him in a gesture of peace, though the pickaxe he held distracted from the gesture. He was surprised at his fellow's reaction. Dale and his friends had been cold, even cruel, before. Now though…the man's face was pure rage. It shone from his eyes, showed in the veins bulging from his forehead, in the clenching of his jaw. Lukys could not understand it.

"You're right!" he said quickly, eyes on the point of Dale's axe. "I *am* nobody. But Romaine is teaching me to fight." Lukys hesitated, thinking fast. "He could teach you as well."

"I already know how to fight, *peasant*," Dale snapped. "Do I need to show you?" He swung his pickaxe in a lazy arc, forcing Lukys to jump backwards out of range.

He stumbled and almost fell. Anger touched him then and he surged back up…

…just as Dale thrust out with the hilt of his pickaxe. The blow caught Lukys square in his midriff and drove the breath from his lungs. He doubled over, gasping. Laughter sounded in his ears.

The sound cut through the pain like a knife, igniting his

rage. Finally he managed to suck in a breath and forced himself to straighten. Dale stood across from him, hands raised as though to accept the cheers of his friends. The smug smile on his lips begged Lukys to take a swing.

Standing almost six feet tall, Dale towered over Lukys. He stood with his feet directly beneath him, just as Romaine had the day before. Clenching his fists, Lukys charged.

Dale saw the danger just as Lukys's shoulder struck him in the chest. Despite the size difference, momentum was on Lukys's side and the other man went down like a sack of bricks, the pickaxe flying from his hands. Grinning, Lukys stepped back, satisfied he'd taught the larger man a lesson…

"Bastard!" Roaring, Dale staggered to his feet, face purpled with rage.

Lukys flinched, fear suddenly touching him as his foe swept up the pickaxe and started towards him.

"Enough." A man stepped between them, hands raised to either side, as though to hold them back.

For a moment, Lukys thought the overseers had finally intervened. Then he realised the man wore the same uniform as himself, the royal blue of Perfugia. The newcomer looked from Lukys to Dale, hazel eyes hard. Light brown hair hung down to his shoulders and he was well-built, shorter than Dale, but no less muscular. It was another second before Lukys recognised the man as another of the noble born recruits—the one he'd knocked over that first day in the plaza, in fact.

A growl came from Dale but the sight of the newcomer gave him pause.

"Travis?" he said, a frown creasing his forehead. "The Fall are you doing?" He tried to shove past, but the recruit held him back.

"I said, that's *enough*, Dale," Travis said, calmly pushing the taller man back.

"The bastard struck me!" Dale spluttered, eyes bulging, teeth bared. He tried to push past Travis again but was rebuffed.

"You insulted him, struck him without warning. You expected the man to roll over?" He waved a hand. "No, never mind. It doesn't matter." Anger shone in his eyes. "Don't you see, Dale? You cling to this belief that we're superior. But look where we are! We all failed, or we wouldn't be in this cursed place." He looked away, seeming to fix on some distant point, beyond the city, beyond the river. "And now that we're here," he continued, his voice suddenly low, "we have greater concerns than your bruised ego."

His words seemed to drain the anger from the other man. For a moment, Dale stood there, hands balled into fists, jaw clenched. Then in a rush he turned away. Lukys let out a breath as he watched the man stalk across the quarry. His heart was pounding in his ears and he was gripping the hilt of his pickaxe so tight his hand had turned white.

Finally he shook himself and turned to his rescuer. The hardness evaporated from Travis's face as their eyes met, replaced by an easy smile. Stepping forward, he offered his hand.

"The name's Travis," he said. "Now, did I hear something about a mighty warrior of Calafe offering to train us?"

❧ 14 ❧

THE WARRIOR

R omaine let out a sigh as he lowered himself onto a boulder and sat back to watch the recruits at their practice. Two weeks had passed since his return from the south, and somehow he now found himself the unofficial instructor for the Perfugians. He now had almost two dozen men and women under his wing; half of the regiments surviving number.

Watching them struggle through the drills he'd set, Romaine tried to keep his face impassive. It was times like these that he was convinced the Gods still watched over humanity, if only to make mischief for their own amusement. How else could he have ended up here, when all he'd wanted was to be alone?

A sigh slipped from his lips and he closed his eyes for a moment, responsibility weighing heavily on his shoulders. When he opened them again, he found Cara standing nearby, one eyebrow raised. He cursed inwardly to have been caught in a moment of frailty, but gestured to join him on the boulder anyway. Their numbers had forced Romaine to move the training to the central plaza, where his activities would be known to all. He was still waiting for the general to come asking after him.

"You're tired," Cara said. An uncharacteristic frown creased her face.

Romaine grunted by way of answer.

"Do you not sleep?" the young woman pressed, frown lines deepening.

"I sleep," Romaine replied, though perhaps that was an exaggeration.

He had taken to sitting atop the walls most evenings, watching the darkness. Waiting was not amongst his talents. He longed to return south, to fight back against the creatures that had stolen his nation, that had taken everything from him.

But while the general had resumed scouting this side of the Illmoor, there had been no more crossings. Fogmore had not even found a new ship capable of making the journey.

Silence fell between them and Romaine turned his gaze back on the recruits. The *clack-clacking* of practice spears rang across the square, drawing the eyes of bystanders, though none had complained so far about the commotion. He'd separated the recruits into two groups to practice drills with shield and spear. One side would attack, running through a series of predetermined movements, while the other matched with the required blocks.

"They seem…slow," Cara said beside him.

Romaine chuckled. "Shouldn't you be out there practicing with them?"

Cara shrugged. She had continued practicing with Lukys at first, but as more and more recruits came asking for Romaine's help, she'd joined them less and less. At least her arm seemed to be healing well. Lukys still changed the bandages regularly, and the last time the bruising had almost vanished.

Silence fell between them again, and shaking his head, Romaine watched as the recruits ran through another drill. Lukys stood in the middle, wielding his spear against a taller man they called Travis. The exercise started with a high stab for the opponent's throat, followed by a spinning riposte, and finally an attacking thrust from the enemy's shield. The two performed the drill well with only minor faults, but even so, Romaine could see Cara was right.

"It's not enough," he murmured, unable to keep the words to himself. "I can't help them. Against ordinary soldiers, with a few more weeks or months, maybe I could make a decent fighting force out of them. But against the Tangata…"

"They *are* getting better," Cara replied, glancing at him. "More than you realise."

As she spoke, a grunt came from nearby as a recruit crashed to the ground. It was one from the attacking group. The thrust of his opponent's shield had caught him in the chin and knocked him off-balance. Romaine let out a sigh.

"You were saying?"

"Maybe you're right," Cara said after a long pause, "maybe you're wrong." A smile lit her face. "But it makes no difference to them. Somehow, you've given them *hope*. Can't you see it in their faces?"

Romaine looked at the Perfugians again, but as the drill continued, more mistakes bled into their exercises. Frustration began to take hold. He sighed.

"I see only fear." He should not have been confessing such things to the woman, but he was in over his head, needed to speak. "Only desperation." He swallowed. "I've heard them, after these sessions, whispering to the Gods, thanking them for sending me." His eyes stung but he forced the words out. "If I have given them hope, it is only a false one."

"All hope is false in the face of desperation," Cara replied. She glanced at Romaine, looking older than her years. "If theirs is a false hope, surely the same must be said for that of humanity. You said it yourself: the Tangata are too fast, too powerful. What hope can there be for your victory?"

Romaine swallowed, but caught in her amber gaze, found he did not have the words to reply. Cara spoke into the silence:

"Yes, they're afraid," she murmured, "and desperate. They know there'll be no ground given in the war to come. And so they learn."

A shudder ran down Romaine's spine as Cara fell silent. They sat together watching the recruits for a while longer, until the ice finally left his veins.

Before the conversation could resume, the sound of approaching hooves rattled from across the plaza. They looked around as a single rider emerged from the main street leading north. It was a fine winter's day and she wore a velvet bodice and slim-cut pants of Flumeeren red rather than furs. Despite her obviously recent arrival, her clothes were untouched by the dirt of the road.

Electric blue eyes swept the square, dismissing the blue-garbed recruits at a glance before continuing towards Romaine. Settling on his green-hued uniform, she heeled her horse towards him. Romaine let out a sigh—he knew a royal courtier when he saw one.

"A Calafe warrior!" the woman exclaimed as she approached. "I did not think any of your kind were left on the front lines."

"Where else would I be, lass?"

The woman's lips twisted in a frown and she scrunched her nose, but did not answer his question. Instead she looked away, eyes fixed on the distance now.

"Where is your general, soldier?" she asked.

Silence had fallen across the plaza at the woman's appearance. Her clothing was of a far better quality than that of any of the citizens still in Fogmore. The rich had fled long ago, packing up their possessions and heading north to escape the coming war. Even without the expensive clothing, her long golden hair and bronzed skin was something of an anomaly amongst the Flumeeren and Perfugian soldiers. They spoke of southern heritage, an oddity in itself given the woman's apparent standing in the Flumeeren court.

When Romaine's reply was not quick in coming, the woman swung back to face him. "I asked you a question," she said curtly.

"Forgive me, lass," Romaine said, taking a step towards the horse, "but who in The Fall are you?"

The woman's mouth fell open at his words, her face turning pale. Romaine only folded his arms and waited. The woman's arrogance probably matched her importance, but not technically being a Flumeeren citizen, he was willing to risk the reprimand. He certainly didn't have the patience to play her games.

"My name is Erika, Archivist to the crown, sent by Queen Amina herself!" The woman spouted the words as though they meant something to Romaine. "And you will show me some respect, Calafe!"

Romaine stifled a sigh and decided it was best to make the woman someone else's problem as quickly as possible.

"My *deepest* apologies, ma'am," he exclaimed, exaggerating a bow. "I had not heard of your arrival. I am sure General Curtis awaits your company with bated breath."

The woman seemed taken aback by his sudden change in conduct. Her eyes narrowed but after a moment she gave a short nod.

"Very well," she murmured, lifting her nose in a way that suggested she was above the apologies of a mere soldier. "You are forgiven. Now, the general?"

"Last I heard he was surveying our defences on the banks of the Illmoor," he said, gesturing in the direction of the river gates. "You should find him there."

The woman faltered, the colour draining from her cheeks. Romaine suppressed a grin. What was this woman doing on the frontier? He watched as she lifted her left hand and clenched it into a fist, and for the first time noticed she wore a gauntlet, though the metal links were too fine to offer any protection. Stranger still, her right hand was bare.

"Was there not an attack here, just two weeks past?" she asked. To her credit, there was no hint of fear in her voice. "What is the general doing outside the walls of this...city?" She said the final word like she could not quite believe the description.

"The Tangata are unlikely to attack in broad daylight, ma'am," Romaine said, attempting to mimic the woman's haughty air. "And the general is eager to bolster our defences. But your fears are...understandable. Perhaps you would prefer to wait—"

"No." The woman drew herself up and set her eyes on the distant walls. "You will take me to the general, now, Calafe. I cannot afford any further delays."

"Very well, ma'am," he murmured, then turned to the recruits. They had stopped their practice at the woman's arrival. It was time they resumed their duties at the quarry anyway. "Off with ya!" he bellowed, gesturing towards the mountains. "We're done here for the day."

The recruits moved off without further complaint. Lukys and Travis waved their goodbyes, grins on their faces, and Romaine nodded back. When they were finally gone, Romaine let out a sigh. Best he get this over and done with. Turning to the woman, he extended a hand in the direction of the river gates.

"After you, ma'am."

⚜ 15 ⚜

THE ARCHIVIST

Erika dismounted in front of the so-called river gates and cursed as her boot immediately sank to the ankle. The ground before the palisade had been churned to mud by the passage of horses and men—but she still could not understand why these gates were being used at all. The report she'd received in Mildeth spoke of dozens of Tangata attacking in the night. She was no officer, but it seemed beyond foolhardy to risk soldiers beyond the admittedly questionable protection of the palisade.

She glanced at the Calafe warrior that had guided her this far and balled her gauntleted hand into a fist. If this was all some joke…No, the man had been insolent at first, but had been the model of good behaviour since learning of her importance. Though she was tempted to have him fetch the general back...

But no, she would be venturing far beyond the wall before long. Letting out a sigh, she nodded to her guide. At a gesture from the warrior, the guards on the gate leapt to remove the heavy locking bar from its brackets. These wore the red of Flumeer, marking them as true soldiers—unlike the Perfugian rabble she had observed in the plaza. Why their island neighbours bothered to send soldiers at all was beyond her when those were the best they could offer. They might have copied the Gemaho and just sent no one at all.

The gates squealed as they swung open, revealing a plain of churned-up mud leading down to the black waters of the Illmoor. A shiver ran down her spine as her eyes continued on. The day was clear and in the distance she spied a hint of green—the banks of Calafe. Enemy territory.

Home.

She pushed the memory away. Calafe was *not* her home. Mildeth, with its towering walls and spiralling citadel and noble queen, that was home.

Forcing her mind to the present, she walked past the guards and out into the sunlight beyond the palisade. The Calafe warrior fell into step beside her but before they could go far, racing footsteps chased after them. To Erika's surprise, another woman ran from the city to join them.

Erika frowned, her stride faltering. The woman wore green, though it was so dark it could have been black, and like Erika she wore pants rather than a dress. Was this the warrior's daughter? No, their complexions were too different. Though they certainly seemed to know each other.

"What are you doing here, Cara?" the man rumbled.

The woman ignored him, instead offering Erika a broad grin. "Cara," she said. Her accent was soft, unlike the warrior's.

"Erika," she said reluctantly, still studying the woman. One of her arms was in a sling, though even that could be an act.

"Don't mind Romaine, here," Cara said lightly, pointing

a thumb at the Calafe warrior. "He's just tired." She swung back to Erika. "So, what brings you here, Archivist?"

The hackles stood up on the back of Erika's neck at the question and she narrowed her eyes. How did this strange woman know who she was? Could this Cara be another of Gemaho's spies? No. She forced the thought from her mind. The woman had probably just overheard, back in the square.

"I'm afraid that's a sensitive matter," she replied coolly, keeping her eyes fixed straight ahead.

The muddy path was treacherous enough as it was without distraction. She glimpsed movement down near the river and was relieved to see the blue cloaks of her fellow countrymen. So the Calafe hadn't been lying, that was something.

Then her eyes alit on something in the river. A vice closed around her heart as she stared at the blackened ruins sitting just above the water level. Even from a distance, she could see it was clearly a ship. A fresh breeze blew across the mudflats, carrying with it the cloying stench of smoke.

"What happened?" Erika croaked, unable to keep the tremor from her voice. There was no sign of another ship; had they truly been so careless as to lose their only vessel for crossing the Illmoor?

"The attack," the Calafe murmured.

"Poor men," Cara added. "They…were kind to me."

"Where…there is another, surely?"

The Calafe shrugged. "Afraid not."

"But I…" Erika trailed off. There was no point spouting secrets to these two. It was the general she needed. She picked up the pace.

As they neared the river, Erica saw that the soldiers were hard at work driving giant wooden spikes into the mud, the sharpened points directed at the water. They had already covered the entire bank and now seemed to be doubling back to add more.

Scanning the ranks of mud-stained men, Erika searched for the general. The men at work did not wear their helmets, though a group standing off to the side looked ready for war. They would be the lookouts. No doubt she would find the general there. Erika started towards them, but a call from the Calafe drew her back.

"Where you are going, lass?" he called, falling back into his informal manner.

"I can find my way from here, Calafe," she called over her shoulder, continuing towards the group of men.

"Glad to hear it," the man's voice chased after her, "since you're heading the wrong way."

Erika came to a stop. "What?" She glared back at him.

The Calafe wore a broad grin as he turned towards the working men. "General Curtis, messenger from the queen for you."

Amidst those working, one straightened with a groan and looked around. Mud covered his face and clothing, though on closer inspection Erika saw this man was older than the others. Grey hair shone through the grime and frown lines marked his forehead. Otherwise, there was nothing to suggest this could be the legendary General Curtis, veteran of a dozen campaigns and hero of Flumeer.

Anger touched Erika as she realised her mistake in trusting this Calafe. A general of such repute would not be here, digging in the dirt. She swung on Romaine and raised her fist, readying herself to release the magic. She would *not* be made a fool of!

"Romaine!" a voice called from the mud. She looked around as the older man strode towards them. "I heard you were busy wasting your time with the Perfugians. What are you doing delivering messenger girls?"

Erika gritted her teeth as a smug smile appeared on the Calafe's face. Exhaling a breath through clenched teeth, she faced the approaching man.

"General Curtis, I presume," she said, drawing herself up. "And I am afraid the Calafe spoke in error. I am Erika, the royal Archivist, not a messenger. The queen sent me on urgent business."

"Did she now?"

The general made a gesture towards the working soldiers. Groans echoed around the work site as the men downed stakes and shovels and wandered towards the lookouts, who were offering waterskins and strips of what looked like beef jerky.

Satisfied his men were cared for, the general returned his attention to Erika. Smiling, he offered his hand.

Erika studied the filthy digits, struggling to keep the reaction from her face, before finally reaching out to accept the gesture—though she only placed her fingertips in his palm. Grime did not bother her, when it served a purpose. But this…any man could be sent to dig in the mud. What was the commander of the entire allied army *doing* here?

"My apologies for the poor welcome," the general went on. "In wartime, there are little resources to spare for luxuries here in Fogmore. My little city must be quite the change from the capital."

"Nonsense, General," Erika replied, forcing a smile to her lips. "I did not get to be the Queen's Archivist without getting my hands dirty."

"I see," the general replied.

His eyes swept her up and down, no doubt taking in her clean clothes and face. She'd been fortunate enough to find an inn with a bathhouse for her last night on the road, though it had taken some convincing to have the innkeeper prepare the waters. Erika had been the woman's only guest in days.

"I must admit though," Erika added. "I did not expect to find the famed General Curtis working in the mud. Surely we are not so short on hands that a common soldier could not be assigned in your place." Despite her best efforts, she could not keep the disdain from her voice.

The general only chuckled. "I am not always so occupied, but at this moment we have little intelligence about the Tangatan invasion plans. There's not much else to do but ready our defences." He paused, but when Erika only raised an eyebrow, his grin spread. "It does me well, to remember my roots as a common soldier, Archivist. And it is good for the men to see their officers are not above a hard day's labour."

"I see," Erika replied, though she did not understand at all.

The queen did not clean her own privy chamber. To do so would be to invite questions of her authority. Had age begun to erode the general's famed military mind?

"In that case," she continued delicately, deciding it was best to leave that line of thought to others, "perhaps my assignment will be of interest to you."

"Oh?" the general asked. "And what task has our illustrious queen assigned to her young Archivist?" As he spoke, he unclipped a waterskin from his belt and upended it over his head. He used his spare hand to wash his face clean.

Erika bristled at his tone, but forced herself to calm. She could not afford to upset this man, not when the success of her mission relied on his benevolence. If he wished to think of her as a youth…she would manage. Perhaps she might even use it to her advantage.

She offered the general an innocent smile. "Through my research, I have found another of the ancient sites," she began delicately. "One I believe has lain undiscovered since The Fall."

"Another of those underground ruins?" the general asked. Wiping the last of the water from his face, he offered the waterskin to the Calafe. The man waved a hand, declining the offer, and the general returned it to his belt. "I thought the queen had abandoned her interest in those dusty old tunnels?"

Erika frowned at his words. "Clearly your knowledge is out of date, General," she replied. "Through my research, the magic of the Gods has been returned to the hands of humanity."

Raising her hand, she clenched her fist, igniting the cold light of her gauntlet. Silence fell over the men at the sight, while nearby the young woman leaned closer, her eyes growing large. The other soldiers were too far off to notice the glow in the bright sunlight. After a moment, Erika lowered her hand and allowed the light to die.

"So you see, General, why my mission is important," Erika murmured. "With magic on our side, the Tangata will be rebuffed, and Flumeer will stand supreme amongst the kingdoms of man." Her heart pounded against her chest as she faced the general, watching for his reaction.

He laughed.

"Archivist," he said after a moment, a grin stretching his cheeks. "The Tangata will not flee from a pretty light show."

"The magic is much more than just *light*—"

"Oh, I know," the general said, waving a hand as

though to dismiss her. "A carrier bird arrived from the capital just yesterday speaking of your demonstration."

"Then why…" Erika trailed off.

"I wanted to see it for myself," the general replied, his grin fading. "Now that I have…" He shook his head. "Archivist, all due respect, but this war will not be won by magic. The ancients thought the same, and look what happened to them—all dead or turned to mindless beasts. No, mark my words, those devices are not for human hands. I'll keep my sanity, thank you very much. We'll win this war the old-fashioned way, with sweat and blood and cold, hard steel."

"I…" What was happening? This meeting was not going at all as she had expected. Why had the queen pre-empted her arrival with a letter of her own? Shaking herself, Erika drew her thoughts together and faced the general. "All due respect to you, *sir*," she said coldly. "That is not your decision to make."

She unclipped her satchel and removed the documents the queen had provided her. Silently she handed them to the general.

"Orders for you to provide me with a squadron to venture south of the Illmoor," she said coldly. "Signed by the queen herself."

Beside her, the Calafe warrior started, his face showing surprise. "*You* want to cross the Illmoor," he gasped.

She faced him, her face carefully blank. "Yes, Calafe. And if you are unable to keep that mouth of yours shut while your betters speak, I would suggest you return to your charges."

The man's face went blank at that, though she could see the rage behind his eyes. She let a satisfied smirk touch her lips. She faced the general again. In stark contrast to the

Calafe, he had shown no reaction to her announcement. No doubt the queen's letter had forewarned him.

"You are insistent on this path, Archivist?" the general asked calmly.

"With all due respect, *General*, we have tried your way." Erika lifted her chin, confidence growing now. "It failed. Calafe was lost. Yet still you cling to your beliefs that the Tangata can be defeated by the sword alone."

"In the south, it was not *my* armies that were defeated, Archivist," the general replied, his voice like ice now. "The Calafe, for all their repute as warriors, were not soldiers. They fought alone, and died for it. There is a reason it was our armies alone who escaped."

His words took the impetus from Erika's argument. She was surprised the Calafe man did not speak up, though a glance in his direction revealed his jaw was clenched tight.

"Perhaps what you say is true," Erika murmured, adopting a consolatory tone, "but the time for caution is over. All weapons must be explored if we are to save our kingdom from destruction. Surely you understand that."

"Do not lecture me on the ways of war, Archivist," the general snapped. His eyes drifted down the riverbanks, to where the burnt ship still lay. "You know nothing of desperation, of what it is to face the Tangata, man to beast." He sighed and looked back at her, eyes sad. "I had hoped to dissuade you from this path. But I see now that was never a possibility." He handed her back the papers.

"Then you will obey the queen's orders?" Erika insisted.

"The Tangata are already in the forests beyond the Illmoor," the general said after a moment. "Romaine was amongst the scouts who encountered them. How many did you lose again, Calafe?"

"Two," her guide rumbled, before adding: "Not including the ferryman and his crew."

"Nor the soldiers we lost when they gave chase and attacked the city," the general added. "I still wonder at that. Why did they come here, throw away lives on an assault that could never have succeeded...?" He trailed off, then shook himself, facing Erika once more. "Your devotion to the Gods has blinded you to reality, Archivist. You would need an army to reach your sacred site. But I will obey my queen, as in all things."

"I *will* be successful," Erika said in response to his doubt. "We will travel fast, set cold camps, fight if we must. It is you who does not see, General." She lifted her gauntlet, gaze lingering on the shining threads of metal that had somehow fused to her flesh. "*This* is our future, our salvation. What lies in those caverns, I must find it, claim it for our queen."

"I will not risk our nation on a fool's gambit," the general continued as though he had not heard her. "This river is the only thing standing between our people and oblivion." His eyes took on a haunted look, before he shook himself and looked at the Calafe. "Romaine, take the Archivist back to the city and have my clerics find her quarters. And have them send a message to Charcity, we will need one of their ships."

"What about my regiment?" Erika insisted as the general made to turn away.

"You will have your soldiers," the general replied curtly. "Until the morrow, Archivist."

❧ 16 ❧

THE RECRUIT

Lukys's shoulders ached as he finished the last trip back from the quarry, barrel loaded high with gravel. It was a thankless task, mining the rock and towing it back to the city to lay on the streets each day, only to watch it be stomped into the mud the next morning. There were simply too many people, too many soldiers, in Fogmore for the unsealed street to be maintained.

What they needed was brick, like they used in Ashura. But the Flumeerens he'd spoken to had laughed at the idea. Their nation was too preoccupied with war to waste their energies on enhancing the city.

So instead the Perfugian recruits marched into the hills each day and gathered gravel.

This trip, Travis had taken the first shift with the barrow, hauling the load through the foothills until they reached the Queen's Highway. That left Lukys with the longer shift, though the way was easier, with less hills and potholes to navigate. Even so, he was glad when they finally entered the shadow of the palisade.

Several others from Romaine's group walked nearby with barrows of their own, but Dale and the others had reached the city long ago. They did not work quarter as hard as Lukys and the others, only half-filling their barrows to make the way back easier. Dale had not spoken to Lukys again since that first day in the quarry, though Lukys had noticed the man watching him.

In a way, Lukys pitied those others. Most of the noble born had spurred Romaine's training, but without the Calafe warrior, they had no hope. You could see it in the way they walked, in how their shoulders slumped and they lowered their heads as they returned to the city. They believed what the general had told them, that they were worthless, a waste of resources best done away with. Only the threat of being hunted down as mutineers kept them in line.

A sliver of despair touched Lukys's heart and he quickly forced his mind from such gloomy thoughts. He had to concentrate on the good. They were getting better, getting proficient with spear and shield. With time, they would become true soldiers, not the frauds they had arrived as.

The only question was, would it be enough, when the Tangata came?

"Why so gloomy, Lukys?"

Lukys looked up as Travis spoke, but before he could speak another voice piped up from nearby.

"He's always gloomy," Cara said as she joined them. A smile took the sting from her words.

Though she rarely participated in Romaine's training now, she did occasionally follow them up to the mine. With her arm, she didn't help much with the work and she rarely spoke to the other recruits, but he and Travis had developed somewhat of a comradery with her.

"You're not eating the same slop as the rest of us," Lukys grunted.

Cara only grinned, though his words were sadly true. Despite their progress, the officers of Flumeer still refused to take the Perfugians seriously. They were barred from the common soldiers' mess hall, and received only the sparest of meals. If there was even any left—Dale and his cohort showed little restraint when it came to saving food for stragglers.

Even worse than the food though was the thought of returning to their barracks. Left in those unlit rooms, there was nothing to occupy their minds but thoughts of what was to come. Alone in a room of dozens, it was strange how those times had come to haunt him. The faint hope that Romaine had given them was little match for those unoccupied hours from dusk to dawn.

"I wonder what that woman is here for," Travis mused as they dumped their load of gravel in a pile inside the gates, to be spread on the roads come morning.

They looked at Cara—she'd followed Romaine and the newcomer after all—but she only looked away.

"Had to be someone from the queen's court," Lukys said finally. "Not like it matters though, she won't be sticking around once the fighting starts."

"You *are* in a bad mood today," Travis replied with a grin. "You're telling me you don't appreciate the presence of a beautiful woman?"

"Ahem," Cara interrupted, a scowl lining her forehead.

"Ahh…" Travis grew red, words failing him for once in his life. Cara punched him in the arm with her good hand.

Lukys laughed as the man looked in his direction. He raised his hands. "Don't look at me."

"Hey, there's Romaine!" Travis said quickly, pointing ahead and changing the subject. "I'm sure *he* can tell us more about our new guest—hey!" he exclaimed as Cara hit him again.

Flashing him a final glare, Cara strode past him and headed for Romaine. Still grinning, Lukys joined her, a sheepish Travis bringing up the rear. Despite her time in the wilderness, Cara was more capable than anyone of putting the noble born in his place.

Lukys spied Romaine sitting atop the palisade, his gaze focused on the southern horizon. They often saw him there in the evenings. He seemed to be waiting for something, as though he expected the Tangata to appear at any moment. Just the thought sent a shudder down Lukys's spine and he directed a quick prayer at the Gods for a quiet night.

"Romaine!" Cara called. Gravel crunched beneath their boots as they started up the steps. At least on the walls it remained long enough to be useful. "How goes the watch?"

A smile touched the warrior's face as he saw them. Slowly he rose from the water barrel he'd been using as a seat. "I'm not on watch, lass," he murmured. "Just like to watch the sun set…" He trailed off.

Lukys glanced in the direction of the river. The sky was clear but for the clouds that clung endlessly to the Mountains of the Gods, and the sun was just dipping towards the distant horizon. Today the fiery glow had an orange tinge. Lukys wondered whether that might be some omen, a warning for rain or snow or another fine day. Distantly he remembered a lesson from the academy. Perhaps if he hadn't failed, he might have remembered…

He shook himself, casting off the memories. The waters of the Illmoor remained brown, polluted by its passage through hundreds of miles of Gemahan farmland. He could just glimpse the trees on the distant riverbanks through the fading light.

"And where are you three headed?" Romaine asked, filling the silence.

"Our mess hall," Travis answered with an easy grin. "Thankfully, we've probably already missed the worst of the pig feed. We wanted to ask you about the woman today—" He broke off as Cara delivered a clean elbow to his ribs.

Romaine grunted. "That one's trouble, if ever I saw it."

"Really?" Lukys asked, his curiosity finally piqued.

The warrior waved a hand. "A worry for the morning," he replied. A frown touched his forehead. "Did you say you'd missed dinner?" He shook his head. "Can't have that. Come, you can dine with me in the soldiers' mess hall."

"Erm…" Lukys exchanged a glance with the others. "We're not allowed—"

"Like The Fall," Romaine interrupted. "You're with me. Come."

He started off down the steps back into town, leaving the three with no choice but to follow. They shared a glance before starting after him. Romaine seemed in a strange mood, and Lukys finally joined Travis in wondering why the strange woman had come. It was bound to be something bad. Surely the queen would not have sent her Archivist so close to the frontier unless it was urgent, not with the Tangata on their doorstep.

His spirits lifted though as they entered the city and Romaine started towards the mess hall. He hadn't eaten a decent meal since they'd arrived—there was no telling what the cooks put in the grey slop served to the recruits; it was barely food.

The temperature plummeted as they made their way

through the darkening streets, the thought of a hot meal drawing them on. It was a welcome sight when the lights of the mess hall finally came into view. The guards on the door gave Lukys pause, but Romaine only offered them a nod, and they said nothing as the two recruits and Cara followed the Calafe inside.

Warmth washed over Lukys as they entered the mess hall. The sight that greeted him did not disappoint. Large tables filled the main floor, most occupied by off-duty soldiers, while on the far wall a large window opened into the kitchen. Two men stood on duty behind the window, serving the soldiers lining for their food. A second counter seemed to be used to return the dirty plates. On another wall, flames burned in two great hearths, casting back the winter chill.

Removing his coat, Romaine gestured for them to hang theirs on a rack beside the door. Lukys sighed as he removed the heavy fur. Travis did the same but Cara left hers on— she didn't seem to like even a hint of the cold. Together they followed Romaine across to the kitchen window. A massive Flumeeren man wearing a grease-speckled apron greeted the Calafe with a grin. Bulging eyes flickered as Lukys and the others approached, before returning to Romaine.

"Your pups?" he rumbled. Romaine grunted, and the cook burst into laughter. "Look like they could use a decent feed." He gestured for them to approach the window. "Come, what can old Dante get you lot? Got some fresh mutton tonight, still hot. Mash too, and 'cauli and 'coli, if vegetables are your thing. Take a plate, help y'selves."

"Thank you!" Lukys gasped.

Travis nodded his own excitement. Plate in hand, Cara was already a step ahead of them. Grabbing utensils of his own, Lukys speared a chunk of meat from the platter, then took a generous helping of mashed potatoes as well. There was broccoli and cauliflower too. Once he might have avoided vegetables, but after the endless slop, he'd go for anything with a green shade to it.

Afterwards, they took a seat at an unoccupied table and Romaine disappeared again. Still taking in their surroundings, Lukys noticed that one of the boulders that lay in the plaza formed part of the mess hall as well—one of the walls had been shaped around the giant stone, rather than moving it.

Shortly, Romaine reappeared with four large mugs and a carafe of some deep red liquid. Curious, Lukys wafted it under his nose and was surprised when he detected the scent of cloves and cinnamon. He raised an eyebrow at Romaine.

"Mulled wine," he replied, a grin tugging at his lips. "Hardly touched my quota these past few weeks so there's plenty to share."

They passed the carafe around, each filling their mugs to the brim, and then sat back to take it all in. Mulled wine was considered a delicacy in Perfugia, a drink they had only enjoyed on special occasions at the academy. Breathing it in, Lukys savoured the rich aroma.

"You're meant to drink it, you know," Travis said, raising his mug to cheers.

"Right." Lukys's cheeks warmed and he chinked his drink with the others before taking a sip.

It was sweeter than what he'd tried during the winter celebrations in Perfugia. Stronger too, though the spice of the cloves covered much of the taste. There was still some warmth in it, and he welcomed the sensation of heat spreading from his stomach. Eating and sleeping in their frigid quarters, it seemed an age since he'd last been truly warm.

"It's good!" Cara exclaimed. She sat across from Romaine and Lukys, with Travis. She lowered the mug only long enough to make her point before taking another swig.

Romaine chuckled. "Did your parents never let you try a southern vintage?" he asked. "The Gods help 'em, there's a reason they spice the stuff here. Undrinkable without it."

"Better than your cooking, Romaine," a man Lukys did not recognise said as he lowered himself down beside Travis.

"That so…Lorene?" Romaine said. There was an obvious pause, as though he had trouble remembering the name. "Don't recall you volunteering to cook during our last trip south of the Illmoor!"

The man grinned but said nothing, only scooped a lump of mash from his plate and took a bite. Lukys and the others looked from Romaine to the newcomer. The Calafe warrior grunted when he finally noticed their confusion.

"This is Lorene," he said. "Joined me on a few scouting trips down in Calafe."

"One, to be exact," Lorene replied, and for a moment his eyes took on a haunted look. "Barely made it back with our lives, too. Though I suppose we did rescue poor old Cara here," he added, gesturing beside them.

"Will you go south with the others then?" Cara asked suddenly, lifting her head from the mulled wine.

Lukys and the others at the table started at the announcement, while Romaine fixed her with a glare. She frowned when he did not reply, before her eyes widened and she muttered a curse.

"Oh, right, that's meant to be a secret."

Beside Lukys, Romaine groaned and buried his head in his hands.

"What The Fall, Romaine?" Lorene hissed, leaning forward. His voice adopted a slight tremor as he went on: "They're sending us into Calafe again?"

The Calafe shook his head. "No," he whispered. "It's that Archivist woman. She wants to go south, find some sacred site of the Gods."

A gasp slipped from Lukys's lips. "*What?*"

In Perfugia, disturbing any relic related to the Gods was a capital offence, one few dared to challenge. All knew what had become of the last souls who'd dared to meddle with the Gods and their magic. Now that Lukys had seen the Tangata himself, he wanted even less to do with such powers. What was the woman thinking, risking her life to seek out such a cursed place?

"She's quite mad," Romaine replied, not understanding the true source of Lukys's indignation, "but she has somehow convinced the queen to support her. The general is to supply her with a regiment. He's not happy about it. I suspect he will ask for volunteers."

Across the table, Lorene let out a long breath, the relief in his eyes obvious.

"She's not *mad*, Romaine," Cara snapped, leaning across the table to glare at the warrior.

"Anyone who wants to go back there is insane in my book," Lorene said cheerfully, raising his glass in salute. Romaine's words seemed to have reassured him.

"Perhaps there is more to her than meets the eye," Cara said softly, before glancing at Lorene. "Besides, *I* want to go back."

Silence fell over the table as they all turned to stare at her. Lukys opened his mouth and then closed it again, unable to fashion a response. Calafe was Cara's home, and true, he couldn't understand what it must be like to lose that, but...

"Don't be a fool," Romaine growled, coming slowly to his feet.

Fool, fool, fool.

Lukys shook his head as the words rang in his mind.

"I'm serious, Romaine," Cara said, standing as well. "I have to go home."

Home, home, home.

"Home?" Romaine gasped. "Home is gone, girl! They took it. All we have left are our lives. Don't throw yours away because some madwoman thinks it's safe to wander around a forest swarming with Tangata."

"You don't understand," Cara whispered, eyes shining in the light of the hearth. Silence had fallen across the mess hall as the other soldiers turned to watch the commotion. "I can't stay here, I have to go."

Go, go, go.

"Don't understand?" Romaine raged. "I understand better than anyone! I forbid it."

"You forbid it?" the young woman hissed, eyes growing dark.

Her hands balled into fists and for a moment it seemed she stood taller. Romaine said nothing, only stared at her across the table. The moment stretched out, punctuated only by the clattering of plates from the kitchen. Finally, Cara gave a curt nod. Without saying a word, she spun and marched from the hall without looking back.

Romaine watched her go, a haunted look on his face, as though he had just lost something dear to him. Finally he closed his eyes, head bowing.

"Piece of advice, lads," he murmured, "if you want to

avoid my mistakes. There's no room in this war to care. About anything. Do yourselves a favour and burn that crap from your hearts now, before it gets you killed."

With that he turned and walked from the mess hall, leaving the two recruits and Lorene sitting looking after him.

THE WARRIOR

Drums pounded against Romaine's skull as he staggered from the barracks and into the street. Silently he cursed the fortified Flumeeren wine. He'd bribed the cooks for an entire bottle and taken it up to the walls. If the watch hadn't found him passed out between the water barrels, he might have spent the whole night up there.

Now he'd almost slept past the roll call the general had announced for noon. He hurried through the streets, head still pounding to the distant rhythm. How long had it been since he'd had *real* wine, from the vineyards of Calafe? Years, surely. It was so hard to find nowadays, impossible in this border city. The Flumeeren stuff was little better than moonshine.

A cold breeze blew down the street as he hurried to reach the central plaza. He barely made it a block before his stomach roiled and he was forced to detour into an alleyway to empty its contents into the mud.

After that he felt slightly better, though there was no way he'd be attempting his daily jog around the palisade. It wasn't just his head that ached; he felt it in his shoulders and back, in his very bones. Maybe it wasn't the wine, maybe time was finally catching up with him. Those who had joined the army alongside him in those early days had retired long ago—those who'd survived, at least. But *he* would not surrender to the creeping erosion of time.

Fool.

The streets began to fill as he neared the square and Romaine found himself searching the crowds for the glint of copper hair. His stomach twisted at the memory of his conversation with Cara. Surely she had not been serious about returning to her homeland? With the light of day she would see sense.

No. He had seen the glint in her eyes the night before. She was determined. A tremor ran down his spine at the thought of saying farewell to the strange woman. He cursed beneath his breath. When had he begun to care for her?

Finally he emerged from the buildings into the central plaza. He was one of the last to arrive, and most of the army's regiments were already in place. With them all standing in line, the differences in discipline was on full display today. Some groups such as the royal guard—the division assigned to the general's protection—stood in perfect rows, eyes fixed to the front, weapons shining in the noonday sun.

Others from the civilian units were only marginally better than the Perfugian recruits, with many slouching against their spears and beards nearly as unkept as Romaine's.

Not being an official part of the army, Romaine himself cared little for Flumeeren regulation. He wandered around the borders of the plaza, seeking out the Perfugian blue.

He found the recruits standing close to the centre of the

plaza, their ranks broken by a large boulder in their midst. They too had no official officers in the Flumeeren command structure—other than the louts that supervised them at the quarry—and so their thirty-seven remaining members stood in a semi-organised mess. His heart lifted as he spotted Lukys and some of his other trainees attempting to impose some order.

Romaine couldn't reach them without forcing his way through the Flumeeren soldiers and causing a stir, so instead he retreated to the edge of the square and leaned against the wall of a nearby building. His eyes slid closed, and he sighed to escape the day's brightness.

Unfortunately, the peace did not last long.

The blaring of a horn announced the arrival of the general. Romaine forced his eyes open and watched as General Curtis marched through the ranks of the soldiers until he reached a cleared section of ground in the centre of the plaza. Only then did Romaine spot the Archivist waiting there. Arms clasped behind her back and lips pursed, the woman was impatience personified.

So eager to get us all killed.

Romaine shook his head. He wondered what the woman would do if none of the soldiers volunteered to join her quest. Indeed, he couldn't imagine anyone being so mad, not after the attack two weeks before.

No one except Cara.

Gritting his teeth, he forced his mind back to the general as the horn sounded again. Armour rattled as the army snapped to attention. Romaine rolled his shoulders, settling his own chainmail into a more comfortable position, and watched as the general leaned in close to the Archivist. Whispers passed between them before he turned back and surveyed the gathered forces.

"Soldiers of Flumeer!" he called, his voice ringing from the walls of the nearby buildings. "Thank you for joining me this fine day. Important works are underway and I saw it fit to ensure you were informed of what is to come."

He paused, looking out over the army, eyes cool. Despite the hangover, Romaine shivered. He had no great love for the general, but he couldn't help but respect him. The man was a veteran after all, had been a general even before Romaine had first signed up as a soldier. Curtis had been one of the few to warn about the Tangatan threat. Maybe if more had listened, the war would have gone differently. Maybe the south would not have been so unprepared, maybe...

Romaine tore himself free of that train of thought. There was no point regretting what had already passed...

"In the coming weeks, the Tangata will attack," General Curtis continued. "The Illmoor is our last defence. If we lose the battle here, Flumeer *will* fall. You have faced the beasts, you know the truth. No one can stand against them on open ground." He walked down the front ranks of soldiers, meeting the eyes of every man in the square. "We do not yet know where they will strike, so we must defend the entire river, man every fort and city, use every resource at our command to protect these shores."

Romaine frowned at the man's words, and noticed many soldiers doing the same. None of this was new. Every soul in the city knew the importance of the Illmoor.

"Of course, you all know this." The hint of a smile crossed the general's face and he turned towards the Archivist. "I say it not for you, but for the sake of this woman here. Like many in the capital, with its learned academics and bureaucrats, she thinks this war can be won with myths and fairytales."

The Archivist's face darkened at the general's words, but to her credit, she stared him down. Chuckling, General Curtis offered her a nod before facing the army once more.

"Sadly, I have failed to convince her of the reality of this world. She insists on endangering our very existence with her daydreams. She would have us venture beyond the Illmoor in search of ancient magics!"

Murmurs spread around the square at the announcement, shock showing on soldier's faces. The Archivist's mask slipped as she stepped up to meet the general, giving way to rage.

"I come on the *queen's* orders," she hissed, loud enough for the entire plaza to hear. "It is not your position to question her, *General*."

She pointed a gauntleted finger at the man. Recalling the light she'd summoned earlier, Romaine shivered. Somehow, that strange magic disturbed him almost as much as the Tangata themselves. Even so, Romaine was impressed at the woman's defiance. He looked at Curtis to see how the general would react.

"Fairytales, as I said," Curtis continued as though the woman had not spoken. "I will not allow Flumeer to fall for the sake of a woman's fancy."

"I will have my soldiers, General," the Archivist snarled.

"Ay," the general rumbled, "the Perfugians will accompany you south."

For a moment, Romaine didn't think he'd heard the general right. Silence fell across the square at his words, every soldier staring in disbelief. Curtis couldn't be serious. A journey beyond the river would be difficult for the hardest company of soldiers. For untrained recruits, it was suicide!

"The Perfugians...what...you cannot...no!" the

Archivist stuttered into the silence, all colour draining from her face.

"Yes," the general replied calmly. "I will not compromise our borders by sacrificing good soldiers to a lost cause. So you will be joined by a lost cause of their own. That is my final decision."

"I will petition the queen!"

"Do what you wish, Archivist." The general's eyes shone. "Though regrettably, our last carrier pigeon departed this morning. If you wish to dispute my interpretation of the queen's commands, you will have to send a runner for a clarification."

"But…that could take weeks!" the Archivist exclaimed. "The Tangata could have occupied the site by then."

"I suggest you be content with what you have been offered then, Archivist," the general replied, a smug smile on his lips.

"Bastard!" the Archivist screamed. She lifted her magic gauntlet as though to strike the general down, then seemed to think better of it.

Romaine stood frozen on the edge of the plaza, staring as the two faced one another down, still reeling. Lukys, Travis and all the others who had turned to him to save them, they would soon be marching to their deaths, doomed to die alone in the frozen forests of his homeland. He had failed them.

A shudder shook him and he cursed himself for a fool. He had learned this lesson, hadn't he? Long ago, again and again. Was he fated to always repeat the same tragedy, always too weak, too slow to save those he cared for?

"Very well, General," the Archivist said finally, the calm mask falling back into place. "Though know this: when I return and win my place at the queen's side, you will know the full weight of my displeasure."

"That is a risk I am willing to take," the general replied, staring her down, "for my kingdom."

"You damn us all with your cowardice," the Archivist spat back, her composure cracking once more. "What lies beyond the Illmoor will change everything."

"Then you had best make yourself ready for the journey," the general replied. "We received word from Charcity this morning. Your ship will arrive in the night. You sail at first light."

The woman matched his glare for a moment longer, then her shoulders slumped and Romaine knew she was defeated.

"Will you at least provide us with scouts?" she murmured. "Someone who knows the land? Calafe was a wilderness even before its fall. I *must* have a guide to show us the way."

"No—"

"I will go, General," Romaine said, striding forward through the ranks of soldiers.

His heart pounded in his chest as he walked past Lukys and the other recruits. Their faces were white with terror, though to their credit they had not tried to argue. Perhaps they were simply too shocked to put up a fight. He caught a glimpse of Lukys's face amongst the others, saw the flash of hope that appeared in his eyes, and quickly looked away.

The Archivist looked surprised as he walked up. She stepped towards him, words of gratitude spilling from her mouth, but Romaine waved her away. He wasn't doing this for her. His eyes caught the general's.

"Are you sure you wish to do this, Romaine?" Curtis murmured, stepping in close. Romaine only nodded, and he sighed. "Very well. I will place you in command of the regiment. I know you have been training them. Perhaps your presence will give them a chance to survive the woman's madness."

"Thank you, sir," Romaine said shortly. He understood the man's reasoning, cold as it was. Maybe under other circumstances he could have agreed with his decision…maybe.

The general nodded, and turning to the rest of the army, he barked the dismissal. Steel rattled as the soldiers filed from the plaza one line after the other. The general watched them for a while, then glanced at the Perfugians. For a second, Romaine thought he glimpsed regret in the general's eye. Had this been a bluff, to force the Archivist to abandon her task? If so, it had failed.

Finally only the Perfugians remained. Glancing one last time at Romaine, the general offered a nod. Then he turned and marched from the square. The Archivist went next.

Then Romaine was alone with the Perfugian recruits. Turning, he found himself looking into the youthful eyes of Lukys.

"I thought you said not to care?" the recruit whispered.

❧ 18 ❧

THE RECRUIT

"I thought you said not to care?" Lukys croaked as Romaine turned towards him.

Standing in the front ranks of his regiment, Lukys couldn't keep the horror from his face as Romaine met his eyes. His heart was pounding in his chest, his ears still ringing. It couldn't be true, couldn't be happening…

They were doomed.

"Who here is afraid?" Lukys flinched as Romaine looked away from him, speaking instead to the entire regiment.

Standing at the head of the column, the warrior's red-streaked eyes swept the gathered recruits, seeming to take them all in at once. Lukys wondered what game the man was playing. Every single Perfugian, even Dale, was trembling in his boots. Surely he could see that.

No one spoke, and after a moment, Romaine began to pace up and down the line. That continued for a while. Every man and woman in the regiment watched the warrior, until he came to a sudden stop, and looked at them again.

"I'm afraid," he said unexpectedly, voice soft. "Many of you already know me, but for those who don't, I am a warrior of Calafe. Tomorrow we will be marching into my homeland." He paused, lowering his head, though Lukys still saw the sadness in his eyes. "But it is no longer my home. It has become enemy territory, the home of our nightmares."

He started to pace again, though now his eyes were on them. He spoke as he walked: "As of tomorrow, we will be brothers and sisters in arms. If we are to stand any chance of surviving, we must trust each other. Even with our deepest, darkest fears." He stopped mid-stride, looking at them in earnest now. "My name is Romaine, and I am afraid of what we will face on the morrow. But that fear will not stop me."

Lukys swallowed as he locked eyes with the warrior. A shudder passed through him and before Lukys knew what he was doing, he stepped forward. "I am afraid."

A snigger came from somewhere behind him, but already another voice was emerging from the ranks of recruits.

"I'm afraid." Lukys smiled as Travis stepped up beside him, head held high as he looked back at their fellow Perfugians. "But I will not run from it."

"I am afraid as well."

Others followed, then all the recruits who had trained under Romaine, and others too, those who had not joined them, but perhaps had wished to, if only they'd found the courage. The laughter that had come from Dale and his friends died away, drowned out by the whispered admissions. Lukys glimpsed anger in his rival's eyes.

"Very good," Romaine spoke again from the front ranks. "Then we will face our fears together." He drew in a breath. "Well, we only have the day. I will not press you—we will need every ounce of strength for what we find in my homeland. But I must know your capabilities."

Whispers went through the recruits as they exchanged glances. Even those who had not joined Lukys knew about the gruelling training regime Romaine had subjected them to.

"Enough!" Romaine's shout rang from the walls of the nearby buildings.

Silence was instant.

"Enough," the warrior repeated, folding his arms across his chest. "We've wasted too much time already. You lot." He indicated the recruits to his left. "Break off, you will be the defenders. And you." He gestured to the right. "The attackers."

Lukys and those who had worked with Romaine leapt to obey, but the rest stood staring at him until he barked, "*Now!*"

Terrified, the recruits stumbled over one other in their haste, and the square rang with the sounds of confusion. It was only when they'd gathered into the two groups that Lukys realised what Romaine was saying. Attackers and defenders? But they didn't have their practice spears. The regiments had come in full parade dress—full chainmail armour and shields and spears. Sharp. Deadly.

Before he could ask what Romaine planned, the warrior issued fresh orders:

"Form up, two ranks deep, shields to the front," he bellowed.

This time the recruits were quicker to obey, though their movements were still clumsy. It was obvious the manoeuvre would have failed in a true battle. Lukys tried to suppress his frustration as the recruits to either side jostled him. He was in the defending group, while Travis had ended up in with the attackers. Both were trying to inject order to the chaos, but it was an exercise in futility.

Finally the two groups stood facing one another, each two lines deep. Romaine strode down the length between them, surveying the Perfugians with a professional eye. Lukys smiled as he saw Dale in the other group. At least he would not have to fight alongside the man.

"Put down your spears," Romaine said softly as he stepped away from the two lines.

The clatter of wooden shafts falling to the dirt followed as the recruits released their weapons. Lukys frowned—they'd only just begun in the last week to practice with shields.

"In this exercise," the warrior continued, "you'll use only your shields. They will be your most important weapon against the Tangata. Stand together, and you can neutralise the enemy's strengths."

A burst of laughter came from the group of attackers. "No wonder your people are dead," Dale snarled, pushing past his fellows to stand at the front of the line. He still held his spear. "Why should we listen to you, Calafe? I heard only the cowards escaped the Tangata with their lives."

To Lukys's surprise, there was no rage in Romaine's eyes as he faced Dale, only pity. "Because I'm your only hope of surviving what is to come," he said coolly.

Dale snorted. "Think I'd rather take my chances with the madwomen, if you think we can defeat the Tangata with a shield."

Romaine stared at the man for a long moment, then

turned and walked to where Lukys stood. "Your shield," he ordered.

Lukys handed it over without a word and the Calafe nodded his thanks. Returning to stand before Dale, he nodded at the recruit.

"Go ahead, soldier," the Calafe said quietly. "Take your best shot."

"I…"

Dale's eyes showed reluctance and despite his bravado, he hesitated. Romaine held only a shield, and Dale's weapon was not some blunted practice stave. Then his eyes narrowed and he seemed to make up his mind. With a roar, he let his own shield fall to the ground, then he rushed Romaine, the razor-sharp blade aimed for the warrior's throat.

To Lukys's surprise, Romaine did not attempt to evade the attack. Instead his stance deepened, bracing his body behind the shield. As Dale neared, he surged forward, taking the recruit by surprise. Off-guard, there was no power behind Dale's blow and his spearhead deflected harmlessly from the wooden shield.

Then Romaine drove the steel-capped rim of his shield into Dale's midriff. Breath hissed between the recruit's teeth and the weight behind the blow put him flat on his back. Lukys winced at the muffled *thump* of Dale hitting the ground.

"The time for games is over," Romaine announced, facing the other recruits.

At his feet, Dale was still straining to catch his breath. Sharing a glance with the Calafe warrior, Lukys couldn't help but offer a satisfied grin. It was about time someone taught the man a lesson.

"Lukys, to the front!"

Lukys jumped as Romaine called his name. After a second's hesitation, he hurried forward, and Romaine returned his shield. Then he gestured Travis forward. He took the shield and spear from him, before sending the man back to the watching ranks.

"Your second strongest weapon is each other," he went on. "A shield is not enough against a creature with the strength to tear you limb from limb. Unless we all stand together, we will die alone." He gestured to Lukys and Dale, who had recovered his spear and managed to stand. "If you want to survive, you must fight together."

"What?" Lukys asked, glancing at Dale.

The man looked just as disgusted at the thought of working alongside Lukys. "You can't be serious."

"Deadly," Romaine replied, then stabbed out suddenly with his spear.

Lukys cried out as the point hammered against his shield, leaping back. Instinctively, he tried to parry with a spear he did not hold. A curse slipped from his lips as alone, Dale charged Romaine. The Calafe caught the charge on his shield and turned the blow aside, then kicked out with a heavy boot, tripping the Perfugian recruit and sending him crashing back to the ground.

"I said *together!*" Romaine bellowed as Dale struggled to his feet.

Panting, Lukys shared a glance with his rival. Without speaking, they took a step closer to one another, Dale on the right with spear held in a two-handed grip, Lukys standing so that the shield could cover them both. A grin split Romaine's face as he advanced on them again.

This time when the Calafe attacked, Lukys stood his ground, using the shield to deflect the spear tip away from Dale. Immediately, the other man thrust out with his weapon. The two-handed grip delivered a powerful blow and Romaine was forced to retreat to avoid being caught by the razor tip. Even in full chainmail, these were live weapons and the risk was real.

Lukys and Dale advanced, doing their best to match one another's strides. Romaine laughed and attacked again. This time Lukys thrust out with his shield the way Romaine had done, turning aside the blow and catching Romaine's shield with his own. A cry came from Dale and he leapt forward, driving his spear for a gap that had opened in Romaine's guard. Lukys's heart lurched in his chest as he realised the blow would surely land.

Quick as a cat, Romaine released his shield, causing Lukys to stagger as the pressure went off his own shield. Still moving, Romaine twisted and narrowly avoided being impaled. The spear spun in Romaine's hands, seemingly an extension of the warrior's own arm, and too late Lukys saw that Dale had stepped beyond the protection of his shield. There was a sharp *crack* as Romaine slammed the butt of his weapon into Dale's chest.

Paling, Dale staggered back, exposing Lukys to Romaine's next attack. He opened his mouth to cry out, but instead found himself staring down the shaft of a spear pointed at his face.

"Together, you had me on the defensive," Romaine said calmly as he lowered the spear and giving it back. He offered Dale a hand. To Lukys's surprise, the recruit accepted. "When you separated, you were defeated."

Turning, he faced the rest of the recruits. "Let that be a lesson to all of you. It doesn't matter how skilled any one of you are, nor how strong or fast your opponent. Stand together, and you can defeat anyone."

Perhaps it was only Lukys's imagination, but it seemed

that Romaine's words lit a spark in the eyes of his fellow Perfugians. Smiling, he looked at the Calafe warrior. But instead of confidence, Lukys thought he glimpsed despair on the face of the warrior. A second later it was gone, but still it gave Lukys pause. His heart throbbed in his chest as he lowered the shield and stepped towards the warrior.

Romaine turned away. "We're all afraid of something," he said softly to the men and women gathered before him. "I can't promise that all of you will survive what is to come. But if you stand with me, together as one, I promise you will have a chance." He drew in a deep breath. "Now, form up!"

❧ 19 ❧

THE ARCHIVIST

E rika tapped her foot gently on the muddy street. She stood before the river gate, rage boiling through every part of her, waiting for her "regiment" to arrive. Bad enough that the general had betrayed her, worse that the Perfugians were *late*. Again, she wondered whether she was making the right choice, gambling her entire expedition, her *life*, on thirty-seven untrained soldiers and a warrior of Calafe. Perhaps she should have sent the message to the capital and risked the delay.

No, she couldn't wait. This was her last chance to discover the true magic of the Gods. She could almost *feel* the power throbbing in the palm of her hand as she clenched and unclenched her fist, but the gauntlet was but a taste. True magic awaited her in the south, she was sure of it. If only she could reach the ancient site before the Tangata swept through the land.

A shiver ran down her spine, though she couldn't have said whether it was from nerves or the cold. It was still dark inside the walls of the town and fresh snow had fallen during the night, leaving a thin layer of white on the slate rooftops. Erika wrinkled her nose as she looked down the torch-lined street. One thing was for sure: she wouldn't miss this damned city. Better the wilderness, the open trees and forests…

The rattle of footsteps finally carried to her from around the corner and she released her breath. They should have already been boarding the ship, but of course the Perfugian regiment would be delayed. Doubt assailed her yet again, and she found herself thinking about that third option, about the strange woman who had accosted her in the countryside…

No, they tried to kill you!

A flash of blue appeared at the end of the street as her regiment marched into view. She straightened her shoulders, determined to make the most of what she had. Almost forty heavily armed soldiers. A Calafe warrior who knew the land. A magic gauntlet that could kill a man with a thought.

No, there was no reason to panic. The general might be determined to see her fail, but Erika would not allow his failures to be her own. She would succeed, would return with the power mankind had sought for centuries. Then the general would know her wrath.

Erika shook herself, forcing her thoughts back to the present. This was no time to get ahead of herself. She must focus on the mission at hand. Watching the approaching recruits, she was relieved to see the Calafe at their head. And the Perfugians seemed to be moving in step now, rather than tripping over one another as she'd glimpsed her first day in the city.

Turning to the city guards, she nodded for them to open

the gates. They said nothing, and she did not miss the disdain in their eyes. But after a moment they turned and set to removing the locking bar.

There was no sign of the general, though Erika had to admit, she was pleased at his absence. She wasn't certain she could contain her rage if forced to face him again. Though no doubt it was a sign of disrespect to the Perfugians that he had not come.

Taking the reins of her horse, Erika started towards the gates as her regiment drew near.

"Not bringing a weapon, Archivist?"

She looked around as the Calafe drew alongside her. He too led a horse, though they would be the only two mounted on this expedition. Yet another factor that would slow their journey. She caught his gaze on her empty belt strap, and smiled.

"I don't need one," she replied, flashing her gauntlet.

He nodded, though doubt still lurked behind his eyes. The demonstration earlier had not been enough to convince the general of her power; why would it be any different with this man? Regardless, she started towards the gates, then noticed the Calafe had stopped and was looking back into the city.

"Forgotten something, Calafe?" she asked.

"What?" he replied, glancing at her. Then he shook his head. "No, let's get going. The sun will be up soon."

Erika frowned at the man, confused by his reactions. Had she missed a madness in the warrior that might jeopardise her mission? If so, it was too late now—they would not make it far on the other side without a guide. Together they walked through the open gates.

Below, a galley now bobbed against the riverbanks,

gangplank already in place to see them aboard. It was larger than the burnt-out husk that lay downriver, and had probably once been used to trade goods up and down the Illmoor. Those days were long gone; now such vessels were used for the defence of the frontier.

Leading her horse down the winding path to the river, Erika noted that the stakes the general had been planting now sprouted in four or five rows along much of the riverbank. The enemy would not be able to charge the palisade so quickly if they came again, though there was still a good eighty yards of open ground left to stake.

Five minutes later, Erika stood at the railings of the galley, watching as the Perfugian recruits made their careful way up the gangplank. She took the chance to examine them more closely, and found herself pleasantly surprised. Each wore full chainmail and carried shield and spear. They looked impressive in their full kit, almost like real soldiers, and she found herself hoping the general's assessment of them might yet be proven wrong.

The ship quickly became crowded as the Perfugians struggled to find space where they would not be in the way of the sailors. They were almost all aboard when shouts carried down from the city walls. Spinning, Erika scanned the currents swirling around them, thinking the guards must be shouting a warning. But the waters were empty, and a second later the pounding of horse hooves carried to her ears.

Looking towards the city, she watched as a rider erupted through the gates. The young woman, Cara, appeared on the back of a black gelding. Riding at full gallop, she directed the horse down the path towards the last of the Perfugians on the banks. Just as she was nearing the shore, more shouts carried down from the fort, then a fresh group of men came running through the gates.

On the shore below, Cara leapt from the horse's back, and taking it by the reins, led it through the last few recruits still on the shore. Only as she started up the gangplank did Erika realise what the woman intended. Suddenly suspicious, she pushed her way through the crowd on the deck, while the last of the Perfugians followed Cara aboard.

"Looks like that's all of us!" Cara was saying as Erika reached her. The young woman wore an easy grin and her injured arm was no longer bandaged. "Think we'd better get on our way?"

"What The Fall are you doing here?" Erika gasped, looking from the woman to the men still racing down the path towards them. Something was very wrong here. Why would this woman want to get *on* a ship heading into enemy territory? Not unless…she was a spy!

She spotted Romaine standing nearby. "Calafe, get your blasted daughter—or whoever she is—off my ship!"

The smile fell from Cara's face at her words. Romaine stepped forward, his lips drawn tight, frown lines marking his forehead. Drawing herself up, Cara swung to face him, her face betraying nothing of her thoughts. A strained silence stretched out between them.

"Didn't know you could ride," Romaine grunted finally. "How's the arm?"

Cara's shoulders sagged, as though in relief, and the hint of a smile returned to her face. "Better," she said with a nod, then: "And I'm a fast learner."

"Good." Romaine nodded. "You can help me scout the way."

"Scout…" Erika pushed forward to stand between them. "What in the Gods is going on here?"

"Archivist," Romaine said, "Cara is not my daughter, but she is of Calafe. We found her on our last scouting trip south of the Illmoor. She was injured in a Tangata attack, so we brought her back, but...she did express to me her wish to return."

"Oh...*what?*" Erika exclaimed, too shocked by this new piece of information to form a response. She managed to shake her head. "But...even so...we cannot afford...any liabilities on this journey. I cannot have an untrained woman slowing us down."

"She survived for months alone in enemy territory," Romaine replied, speaking slowly. "I think you'll find she's anything but a liability."

Erika glanced from the young woman to the men still racing down the slope. It didn't look as though Cara had asked permission to take her horse. If the soldiers came aboard, there would be yet more delays. Grinding her teeth, she turned on the ship captain.

"Push off, Captain!" she ordered. "Time we got underway."

The man hesitated, his eyes flicking to the approaching soldiers, but a bellow from the Calafe warrior sent him into action.

"Heave hoe!" he bellowed, moving to the tiller at the rear of the ship. "Get that gangplank aboard!"

The half-dozen sailors raced to obey, taking hold of ropes attached to the plank. As it lifted from the mud, the ship immediately began to turn, the currents taking hold. The sailors stowed the plank alongside the railing then turned to their oars. Sixty tonnes of wood and metal surged out into the currents as the captain called the timing.

Shouts chased after them as the soldiers reached the

shore, but they faded quickly as the river drew the galley downstream. The Perfugian recruits clung to whatever they could as the ship lurched, swinging to the south, before turning more slowly to face upriver. Groans came from the sailors as they began to row against the current.

Erika nodded her satisfaction. She had told no one the exact location of her ancient site, but the captain knew to drop them several leagues upstream. Still unsure whether she'd done the right thing, she looked back at Cara. Finally, the full weight of Romaine's words struck her. This woman had been *alone* in Calafe?

The new information forced a reappraisal of the woman. Anyone who could survive a winter in the wilderness, let alone in Tangata territory, was surely a force to be reckoned with. Her heartbeat quickened as she realised the woman could be an asset. Perhaps Cara even knew something of their destination.

Erika was already reaching for the map in her satchel before she thought better of it. It would not be prudent to speak of their destination in front of the captain and his sailors—who knew where else Gemaho might have agents? Better to wait and talk with Cara and the Calafe warrior privately.

Moving to the bow of the ship, she eyed the way ahead. The waters of the Illmoor raced past, the galley surging with each beat of the sailors' oars. There was a mist today, a heavy, clinging cloud that tasted of winter, and ahead the river vanished into the white. There was no seeing what lay beyond; all she could do was trust the captain knew where to go.

"Nervous?"

Erika started as the Calafe warrior appeared alongside

her. His eyes were distant, focused as hers had been on the drifting mist, as though he could already see the lands that awaited them. A scowl crossed her face.

"None of your business, Calafe."

"My name is Romaine," he replied, though his gaze did not flicker.

"What?"

This time he turned towards her. Their eyes met and Erika swallowed despite herself. There was a darkness in those steel-blue orbs, a silent grief, an awful anger that promised retribution.

"It is traditional to call a man by his name," he said, voice not rising above a murmur.

Erika opened her mouth but the retort died on her tongue. He was right. Alone of all the soldiers in Fogmore, this man had volunteered to join her expedition. He was risking his life to help her—the least she could do was treat him with respect. She let out a long breath, swallowing her pride.

"My apologies, Romaine," she said, inclining her head. "I am thankful for your help."

A grim smile appeared on the warrior's face. "Thank me when we make it safely back to Flumeer. For now, I'd be happier to know what exactly that gauntlet of yours can do."

It was Erika's turn to smile. "On that, you will have to trust me, Romaine," she replied. "Let it be enough to know its effects are…unpleasant for those who cross me."

Romaine raised an eyebrow at that, but to her surprise he did not press the matter. His eyes returned to the mist. "Can't say I trust such magic," he murmured, "but after that last attack…I have a feeling we're going to need every weapon we can get on the other side."

Instinctively, Erika followed his gaze. The brave words of a few moments before turned to dust on her tongue as the mists began to lift. Dark trees appeared to the starboard of the ship, fog still clinging to their twisted branches.

Calafe waited.

20

THE WARRIOR

The forest was silent as Romaine guided his horse carefully between the trees, taking care to avoid the deep drifts beneath the trunks. There was no path here and with the tall pines stretching up around them, Romaine was navigating by instinct. At least the Archivist's map had been detailed—they were making for a plateau in the foothills. The area was beyond their usual scouting routes, but Romaine hoped it might be far enough east to avoid any Tangatan forces marching north.

He marked a tree with a cross as he rode past, then glanced back to check on Travis. They had decided it would be best if he and Cara did not scout together. Someone needed to ride ahead to check for ambushes and ensure the way was passable, but not the both of them. This way if the worst happened, the main party would still have a guide to get them back to Flumeer. Romaine had asked Travis to join him on Cara's horse instead, to be a runner between the groups should they encounter the Tangata.

The recruit offered a nod and Romaine returned his

gaze to the way ahead. If the horses were struggling with the snow, he didn't like to think how Lukys and the other recruits were managing. Marching through the snow, in the dead of winter, was not an enviable task.

At least there had been no sign of Tangata tracks so far. That could not last. A party of forty men and women could not go unnoticed forever. The Archivist was bargaining on their force being too large for a Tangata pair to challenge. The beasts would need time to gather more of their fellows to tackle the Perfugians. With luck, they would be long gone from Calafe before then.

At least, that was the hope.

The *thump* of snow falling came from off to their right. The hiss of inhaled breath followed from Travis, and even Romaine tensed, gaze sweeping the undergrowth. After a moment he shook himself and shared a grin with Travis. The recruit smiled back, though it did not reach his eyes. Romaine couldn't blame him. The Perfugian was in unknown territory now.

Even Romaine was struggling to find the usual peace he felt at returning to his homeland. The heady scent of pines was all around and the familiar trees stretched above, untouched by the axes of man. Gone was the cloying stench of smoke and human waste, the incessant pounding of hammers and clashing of practice weapons. This was his home, heavy with the silence of winter…

And yet…he felt something had changed. There was an edge to the air now, one Romaine had not felt before, not even when fleeing the Tangata on his last visit.

The two rode on, what little they could see of the sun through the canopy stretching higher into the sky, but still the source of Romaine's anxiety escaped him. Finally the trees began to thin, pines giving way to spruce and hemlock, and eventually beech. As the sun dipped back towards the horizon, clouds appeared to obscure the sky, and Romaine guessed it would snow again that night.

Thankfully he knew of an abandoned village slightly higher in the foothills. Now that the trees had thinned, he could use the mountain peaks for navigation, and tugging on his reins, he adjusted their path. The village would not be as far as the Archivist had wished to reach on their first day, but with the snow growing thicker, Romaine doubted the recruits could keep pace with her schedule anyway.

He and Travis reached the village several hours before dusk. Here the forest had been cleared to make way for stone cottages. Though there were only a dozen in total, each had been built from rocks of different sizes, likely taken from a nearby stream. The stones had been placed together like a jigsaw to form a whole, and mortar added later to make them whole.

The place had been abandoned less than a year before, but already signs of deterioration had set in. The thatched roofs of several had collapsed beneath the weight of snow, and saplings now grew amongst the stones, as the forest sought to reclaim what had been taken.

With Lukys and the others still some hours away, they dismounted and set about making the place ready. In the end, eight of the cottages were habitable, though Romaine had Travis climb up and dislodge the snow from atop several. Then they set about collecting firewood. They would not risk the smoke during the day, but once the sun set, the flames could be hidden inside one of the buildings.

"It's strange," Travis said when they finally stopped to rest.

They were seated on a stone bench outside one of the cottages, and rummaging in his saddlebag for the beef jerky,

Romaine almost missed what the recruit had said. Finally finding the right package, he drew it out and tossed Travis a piece before claiming a strip of his own. He took a bite before looking at his companion, one eyebrow raised.

"What's strange?"

Travis shrugged, then grinned. "It's just this place," he replied, "it almost looks...*normal.* I thought the Calafe were nomadic."

Romaine snorted. "That's what the Flumeerens think as well," he grunted, then tore another bite from his jerky. "It was always more a general dislike of cities," he answered at last. "Places like Fogmore and Charcity and Mildeth, they fight to keep nature out, to separate humanity from the land that bore us. Though, there *are* many of us who prefer a life in the forests."

"And this?" Travis asked, gesturing to the cottages.

Romaine snorted. "Winter houses," he replied. "Even for us, the winter is no time to be walking around in the forest."

"Oh really?" the recruit asked sarcastically. "You should have said something earlier—I *never* would have come had I known."

Despite himself, Romaine chuckled. "This is nothing yet," he said, gesturing to the nearby trees. "Once we get onto the plateaus, the winds blow straight off the mountains. There'll be no shelter our last night, not unless we get lucky and find the Archivist's ancient site quickly." He paused. "Which seems unlikely, given it hasn't been discovered in a millennia."

"Half a millennia," Travis replied absently, then when Romaine raised his eyebrows, continued: "At least, that's what they teach us in the academy: that The Fall took place five centuries ago."

"Useful," Romaine said wryly.

"It would make the Gods slightly less ancient than some would have us believe," he replied, though his tone made it clear he was sceptical. He paused, then glanced his way, eyes shining. "Have you ever seen them?"

"Who, a God?"

Travis nodded, though given his nature, Romaine still wasn't entirely sure he wasn't joking.

"Where would I have a seen a God, lad?"

"Up there!" he exclaimed, pointing. Through the tree-tops Romaine could still make out the highest peaks of the mountains. "That's where they're meant to live, right? I always thought the Calafe must have some secret knowledge of them, living so close."

"Afraid not," Romaine replied, though Travis's words sent a tremor racing down his spine. "The Mountains of the Gods are forbidden, even to the Flumeeren and Gemahan. No one goes there—or at least, no one that does ever returns." He frowned. "Isn't it the same way, with the ancient sites you've found in Perfugia?"

Travis shrugged. "Yeah, but those are different. The Gods left those. Besides, we fear those places...we're taught that the Gods didn't want to *cause* The Fall. It was an aftereffect of their magic, when they tried to destroy the Tangata."

"They failed," Romaine replied, then shrugged. "Though I suppose the reason hardly matters, after all this time."

"It matters to me," Travis murmured, his tone changing, becoming serious. His eyes drifted to the mountains. "I've always been fascinated by them."

Romaine grunted. "Perhaps you should talk with the Archivist."

"Perhaps I will," he replied, "though...I think Erika is

only interested in their magic, rather than the Gods themselves." He fell silent.

"There are rumours," Romaine offered after a moment, "legends, from those who claim to have seen the Gods."

"Really?" Travis asked quickly. "What do they look like?"

Romaine sighed, already regretting speaking up. "There are some who claim they're giants," he rumbled, "that they look like us, with human features, but standing as tall as the great redwoods of southern Calafe."

Travis snorted, the excitement draining from him somewhat. "Seems unlikely. I've seen sketches of these ancient sites the Archivist is so interested in. Some of the tunnels could barely fit a human."

"True." Romaine smiled despite himself. "Though perhaps their magic allows them to change shape."

The recruit nodded, and after a moment, Romaine continued.

"Others claim the Gods exist now only as spirits. That they retreated from the physical world after The Fall, in shame for what they had unleashed. More still claim they soar high above, up amongst the clouds, watching us even now."

Travis glanced upwards at his words, as though they might even now catch a glimpse of the Divine. Then a sheepish smile appeared on his lips and his gaze returned to Romaine.

"Our priests say the same," he replied.

"Who knows, lad?" Romaine waved a hand. "I haven't seen them. Though...I find it hard to believe they're watching. Not with the Tangata invading our lands, murdering... families, innocents."

The smile slipped from Travis's lips. "Maybe...maybe

they fear using their magic again, lest they bring about another Fall?"

"Another few years like the last, and humanity will be doomed anyway." Romaine shook his head. "The Flumeerens believe the Tangata are a test, to show whether we are worthy of the Gods' return." He forced himself to laugh. "Trust them to find something divine in the act of war."

Travis said nothing at that, and he saw the man's eyes had returned to the mountains. Romaine let out a sigh, unwilling to stomp any further on the man's dreams. Let the Perfugian recruits pray for deliverance. It could hardly hurt.

"So," he said, deciding at last to change the subject. "Has anything happened between you and Cara yet?"

"*What!*" Travis exclaimed, head swinging around so fast it must have given him whiplash.

Romaine chuckled but did not elaborate further.

"I…what…" he trailed off, his cheeks growing bright. A sheepish look crossed his face. "No. Ah…who else knows?"

"Relax," Romaine replied, still grinning. "I don't think anyone else has guessed. Too busy worrying about the Tangata, no doubt."

Travis nodded, though he still seemed worried. Finally he stood and began to pace up and down in front of the building.

"That's it isn't it?" he said at last. "We have bigger things to worry about. I shouldn't be getting distracted by…things!"

Romaine suppressed another bout of laughter. "Ah lad, you've got a lot to learn."

Travis scowled. "I didn't see a Calafe wife back in Fogmore."

Ice gripped Romaine's chest at his words and he sucked

in a breath, struggling to control a rush of rage. Exhaling slowly, he forced aside the pain.

"That's...personal," he said softly.

Travis looked up sharply and his eyes widened at the sight of Romaine's face. He opened his mouth to speak, but Romaine spoke over the top of him:

"Look lad, it's never the right time, okay?"

The recruit hesitated, but after a long moment, he nodded. Silence fell between them once more, and Romaine leaned back against the stone wall of the cottage, eyes on the sky. The clouds were growing darker. It would start to snow soon, and with night approaching, he hoped Lukys and the others were close.

As though summoned by the thought, the distant whinny of a horse carried to them on the breeze. Letting out a long sigh, Romaine levered himself to his feet and glanced down at Travis.

"Coming?"

Travis started as though he'd been caught unawares. A frown twisted his lips as he glanced at the trees, and his shoulders slumped.

"It's just...I failed, you know?" he murmured, slowly coming to his feet. "At literally *everything*."

"Forget the past, lad," Romaine sighed. "We've all failed at...something. That's no bad thing—so long as you learn from it. And from where I sit, you've done well these last weeks."

"If you say so..." Travis trailed off, then laughed. "Ah well, she probably wouldn't go for a city boy like me anyway."

"You'll never know unless you ask," Romaine replied, stepping past the man. "Now come on, they'll be tired from the trek."

He started down the slope towards the path they'd taken. Already movement was visible amongst the trees. Stones crunched a moment later as Travis followed. A smile touched his lips. The man had a good heart—

Romaine stumbled as realisation struck him; he suddenly knew what was off, the edge he'd felt ever since crossing the Illmoor. It wasn't something that had changed in Calafe at all.

It was him.

Always before when he'd come on these scouting trips, it had been with Flumeeren soldiers. Strangers. He didn't care whether they lived or died.

"Godsdamnit," he whispered to the winds.

This time, he cared.

🦋 21 🦋

THE RECRUIT

Lukys marched at the head of the column for much of their first day. Cara walked at his side, helping to pick out the marks Romaine and Travis had made for them to follow, though she said little. Returning to Calafe seemed to have left her lost for words. Lukys didn't press her—after all, how would he react in her situation? He could hardly imagine Perfugia falling, let alone returning after his land had been claimed by the enemy.

Unfortunately, the conversation was little better with the one who came behind them. So far, the Archivist had shown little interest in anyone but Romaine and, briefly, Cara. As for the rest of them…Lukys had spent enough time around the noble born in Perfugia to sense when someone thought herself above him.

As the day stretched on, the silence began to weigh on Lukys. Occasionally, he wandered back down the line of recruits, checking on their progress. Speaking with the others at least helped to dissolve some of the burden that grew in those silent hours.

It seemed to help the other Perfugians too. Despite their brave words the day before, many marched with their heads down, while others stared at the trees to either side of the thin trail, open fear on their faces. When he addressed them, they would look at him in fright, as though he were announcing the Tangata were upon them. Then their eyes would show recognition and their shoulders would relax, and they would nod and comment about the snow or their boots or the blasted Archivist sitting on her horse.

Lukys did his best to encourage them, though at times he felt it was more for himself than the others. In Romaine's absence and the Archivist's lack of interest in anyone but herself, he felt almost responsible for his fellow Perfugians. There was a voice in his head, whispering that he should have done more back in Fogmore, should have convinced them all to train together.

At midday he called a stop. That was probably the Archivist's responsibility, but she didn't seem interested, and several of the recruits looked close to dropping on their feet. Groans whispered through the trees as men and women lowered themselves to the ground and took out packages of food.

It disheartened Lukys to see their exhaustion. Despite the snow, the trek had been easy compared to their overland hike through Flumeer. The ground had climbed gently so far from the river, but from the path Romaine had outlined before setting out, soon they would start into the foothills. How would his fellow Perfugians manage that climb if they struggled on the flat?

Unfortunately, it wasn't long before the Archivist grew impatient and they were forced to continue. With their late departure, Erika was eager to press on and recover lost time.

Never mind that she rode a horse while the rest of them walked.

They set off with Lukys still in the lead, Cara and the Archivist close behind. It wasn't long, though, before Lukys dropped back again, standing to the side while the others continued. Cara lingered though, amber eyes watching him.

"You worry for them," she murmured.

Lukys shrugged. "Maybe." They started walking again.

Cara frowned. "They're not your responsibility."

"No," Lukys sighed. "Maybe I'm not doing it for them though."

The woman's frown only deepened at that and Lukys continued before she could speak, "Maybe I'm just trying to convince myself of something."

"Convince yourself of what?"

"I'm not sure," Lukys replied, then grinned. "I'll let you know when I figure it out. Go on, I'm going to talk with some of the others."

He waved her on and turned to wait for the rest of the column. Cara lingered, but after a moment she nodded and hurried to catch up with the Archivist.

"Bradbury, how's your legs?" Lukys commented as he fell into step with another of the recruits.

It was a moment before his new companion responded. "What?"

Lukys forced a smile and tried again. "Your legs, man! How are they?" he said, adopting a false bravado. "Mine feel as though they're about to fall off."

Bradbury stared at Lukys for a long moment, then returned his eyes to the road. "They're fine."

A sigh escaped Lukys's lips. Clearly this wasn't working. He needed to jerk the recruits out of this stupor that had come over them since entering Calafe.

AARON HODGES

"Shame we can't just give up, hey?" he continued. "Seems as nice a place as any to set camp, but what do I know. Good thing we've got Romaine, he'll know the best place to stop. This forest is probably infested with wolves or something!"

"Wolves!" Bradbury gasped. Eyes wide, he glanced around, as though the beasts might be creeping up on him at that very moment. "There are *wolves* in this forest?"

"Ahhhh." Lukys cursed inwardly at the fear in the man's face. "Maybe, but don't worry, don't you remember biology class? Wolves don't bother humans."

"That's not what the old tales say!"

"The old tales say a lot of things." Lukys slapped the man on the back. "Remember that one claiming the Calafe are part Tangata? Well, you've met Romaine, right? Does he look like one of those beasts to you?"

"I...no..." The recruit trailed off, before adding, "Though he *is* ferocious."

Lukys forced a laugh. "And he's on our side," he said. "Something to be thankful for, right? And look, the trees are beginning to thin, you can even see the mountains! I'm sure it won't be long before we catch up with Travis and the old Calafe."

With that he gave Bradbury a final nod and strode back up the line. Approaching the front of the column, he saw the Archivist had dismounted and was taking a turn at walking. Even more surprising, Cara sat on her horse, a large piece of paper held out before her.

"You see the red star?" Erika was saying.

"Where did you get this?" Cara murmured, eyes wide as she stared at the unfurled paper.

"One of the ancient sites," the Archivist replied. "Do you recognise the area?" Her voice took on an excited tone.

212

Drawing closer, Lukys saw that the paper Cara held was in fact a map. His heartbeat quickened as he realized this must be the relic the Archivist had discovered, the one directing them to the undiscovered site of the Gods. Lukys still loathed the thought of stepping foot in those ancient tunnels, of desecrating what had once been a sacred place of the Gods…

Sacred, secret, death.

…a shiver ran down Lukys's spine. The Archivist said that reclaiming the magic of the Gods was the only way to save humanity…but Lukys hadn't missed the glint in the woman's eyes when she spoke of that magic. She wanted more than just protection; she wanted *power*. His gaze was drawn to the gauntlet on her hand and he swallowed. Rumours had swirled amongst the recruits as to what it was, but Lukys knew. Romaine had told him.

It was another artefact, one with true magic. A weapon.

"It is…close to my home," Cara said hesitantly. "Though…I do not know the terrain well."

At least Cara was talking again. She seemed fascinated by the Archivist, though Lukys couldn't see why. Perhaps it was the novelty of meeting a Flumeeren aristocrat, or the woman's study of the Gods. Either way, the interest had not seemed to be reciprocated until now.

"May I see?" Lukys asked as he joined Cara on the other side of the horse from the Archivist.

"Why?" Erika asked sharply. She grasped the reins, as though suddenly fearing Cara would flee.

Lukys raised an eyebrow. "I don't know the terrain. It would be good to know what to expect if we're to protect you, Archivist."

The woman stared at him across the horse, as though if

she looked long enough, she might read his mind. Finally, she shrugged and gestured her permission.

"Careful," Cara murmured. Dismounting, she handed it over to him. "It's…old."

"No kidding," Lukys replied as he took it from her hands.

He unfurled the map as he walked, taking care to keep one eye on the uneven ground. It surprised him to see that colours filled the paper, greens and browns and blues and whites and many more. A quick glance suggested what he held was more painting than map. Certainly it was nothing like the charts back in the academy. Those were all black lines and empty spaces on yellowed pages.

As he inspected the mixtures of colours, landmarks started to leap at him from the page. There, a large mass of green and white set apart from the rest, surrounded by blue. He could not read the names on the map, but it had to be Perfugia. He followed the coastline south, amazed at the detail the ancients had captured, until he found a great river. Its position had shifted, but it could only be the Illmoor. Further inland and to the south, he found the red star the Archivist had mentioned.

"This is where we're going?" he asked.

Stepping back into the saddle of her horse, the Archivist ignored him, but Cara leaned closer.

"Yes, I…think it is a part of the foothills." She frowned, brow furrowing. "That dark green, I think that means it was forest, but there are no trees there now."

"I see," Lukys murmured, his eyes continuing. "Then these here must be the Mountains of the Gods?"

"I…" Cara hesitated, glancing at Lukys then up at the Archivist. Swallowing, she nodded. "I think so."

"Yes, it has to be," he continued excitedly, pointing to

white and grey blotches on the paper. "You see these lines? They circle around the white spots—those must be the peaks. The closer they come together, the steeper the slope. They're called—"

"Contours," the Archivist interrupted from her horse.

Lukys glanced at her. "We learnt about them at the Perfugian academy. But…" He hesitated, glancing back at the map. "I've never seen any so detailed." Then he frowned, noticing something else. There was another red star. "And this…there's another site, in the Mountains of the Gods themselves."

No, no, no!

On her horse, Erika chuckled. "You look like you've seen a ghost, Perfugian."

"I…but…" He swallowed. "If this is truly a map of their sacred sites, you realise…"

"*No!*" Cara exclaimed unexpectedly. Before he could react, she snatched the map from his hands.

"*Careful,*" Erika hissed, swinging her horse in front of them. "The boy is right, that star could be the home of the Gods *themselves!*" She dropped from the saddle and almost stumbled. Cursing, she caught Cara by the arm. "Gods, woman, I did not think the Calafe so superstitious."

A tremor shook Cara as she clutched the map to her jacket. Even Lukys found himself shaking. If what the Archivist suspected was true…*Gods,* surely that was blasphemous knowledge? To know where the Gods themselves lived…

"But it's *forbidden!*" Cara whispered.

"Definitely not a good idea," Lukys said at the same time.

"Oh, calm down," Erika said, rolling her eyes. "We're not actually *going* there. The queen has prohibited even speaking of it." She paused, then muttered another curse. "I should have known better than to show you the map. Quick, give it back." Lips pursed, she held out her hand to Cara.

The woman bit her lip, glancing to Lukys then back to the Archivist. Finally she nodded and handed over the map. Erika rolled it back up and slid it into a metal cylinder before placing it in her knapsack. A grin touched her lips as she looked at them again.

"Our superstitions never cease to amaze me," she murmured. "Don't you see? The Gods *left* this for us to find. It is an invitation. They *want* us to come to them." As she spoke, she lifted her gauntleted hand and clenched it into a fist. "Though of course, only the worthy will be welcomed."

A faint light seeped from the woven steel.

It turned Lukys's insides to ice.

22

THE WARRIOR

Romaine groaned as he lowered himself onto the wall at the edge of the village and watched the recruits going about organising their camp—although there wasn't much organisation to be seen. A watch had been set to keep eyes on the forest, but otherwise the Perfugians were doing a poor job of dividing up the eight habitable cottages between them.

Given that the general had put him in charge, Romaine probably should have taken more responsibility, but his mind was occupied. On other scouting trips, he had rarely gone a day without glimpsing signs of the Tangata. That was why they'd spent so little time this side of the Illmoor. So far though, there hadn't been a whisper, not even a boot print in the snow.

After the attack on Fogmore, he'd half expected these forests to be crawling with Tangata. Yet now they found northern Calafe empty. The enemy's tactics often seemed incomprehensible, but this was stranger still. The assault, though made up of at least a dozen Tangata, had never stood a chance of taking the city. Curtis had assumed it had been a precursor, a probe before a greater force attempted the crossing.

Now, though…could the attack have been punitive? Romaine and the scouts had killed two of their number… but no, the Tangata were prone to rages, but they rarely threw lives away on hopeless causes.

Romaine found himself shaking his head. He could make no sense of it. And that worried him.

Movement came from nearby, and Romaine looked up to see Cara approaching. The frown on her face was a mirror of Romaine's own, and he couldn't help but smile at the sight.

"Why the sad face, lass?" he asked as she walked up.

Cara started at his voice, then gave a shrug. Romaine gestured for her to join him on the wall.

"I thought you'd be happy, being back here. This is what you wanted, isn't it?"

"I…coming back is not what I imagined." She rolled her shoulders, eyes turning to the sky. "I never expected…" A sheepish smile tugged at her lips. "To make friends."

A lump lodged in Romaine's throat as she echoed his earlier thoughts, but he pushed it aside. "You're still young, lass," he replied. "Nothing wrong with making a few friends."

Cara sighed, shifting slightly on the wall. It had been constructed in the same manner as the cottages, rocks fitted one on top of the other, though no mortar had been used here. It made finding a comfortable position difficult, and Cara spent a long moment wiggling before settling again.

"I…I have to go, Romaine," she whispered.

"What?" His heart gave a painful throb. "Go *where?*"

"I told you," she murmured, still looking at the sky,

anywhere but at him, it seemed. "I have to…find my family."

"You're sure…" He trailed off, not wanting to finish the sentence, but it had to be said. "You're sure they're still alive, Cara?"

She shrugged, not saying anything, but he could see the darkness in her eyes. She didn't know. Maybe she even thought them dead. But until she saw, until she knew for sure…a spark of hope would live on. Romaine knew that feeling well. For too long he had clung to it, like a man clutching to a jagged ledge, knowing it could not save him, and yet…unable to let go.

Living torture.

"I understand," he said at last.

"Why am I not surprised!" Romaine looked up to see Travis approaching.

The recruit whistled as he walked; of all the Perfugians, he alone seemed to be unaffected by their predicament. At least outwardly. Romaine's heart twisted as he recalled their earlier conversation about Cara.

"Leave it to the Calafe to skirt work," Travis continued as he reached them, grinning. "Where do I sign up?"

Romaine grunted. "When you lose your kingdom, we'll talk."

"I…ah…sure…"

The recruit trailed off, looking awkward, and Romaine laughed. "Come and sit, lad," he said, gesturing to the wall.

A smile lit Cara's face as Travis sat beside her, though now Romaine did not miss the edge of sadness that crinkled the corners of her eyes. He sighed. The lad deserved to know…

"So when will you go?" he murmured softly, looking at Cara, "Looking for your family, I mean."

Cara stiffened at his words and she flashed him a glare that could have melted stone. Beside her, Travis looked from Romaine to Cara, a frown twisting his lips.

"You're leaving?"

Biting her lip, Cara looked at the young man, and nodded. "I have to," she said. "My family…I can't stay with you."

"I…see." Travis swallowed, his Adam's apple bobbing up and down. "Of course…"

He trailed off, and an uncomfortable silence fell between them. Romaine cursed inwardly. It had needed to be done, but he should have let Cara broach the subject. After a few minutes, Travis let out a sigh and rose.

"Well…I'd better see if the others need any help," he said, rising. He flashed a smile, though even to Romaine it seemed forced, then wandered back towards the village.

Flashing Romaine another glare, Cara leapt to her feet and chased after him. She did not glance back.

Letting out a sigh, Romaine rose and set off along the waist-high-wall that marked the perimeter of the village. The sun had set and he wanted to check on the lookouts he'd set before it grew completely dark. All were where he had left them.

He found the last standing nervously watching the forest, spear and shield held tight to her chest. Recognising her as one of those who had been training with him, he waved her over.

"Go find yourself some food, lass," he said. "I'll take the watch."

"Are you sure?" she asked, though her expression revealed her eagerness to be away from the trees.

Romaine nodded. "Go, I could use the quiet."

She left, leaving him alone with the night. Letting out a

groan, Romaine took her place on the wall, his joints popping. Cara would get over her anger, if she did not leave immediately. She'd said the ancient site was close to her home; he hoped that meant she would stick around at least another day.

Overhead, moonlight touched the sky, setting the distant mountains aglow. They hulked like giants on the horizon, reminding him of the stories he'd told Travis. Perhaps that was the true source of the Calafe legends. Had their ancestors after The Fall come to see those hulking peaks as Gods, passing down tales until modern men viewed them as the birthplace of the Divine?

He almost preferred the idea. For if the Gods truly roamed those remote peaks, how could he not but hate them? It had been their magic, stolen or otherwise, that had given birth to the Tangata. Yet if the legends were true, instead of aiding humanity, the Gods had cast them down, abandoning them to the darkness.

"We lit the fire where you said," came Lukys's voice from the darkness. A second later the recruit appeared, face lit by the cold light of the moon. He held out a bowl made from bark, something Romaine and Travis had prepared before their arrival. "Gruel?"

Romaine nodded his thanks, then took a spoonful and almost spat it back out. It was saltier than jerky. Managing to swallow the mouthful, he set the bowl aside.

"Travis…isn't much of a cook," Lukys said. He hesitated, standing in the darkness, eyes on the trees. "Cara…told us."

"Is she okay?" Romaine asked, turning his eyes towards the trees.

Lukys shrugged and took a seat beside him. "She's fine. Travis will be alright," he hesitated, flicking a glance in

Romaine's direction. "It's the rest of them I'm worried about. I tried to encourage them today, keep their spirits up. I don't think it helped much."

Romaine grunted. "They don't need mothering, lad," he said. Reaching up, he took the axe from its sheath on his back and held it up. Its twin blades shone in the moonlight. "They're not children; you can't tell them everything is going to be alright. They know it's not. Chances are, some of us are going to die before this journey is done."

"Then what do I do?" Lukys whispered. "They're terrified, on the verge of giving up. How do I hold them together?"

A sigh slipped from Romaine's lips. Lukys was taking too much on his shoulders, but then…what else could he do? Romaine couldn't do everything by himself. Someone had to step up.

Taking a firmer grip on his axe, Romaine drove its twin points into the earth. Lukys flinched, but did not look away as their eyes met.

"Show them your strength," Romaine said quietly. "When everything is dark, soldiers need to believe in their commanders—even if they don't believe in themselves."

Lukys swallowed, his eyes wide in the darkness, but finally he nodded. "I understand," he murmured. "I'll do my best."

"That's all anyone can ask, lad," Romaine replied, his heart swelling as he saw the resolve in the other man's eyes.

An image flickered into his mind, of another boy, eyes staring up from a bed of snow. He clenched his fist closed around the hilt of his axe, trying to keep the pain from his face.

"You want me to take over the watch?" Lukys asked.

Romaine raised an eyebrow at the young Perfugian. "You think I'm too old to look out for a few Tangata?"

A wry grin appeared on Lukys's lips as he stood. "Just being polite," he replied, "but since you're apparently happy to sit here in the cold, I think I'll go see if our second cooks any better." He raised a hand in farewell, then turned and disappeared into the darkness.

And Romaine was left alone with his pain.

THE RECRUIT

Mountains in a grey sky.
     A blood-red moon.
Stark slopes of rock.
Screaming in the earth.
Desperation, despair, lost.
Then…hope!
Life!
A flash, then an image, not like the others…
Colourful, blue and green and white and grey.
Lines of black.
A star of red.
Life!

Lukys gasped as he jerked awake, sitting bolt upright. Curses came from alongside him as the two recruits he shared the tent with mumbled in their sleeping rolls, though neither woke.

Clutching at his chest, Lukys strained to see in the darkness, but no light penetrated the heavy canvas. The sun had not yet risen, and finally he lay back against the hard ground, trying to force his mind to calm. The dream was already fading, though it had seemed so vivid, almost real. He could not have said why, but it left him feeling disturbed. It must have been his exhaustion.

They had marched hard their second day, leaving behind the forest and moving into foothills. Despite the lack of trees, there the going had become harder, as the recruits were forced to scramble up slopes of loose gravel. Even the flatter sections were inundated with spiked shrubs that would catch at their clothing and tear their skin, until they were forced to use knives to cut their way free.

It would have been even worse if not for Romaine's scouting. Travis had ridden with the Calafe again, though at times the column had caught them as they backtracked from a false slope. Thankfully, their efforts kept the rest of them from hiking up the wrong hills; otherwise, Lukys doubted there would have been a single Perfugian on his feet by the end of the day. There had been a collective groan of relief when they'd finally spied Romaine and Travis waiting for them at a notch in the hillside.

Romaine said they would reach the Archivist's plateau by dusk the following day. Though it was half a day behind the Archivist's schedule, Lukys was just glad they still hadn't encountered any of the Tangata.

Finally realising he wasn't going back to sleep, Lukys stifled a moan and slipped out of his bedroll. Unbuttoning the tent flap, he pulled on his boots and stood, closing things again behind him. Then he went searching for one of the lookouts.

The night was clear, though the air was so cold it hurt to breathe. He shivered as he saw the moon overhead, recalling the scarlet globe from his dreams, though here it remained a brilliant silver. It illuminated the dusting of snow on the ground, left over from the fall they'd had the night they'd stayed in the village.

Though Romaine had chosen the campsite for its shelter, a light wind still blew through the valley, raising goosebumps on Lukys's neck. He pulled his fur cloak tighter around himself, then froze as a noise carried to him on the breeze. Suddenly alert, he scanned the hillside around the tent, but in the darkness, it was difficult to tell rock from enemy.

Movement flickered in the shadows. Lukys was about to cry out a warning when the sound came again. Voices. The hairs on his neck stood on end. The Tangata did not speak, but who would be out here in the night? Heart racing, he crept through the lines of canvas tents, eyes fixed on the point he'd seen movement.

"Lukys?"

He started as a whisper came from nearby, reaching for the dagger on his belt. His hand was on the hilt when he realised it was only Cara. Letting out a long breath, he released the blade. For a moment he thought she'd been the speaker, then the whisper of voices came on the breeze again.

"*Quiet,*" he hissed, eyes returning to the hillside. Had they heard her? Stepping closer, he raised a finger to his lips. "What are you doing out here?"

Her eyes widened. "I…couldn't sleep?"

Lukys frowned. "Are you leavin…"

He trailed off as the whispers came again. This time Cara heard them too and swung around, eyes fixed on the darkness. "What are they doing up there?"

"They?"

"Some of your recruits," she replied softly.

Squinting into the night, Lukys cursed, still unable to

spot the speakers. "I don't know," he murmured, "but we'd better find out. Come on."

He started forward, crouched low to the ground and taking care not to disturb the loose stones as he moved. Cara followed, her step so light he had to keep checking to know where she was. The voices came from further up the valley, on the slope that sheltered the camp from the mountain winds.

There was meant to be a scout posted nearby, but they found the position empty. Lukys cursed. If they couldn't even trust the other Perfugians to keep watch…

"…only a…of em."

Lukys froze as the voices grew louder, allowing him to recognise several scattered words. Beside him, Cara froze, casting an uncertain glance in his direction. He bid her to wait. Blood pounded in his ears as he strained to hear the rest of the conversation.

"…you seen…that axe…"

Still unable to make out all the words, Lukys crept closer, trying to make sense of them.

"Better than the Tangata!" a man exclaimed, far louder than the others.

Whispers hissed in the night as others quieted him, then silence. Lukys held his breath as he sensed movement above, then a flash of white as someone peered out from behind a boulder and looked down the slope. Crouching lower amongst the rocks, Lukys prayed for Cara to do the same. He wasn't sure what the recruits above were planning yet, but it couldn't be anything good.

A moment later the recruit retreated and the conversation resumed.

"You know they're out here," the last speaker continued in a softer tone. "We've been lucky so far, but how long is that going to last? Sooner or later the beasts will find us. I don't want to be around when they do."

"I dunno…" another argued. This time Lukys recognised the speaker—Bradbury. "You think we can survive without them? The Tangata aren't the only things in these woods, you know…"

Another of the recruits laughed. "You still on about them wolves, Bradbury?"

"We have to go," the first voice repeated.

"What about the Archivist? If she makes it back, we'll be branded as traitors."

"Then we make sure none of them make it back."

Silence answered the speaker's words. Below, Lukys's heart pounded against his chest. He shared a glance with Cara. Her eyes were wide, shining in the moonlight, and he swallowed. They were talking about a mutiny, though from here he could not tell how many.

"We say the Tangata attacked," the speaker continued. The other's silence seemed to have made him bold. "No one will question it. You heard the general, he already thinks this is a fool's errand. Mark my words, he'll be thankful any of us returned!"

Lukys's shock turned slowly to anger. How dare they! Romaine had volunteered to come, to protect them all, yet these recruits planned to murder him. He clenched his fists, though he knew he could not risk a confrontation. With only his knife and Cara for support, he'd be quickly overwhelmed.

He rose and slipped back towards the camp. If they could raise the alarm, the traitors would not have a chance to enact their plan—

The moon slipped behind a cloud, plunging the night

into utter black. He cursed, stumbling on the uneven ground…

Crack.

His foot struck a rock, sending it tumbling down the slope. Lukys froze where he stood, praying the darkness would shield him…but then the moon reappeared overhead, casting its silver light across the valley.

"*There!*"

Stones rattled above as shadows raced towards him. Stomach twisting in knots, Lukys looked in the direction of camp. They'd come farther than he'd thought. No way he'd make it before the recruits overtook him. He looked at Cara.

"Go warn Romaine," he murmured.

Cara glanced at the approaching shadows, eyes wide, face pale in the moonlight. For a second it seemed she would do as he said. But shuddering, she pulled her cloak tighter around herself and faced the traitors. Lukys nodded. It was probably too late for her to escape anyway.

The traitors slowed as they approached. There were a dozen of them, each armed with their spears, though they didn't wear armour. They spread out around him, weapons at the ready.

"Lukys," Bradbury gasped, his weapon held awkwardly to his chest.

"Of course." Another recruit pushed past the man, a sneer on his lips. It was a moment before Lukys recalled his name—Dyge. "Little bastard, always sticking his nose in other people's business."

Lukys scanned the ring of Perfugians, noting those who seemed doubtful, others who looked ready to run him through. Dale stood amongst the circle, though for once he did not appear to be the ringleader. Drawing in a breath, Lukys faced Dyge.

"Quite the commotion you lot are making out here," he said softly, fighting for calm. "Think you'd best return to your tents, before you catch your death."

"Is that a threat, peasant?" Dyge snarled, stalking forward until they stood face-to-face.

Lukys did not flinch away. "It's a cold night," he said, spreading his hands. "Anyone with half a brain should know to be in his bed."

Whispers came from around the circle as those who had looked uncertain shared glances.

His foe only growled and grabbed Lukys by the front of his shirt. "What's the matter?" Dyge laughed. "No Calafe warrior to come to your rescue?"

Lukys calmly looked from the man's hands to his eyes, though inwardly his heart was racing. His hand crept to his belt as he spoke. "Release me."

"Like The Fall," Dyge snapped. Then he grinned, the gesture a cold, hungry look. "You know, I think you were right. In this cold, you might just catch your dea—"

He broke off as Lukys pressed the point of his knife into the man's groin. Dyge's mouth opened but Lukys pushed the knife harder.

Death, death, death.

"I suggest," Lukys said again, "that you return to your tent."

"I…" Dyge swallowed, then nodded eagerly. "Yes, you're right. I think I'll do that." He released Lukys's shirt and raised his hands, gesturing at the knife.

Lukys lingered, holding the man's gaze before finally drawing back. Dyge licked his lips, still appearing nervous, while Lukys turned to look at the others.

"We're all afraid, remember," he said, "but our only

hope is to stay together. Alone, we don't stand a chance out here."

The others said nothing, unable to meet his eyes, and Lukys nodded his satisfaction. In silence he shared a glance with Cara, then led her towards a gap in the circle.

"I'd rather die alone than stand with the likes of you," Dyge's voice came from behind them.

Die, die, die.

Lukys spun, knife still in hand, but his foe now held a spear. The razor-sharp point flashed for Lukys's throat…

…and was knocked aside as another recruit leapt to his aid. A roar of anger came from Dyge, but before he could bring his weapon around to attack again, the newcomer slammed the tip of his spear into the man's chest.

A stunned look appeared in Dyge's eyes as he looked up at the recruit that had stabbed him.

"Da…Dale?"

Blood burst from his lips as Dale yanked back his spear, allowing the traitor to slump to the ground. He stepped back, eyes still on the body, spear clutched at the ready. Lukys could only stare at the man, unable to believe it had been *Dale* who had come to his rescue.

Finally Dale lowered his spear. He still did not look at Lukys, but instead turned to face the circle of recruits. They stared back at him, open fear on their faces.

"Dyge was a fool," he said softly, "and if any of you think the same as him, you're fools as well. None of us would last a day out here without the Calafe. The Tangata would have you by suppertime."

"The Tangata will have us anyway," Bradbury said, looking despondent.

"Maybe," Dale replied. Finally he looked at Lukys. "But I'd rather die with honour than as a traitor."

"Dyge was the only deserter here," Lukys said, his voice hard. He ignored the others who'd looked ready to murder him—they could not fight them all. "Go back to your beds and speak no more of this."

The eyes of several flickered to Dyge's body, and Lukys caught a glimpse of anger there. But it faded as they looked again at Lukys and Dale and Cara, giving way to resignation. Without further word, they collected up their spears and started off towards the camp.

Lukys let out a long breath as he watched them go, and allowed the mask to slip. He swallowed, legs suddenly trembling as he realised how close he'd come to death.

"Thank you," he said, offering a hesitant smile to Dale.

The young noble grunted. "Don't take it personally," he replied. "Like you said, doesn't matter if we're friends or enemies. We need to stick together this side of the Illmoor." With that he turned and followed the others, leaving Lukys standing alone with Cara.

They stood there a while, saying nothing. Lukys stared out into the darkness, replaying the moment again and again. Inevitably, his gaze was drawn to the body of Dyge. He'd underestimated the man—but had it been his hatred, or his desperation? A shiver ran down his spine and he forced himself to look away.

"I'm sorry," Cara whispered, drawing Lukys's gaze.

She stood with her arms wrapped around herself, eyes staring into the distance, tears streaking her cheeks. Surprised, he shook his head.

"Sorry for what?"

"I should have stopped him," Cara whispered. Her amber eyes flickered to Dyge's body, shining in the moonlight. A shudder went through her. "So much...blood."

Blood, blood, blood.

"Hey, it's not your fault," Lukys exclaimed, stepping close and opening his arms to hug her.

She flinched away, eyes wide, and he remembered her fear of being touched.

"Sorry," he said, turning his hands palm out. Then he smiled. "But I'm okay."

Cara watched him for a long while before responding with a nod. "Okay." She yawned, stretching her arms, before a grin appeared on her face. "Guess we'd better head back to camp then." She gestured at the mountain slopes around them. "Who knows what else is out roaming in the moonlight?"

Lukys started as his dream came rushing back to him, the scarlet moon, the shadows rushing across a barren slope, the thumping of blood in his ears.

Not seeming to notice, Cara started off towards the camp. Lukys followed after a moment's hesitation, though his mind was elsewhere, lingering on the dream, on that moon. The same moon that hung above them, though without the red…

…he glanced back towards where Dyge lay, though in the darkness he could no longer make out the body.

Nor the blood that now stained the rocks.

❧ 24 ❧

THE ARCHIVIST

Impatient to be going, Erika had the Perfugians break camp in the dark so they could be on the road at dawn. She was surprised there had been no complaints, though there had been a sullen mood about the soldiers as they set off. Too bad; they were already half a day behind schedule —she'd wanted the afternoon to explore the area, hopefully find the unknown entrance.

Perhaps if the recruits increased their pace, they might still reach the site with daylight to spare. She sought out the young man who seemed to take on the role of officer while the Calafe was absent. What was his name...Lukys! She spotted him marching at the front as usual and edged her horse alongside him.

"Lukys," she said, drawing his attention. Eyes ringed by shadow glanced at her from the road, and she hesitated a moment before continuing: "Your soldiers need to pick up the pace. I want to reach our destination before we lose the light."

A groan came from behind her, but Erika ignored the other recruits.

An extended moment passed before Lukys shook his head. "No," he said, and returned his eyes to the road.

"What…" Erika's mouth fell open, shocked at the man's disobedience. *She* was in charge here, not this upstart of a soldier. Clenching her fist, she took control of her emotions. "That was not a question, recruit," she said, voice cold now.

"I know," the man replied, eyes fixed straight ahead.

"Then just what do you think you're doing?" Erika hissed, losing control despite her best efforts.

"Keeping us all alive," came the response. He glanced in her direction. "With all due respect, *Archivist*, you don't have a clue."

"How dare—"

"I dare!" the recruit snapped, swinging on her. She flinched in the saddle and tried to pull away, but he snatched the reins, bringing the horse to a stop. Angry eyes glared up at her. "I dare, because if you push them any harder, we'll have a mutiny on our hands." He sucked in a breath, and seemed to calm somewhat. Releasing the reins, he stepped back. "If you didn't notice, we're already a man short today."

He started off again, leaving Erika sitting stunned on her horse. Cursing, she shook herself and kicked the beast after him.

"What do you mean, a mutiny?" she hissed.

"It's taken care of," Lukys replied, eyes ignoring her again.

Erika swore beneath her breath, but decided it best not to press the man. Suddenly, she wished Romaine had not ridden so far ahead. Clutching her fist, she sought out the power of the gauntlet, feeling its warmth as it began to glow. She let out a long breath, the pressure in her chest relenting a little. It came racing back as she remembered the forty-odd soldiers marching behind her. Even with the magic of the Gods, she could not fight them all.

"Are you okay, Erika?" Cara asked, approaching on Erika's left.

"I'm fine," she said shortly. Clutching her reins close, Erika tried to quell her racing heart.

Laughter came from the Calafe girl. "You look like you woke up on the wrong side of the tent." She leaned closer in a conspiratorial manner, eyes dancing. "Or just found out about the excitement in the night."

"I…" Erika glanced sharply at the woman. "You were there."

Cara only shrugged and began to whistle.

Erika opened her mouth, then decided it was best to forget about the whole thing. She couldn't cope with the strangeness of these people. The Perfugian spoke of a missing man and walked as though he carried a boulder on his shoulders, and meanwhile the Calafe woman…whistled?

No wonder Erika's mother had decided to return to Flumeer after her father had died. If all the Calafe were as strange as Cara, or stoic as Romaine…not to mention the boredom of life in this wild, untamed world. Erika couldn't understand how anyone could live in a village such as the one they'd camped in for the night, so far from the pleasures of civilisation.

Sure, she had enjoyed that life as a child, when the forests and mountains had been an unending land of adventure…but children were easily entertained. A true Flumeeren could never have been happy with such an existence.

The weather warmed as the day passed on, melting the

last of the snow from the slopes—and turning the ground to mud. To Erika's frustration, their progress slowed further, though she decided to keep her mouth shut for the moment. By the time the column stopped to lunch, they had barely covered five miles.

Erika was just dismounting when a distant sound carried down from the slope they were about to traverse. Lukys was on his feet in an instant, swinging the shield from his pack and holding his spear at the ready. A moment later the noise resolved into hoofbeats as a rider topped the crest of the nearby hill.

The man, Travis, riding hard.

"Perfugians, at the ready," Lukys bellowed.

The rattling of steel came from behind them as the recruits clambered to their feet and clutched at their weapons. Some even seemed to know what to do with them.

Heart racing, Erika eyed the crest of the hill, reins clutched tightly in one fist. Travis was racing down the slope towards them, seemingly uncaring of the uneven ground. There was no sign of Romaine. She cursed beneath her breath. Had the Tangata finally appeared?

Movement came from the top and Erika released a breath as the Calafe warrior appeared. His axe remained undrawn and he was riding slower than the recruit. She took it as a good sign and edged her horse forward alongside Lukys.

"What is it, recruit?" she called as the woman rode up.

"Travis, are you okay?" Lukys asked at the same time.

The man's face was pale as he pulled to a stop, his horse drenched in sweat. They must have ridden hard and for some distance. Blood thundered in Erika's ears and she wanted to scream as the man sucked in great lungfuls of air.

"Tangata!" he gasped finally.

Erika's blood ran cold.

No, no, no.

It couldn't end like this, not when they were so close, just a few hours from triumph. The secrets of the Gods, of their magic, she could almost *feel* it, pulsing in her fingertips…

…she started as the others looked at her, foreheads creased in concern. Light pulsed from her fist and she realized the magic of the gauntlet had arisen unbidden. Ice touched her chest and she forced herself to exhale. The light faded slowly.

No harm done, she thought, hoping her face did not show her shock. Out loud, she said:

"How many?"

The man swallowed as he met Erika's gaze. "Twenty, at least."

Gasps came from behind Erika and she gritted her teeth. Twenty was an army, far too many for one regiment, even had they been properly trained. A curse slipped from her lips before she controlled herself.

"Where?"

"Heading towards us," the recruit said shortly. "They don't seem to know we're here, but…we're right in their path."

Erika cursed again, though the pounding of hooves as Romaine rode up covered the words. She looked to the Calafe warrior, hoping against hope he would refute the recruit's claims.

"You can put those away," he said as he dismounted, looking past Erika to the recruits formed up behind her. "We're not in danger—yet. They've set camp for the day."

"What is your assessment, Romaine?" Erika said, remaining in her saddle.

"The Tangata are ahead of us," he said as though their

path was clear. "Too many for us to fight. Thankfully we were downwind. The horses sensed them before we did and we weren't seen. But they're definitely heading in this direction."

"We have to turn back!" called a voice from the recruits behind Erika. Others rose in agreement. She ignored them, fixing her eyes on Romaine, waiting for him to continue.

The warrior spread his hands. "I'm sorry, Archivist. We have to turn back, and quickly, or there'll be no avoiding crossing their path."

"Unacceptable," Erika snapped, no longer bothering to contain her anger. "The fate of humanity is at stake. We must press on, whatever the cost."

"The cost will be your life," Romaine replied bluntly.

A shudder went through Erika at his words, and suddenly she was back in the throne room, standing before the queen, subjected to her displeasure.

Do not fail me.

Erika didn't need to ask what would happen if she returned without new treasures. The queen had been promised the magic of the Gods and she would have it— even if it meant cutting the gauntlet from Erika's corpse.

No one else had moved at Romaine's words. They all looked to her, waiting for her to speak, to accept her fate.

"The cost of failure will be my life regardless, Romaine," she said softly, forcing herself to meet the warrior's eyes. "So I will go on, alone if needs be. Maybe I can slip by them, though without you, I doubt it." She hesitated, before adding: "You and I both know how it would look to General Curtis should you return without me."

A moment of silence answered her words, followed by the angry buzz of voices. Erika's heart pounded hard in her chest but she held the Calafe's gaze, determined not to be the first to break.

"Are you truly so selfish," he whispered, without a trace of anger in his voice, "that you would sacrifice us all for your folly?"

Erika lifted her chin, defiant. "I…" She hesitated, the words stumbling on her tongue before she recovered her composure. "For the fate of humanity, I refuse to turn back."

Romaine shook his head. Stepping from the path they had been following, he slumped onto a boulder. Erika was shocked to see the despair in the man's eyes. The Perfugians fell silent as they saw the hero who had led them this far bowed low. A cold wind blew across the mountainside, sending shivers down Erika's spine, but still she did not retreat.

"What if just a few of us cut through the hills?" a voice said from alongside Erika.

She started as the recruit, Lukys, stepped into her path. There was a determined glint in the man's eyes as he faced her, spear held firmly in hand, head high. Where Romaine looked ready to give up, somehow this recruit still radiated strength.

"What are you suggesting?" she asked, intrigued.

"Romaine is right; the entire regiment cannot continue unnoticed. When the Tangata continue in this direction, they'll pick up our tracks and follow. Whatever we do, it will be a race to reach the Illmoor before they catch us." He drew in a breath before continuing. "But they might miss a few of us if we split from the rest and took another trail to reach the site."

"Another trail?" Erika pressed, heart throbbing painfully in her chest. Could there really be another way?

Lukys gestured up the mountain. They'd been cutting across the hillside, making for the pass Romaine and Travis had returned from not long ago. "We've been following the easier passages through the hills," the Perfugian continued, "but what if we cut straight over the mountain?"

Glancing up the slope, Erika wondered if such a thing was even possible. These foothills were mere shadows of the Mountains that loomed beyond, but the slope Lukys had indicated was still steep, and covered in loose gravel. It would be a terrible, dangerous climb. The horses certainly could not pass that way. And even if they reached the top, there was no telling what else awaited. The way down might prove impassable.

She glanced at Romaine, waiting to see what the warrior would say, but Cara spoke up instead: "There is a path down the other side."

Erika's breath caught in her throat as she spun to face the woman. "Truly?" she gasped. "You've been that way before?"

Cara hesitated. Her eyes flickered in her face as she bit her lip. "I've seen it from afar," she said at last. "A path between the cliffs—steep, but passable. I think."

"Then we try it," Erika said, turning to Romaine.

The warrior looked back at her, eyes still hard, and she saw now his anger. He hated her for making him consider this option, for making them take this risk. She didn't care. They had a chance!

"Very well," he said, rising. "Let's be about it then." Turning, he cast his gaze over the column of recruits. "Travis, do you think you could find the way back to the trees?"

The man hesitated, but after a moment he nodded. "I think so."

"Good. You'll take the horses and lead the recruits back to the Illmoor. Leave everything behind you don't need and don't stop except for sleep; once the Tangata find your scent, you can be sure they won't. Once you reach the river, signal the other side. The forts all know to look for us. Don't wait; hopefully the Tangata don't notice our scent, but if they do, we're dead."

Travis hesitated, but after a moment he nodded. Drawing in a breath, Romaine turned to the other recruits.

"Lukys, Cara…" He paused, eyeing the Perfugians lined up across the hillside. The recruits shifted nervously on their feet. "Dale and Groner," he named two of the recruits Erika didn't recognise, "you're with us."

Erika was surprised when the two stepped forward immediately. Romaine had chosen well, but there was another problem. She swung on the Calafe.

"We need more," she said quickly. "To bring back what we find."

"No," Romaine rumbled. "You see that slope, those rocks? A single misplaced step could start a small avalanche. Six will make enough noise as it is; any more would doom us. If the Tangata have scouts out, we'll likely fail anyway. No, you'll have to make do with the six of us."

Erika swallowed, but it was clear there would be no arguing the point. She nodded, and Romaine turned to the others.

"We need to move quickly as well," he said, addressing those that would continue. "Empty out your packs. We'll bring two tents and enough food for three days. Rope, the Archivists tools, nothing more. Whatever space is left we'll need for these artefacts of the Archivists."

They were ready before Erika had finished processing his words. Still reeling from the sudden turn of events, she stepped from the saddle and found her legs trembling. Sucking in a breath, she recovered her knapsack, then looked at the slope again. Loose rocks stretched up at least 600 feet before disappearing over a lip. She swallowed. Could she truly climb that?

"Good luck." The scout, Travis, said from amongst those recruits who were to return.

"Same to you," Lukys replied, and they embraced.

Erika looked away again, feeling inexplicably guilty. Angrily, she forced the emotion aside. There was no room for sentimentality on this journey, not with the fate of humanity in the balance—not to mention the queen's expectations. Letting out a breath, she faced the Calafe warrior.

"Let's be off then," she said shortly. "I'd rather not still be standing here when night falls."

✵ 25 ✵

THE RECRUIT

It was growing dark by the time Lukys and the others reached the top of the slope. Lukys, Cara and Romaine had taken the climb in their stride, but the other Perfugians had struggled, and at points the Archivist had needed their aid to continue. Without her horse, she did not complain about their slow pace at all now.

Thankfully the night was clear, the ground lit by the growing moon, and knowing time was short, they pressed on. High above the forests, ice lay in patches amongst the stones and a cold wind blew across the slope, cutting through even the heaviest of furs.

Romaine took the lead, twin-bladed axe hanging from his broad shoulders. Lukys and the other Perfugians carried spears and their shields strapped to their packs, while Cara had refused a weapon. The Archivist didn't seem to need any but her magic gauntlet.

The sight of the Calafe warrior standing tall in the darkness was reassuring, though Lukys couldn't quite banish the memory of Romaine sitting slumped beside the trail, defeated. The despair that had flickered in the man's eyes…

No.

He wouldn't think of that. Instead, Lukys turned his mind to the landscape. In the moonlight, stark cliffs rose around them, surfaces glistening with ice. Fortunately, the slope had led into a canyon between the rocks. The ground still continued higher as they walked, but more gently now, other than a few sections where jagged boulders blocked the way. In those places they were forced to climb, fingers seeking out cracks in the stone to pull themselves up.

They did their best to keep silent, but at times the very terrain seemed to be working against them. The smallest of rocks dislodged would send dozens of others careening down the slope, and with the canyon walls amplifying the sound, Lukys was sure the Tangata must hear them eventually. Already he was beginning to regret speaking up, though what other options had there been?

Thankfully, Romaine seemed confident that the beasts would not start off until closer to midnight. If they could cross the crest of the hill before then, they would be safe— unless the beasts picked up their trail.

Even so, Lukys couldn't help but jump at every tumbling rock, every shadow and whisper of movement from behind them. In the frigid darkness, it was easy to imagine the creatures stalking the group. The night was their world, after all. Lukys and his friends were only visitors.

He flicked glances at the Archivist as they climbed, wondering what drove the woman, why she had staked so much upon this mission. Did she truly think recovering the magic of the Gods was so important? She clenched and unclenched her fist as she walked, a faint light flickering from her gauntlet. Lukys shivered and looked away.

No, there had to be another way to defeat the Tangata. Surely using the magic of the Gods could only lead them down the same path as ages past, to a repetition of the mistakes that had caused the entire world to fall.

But it was not his place to make those decisions.

His boot caught on another rock and he suppressed a curse as it went scattering away. Thankfully no others were dislodged. It took a moment for him to realise the slope had changed. They were heading down. Movement came from nearby as Cara came alongside him.

"I hope this path of yours is close," he said.

Cara glanced at him, then up at the sky, as though she could read their position from the stars. Her lips pursed. "I don't know."

A sigh slipped from Lukys's lips. "Doesn't matter," he said, "I just hope the Archivist can make it."

Cara glanced back at where Erika was falling behind again. "She's stronger than she looks," she replied.

"You like her, don't you?" Lukys asked.

"She's different," the woman replied with a shrug, then grinned. "You all are."

Despite himself, Lukys smiled. He watched as Cara strode ahead. She moved with more confidence and grace than the rest of them combined, each step barely disturbing the loose rocks on which she strode. Long gone were the days when she'd clutched her broken arm to her chest. How long ago had that been now? No more than a month. The Calafe healed quickly.

They marched on, the ground growing steeper again, though now that they climbed downwards Lukys had to be careful again about where he put his feet. Every mistake sent rocks tumbling down the slope towards the others. The sharper their descent became, the more the danger grew, until finally they were forced to take turns moving down each stretch of the canyon.

Exhaustion weighed heavily on Lukys's shoulders as the night grew late. They stopped for a time to rest, though on the steep slope it was impossible to pitch the tents, and with the threat of the Tangata lurking in the background, they were soon moving again.

Eventually the moon dropped below the clifftops, plunging the canyon into darkness. A moment later, light flashed on the canyon floor as Erika raised her hand. Her gauntlet blazed a brilliant white as she took the lead, outstretched hand guiding the way.

Finally they found themselves standing atop a broad cliff, looking down upon a plateau some six hundred feet below. The Mountains of the Gods loomed overhead, their icy peaks lit by the first hint of dawn. Below, the plateau remained in darkness.

From where they stood, Lukys could see no hint of a path down the escarpment. Indeed, it looked almost sheer. But Cara was insistent, bidding them wait before starting off along the clifftop, her poise making the perilous walk look easy. She returned before long, and led them across to a narrow gap where a section of the mountain had broken away. The rubble left behind provided a steep but not quite sheer, way down to the plateau.

"After you, Calafe," Dale said softly, glancing nervously at Cara.

Her teeth flashed in the light of Erika's gauntlet as she grinned back. "Just try to keep up."

Lukys's heart lurched in his chest as she leapt from the edge. The others cried out, but to all of their surprise, she landed easily on the steep slope. Stones shifted beneath her weight but did not send her tumbling into the darkness. She slid several feet before coming to a stop at the edge of Erika's light. Her face was flushed as she looked back at them.

"Almost like flying," she said, grinning at them. "Are you coming?"

Everyone turned to look at the Archivist. She would need to go next, to light the way for the rest of them. Drawing in a breath, she followed Cara over the edge, making it look far more difficult than the young Calafe had. Rocks tumbled into the darkness with her every step, the sound of their fall echoing from the cliffs.

As Lukys started after her, he saw now why Romaine had insisted on so few. Even with just the six of them they were making far too much noise. Surely anyone—or anything—out on the plateau would hear the falling stones and investigate. At least the Tangata were behind them.

The light on the horizon grew as they continued down, the sun appearing slowly above the peaks, until finally Erika was able to dismiss her gauntlet's magic. Watching her as the glow died, Lukys wondered where the power came from. Sweat drenched the woman's face and she was pale in the dawn light, but that could easily be exhaustion from the night's climb.

As they neared the bottom, Lukys spotted movement out on the plateau. His heart palpitated, and a moment later he saw a dozen heads lift from the alpine tussock. Standing on four legs and covered in grey and orange wool, the strange long-necked creatures watched the group of humans descending towards the plateau. With their slow-blinking eyes and lazy smiles, they were apparently unconcerned.

"Guanaco," Romaine explained as they stopped on an outcropping of rock that gave them a place to sit. "They usually keep to the higher peaks. It was rare to see them, when we inhabited this land…" He trailed off, blue eyes on the distant creatures. "My people consider it good luck to cross the creatures on a journey."

Lukys shivered as he glanced at Romaine. It was easy to forget sometimes that this rugged, untouched land had once belonged to his people.

"They farm them, in the higher pastures of Flumeer," the Archivist said. Her voice seemed sad.

"Bad luck to cage a creature that has set eyes upon the Gods," was all Romaine said.

He rose and started off again. Now that they were close to the bottom, the way was easier and they made good time. Lukys kept one eye on the slope high above as they walked, seeking sign of anything that might be following them.

The earth was dry beneath his boots as he walked, the rocks stained scarlet and orange. Looking at the tussock growing upon the plateau, Lukys wondered how it survived, how anything could live in such a barren environment. Even the last of the snow and ice dried away as they reached the bottom and moved out onto the flat.

The Guanaco finally wandered away at their approach, making for the distant snow-capped peaks. A light breeze blew through the valley and drifted up the slope they had just descended. If the Tangata *had* followed their group, the creatures had their scent now.

"This is it," the Archivist whispered. She looked from the map clutched in her hand to the broad plateau. "It's here, somewhere. Waiting for me."

Lukys swallowed at the glint he caught in the woman's eyes, recalling his earlier assessment of Erika. Whatever the Archivist claimed, she hadn't come all this way just to save humanity. There was a reward in this for her, one that had driven her to risk near certain death.

Just get on with it, he thought to himself.

The sooner they found the ancient site, the sooner they could leave. He still feared the magic of the Gods, and what might happen when they stepped foot in such a sacred place. But the wrath of the Gods seemed an unlikely possibility compared to the ever-present threat of the Tangata.

Lukys flinched as a sudden, brilliant light swept across the plateau. For a second he thought their very presence there had somehow angered the Gods, before realising it was only the sun finally topping the last mountain peak. He glanced around sheepishly and was glad to see no one had noticed his reaction. Letting out a breath, he closed his eyes, basking in the warmth of a new day.

"We'll have to spread out." The Archivist's voice drew him back to their present danger. "Divide the plateau up into sections. Look for anything that looks unnatural, rock formations that are too smooth or horizontal, sections of ground that are too flat."

For once they did as the woman bid. There was no point in arguing, and she was right—they could cover more ground separately. It wasn't like they could fight the Tangata if they appeared anyway. In fact, being apart meant if one was attacked, the others might at least have a chance to escape.

Small consolation if Lukys was the one to be caught.

The alpine grass grew surprisingly tall here, not so high that it obscured their view of any approaching creatures, but enough that it made searching for unnatural rock formations difficult. Lukys could only see the ground within a few yards of where he stood. An hour passed as they made their slow way across the plateau, then another, until Lukys found he was watching the path they had taken down the mountain more than he was looking for the entrance.

If the Tangata had found their tracks, how long would it take—

"*No!*"

Lukys swung around as a scream carried across the tussock grass, high pitched and brimming with agony. Someone was dying, under attack...but how had the Tangata come upon them unnoticed?

The scream had come from Erika. She stood a dozen yards from him, face pale, twisted into a mask of horror. The scream came again, seemingly drawn from the depths of her soul, as though someone had taken a hot poker and stabbed it through her belly.

She stood alone.

Then suddenly she darted across the plateau—and disappeared.

❦ 26 ❦

THE WARRIOR

R omaine cursed as the Archivist started to run, then swore as she vanished, seemingly into the earth itself. He froze, trying to process what he'd seen. The tussock grew up tall here, obscuring the ground. Starting after her, he lifted the axe from his shoulders as he went. Weapon extended, he approached the area where the woman had vanished...

...and cursed again.

"Blasted woman!" he shouted, coming to a stop.

In front of him, the earth had been torn apart, exposed soil and broken rock cast in all directions. At its centre was a shaft of sheer rock, six by eight feet wide. A steel ladder disappeared into the darkness. The Archivist had already vanished into the black.

Shouts came from around him as the others approached. Romaine clutched his axe tight, cursing the Archivist with every expletive he knew. Had she lost her mind? It was clear the Tangata had discovered the site ahead of her. What if more were waiting below, left behind by the group they had seen the day before? There was no other explanation for her actions.

"How did the Tangata find it?" Lukys whispered as he staggered up to the hole.

"They're good at finding underground places," Romaine grunted.

It was true, the Tangata preferred these dark spaces—but there was no way they could have known this was here. Not unless somebody had told them...

"What do we do?" Cara murmured as she approached.

"We get The Fall out of here," Dale croaked, his face pale.

Ignoring them, Romaine crouched beside the broken earth. The Tangata had made a mess of the site around the shaft, trampling back and forwards through the dirt. There was no way of knowing their numbers.

"Nobody move," he murmured as the last recruit, Groner, arrived.

A glare ensured they would obey. Romaine stepped carefully away from the entrance and circled the exposed area. It didn't take long to locate the path the Tangata had taken to reach the site—a broad stretch of tussock had been trampled beneath their boots. There he knelt again, trying to determine how many had passed through. Fresh dirt had been trodden into the flattened grass, confirming his suspicions that the group had left. There was still no telling whether any remained.

Romaine sat back on his haunches. "They left," he said, more to himself than the others. "It was probably the group we encountered. But...why would they leave?"

"Erika needs our help." Cara interrupted his musings. "She's...all alone down there."

"That was her choice," Lukys replied.

"The Tangata are gone," she replied, meeting each of their eyes.

Romaine let out a sigh, then nodded. Coming to his feet, he marched back to where the others waited, shields now clutched in hand, spears pointed at the silent shaft.

"Stand down," he grunted, gesturing over his shoulder at the tracks. "The Tangata already left. Come on, we'd better go fetch the woman."

The others exhaled loudly as they lowered their weapons, the tension that had built amongst them draining away. Lukys shook his head, face paler than normal as he turned to Romaine.

"Do we have to?"

Romaine forced a laugh but did not reply. Sheathing his axe, he stepped past the others and approached the shaft. Despite his reassurances, he was not sure what might wait for them in the dark. None of this made sense. *How* had the Tangata known to come here?

A faint glow was visible far below—the Archivist's gauntlet. He hoped.

"Dale, the torches," he said softly.

The recruit handed his spear to Groner and swung the pack from his back. He searched inside for a moment before coming back out with the torch. Once it was lit, he held it out for Romaine.

Drawing in a breath, Romaine took one last look at the sun. Then he grasped the flaming torch and swung over the side of the shaft. An icy cold wrapped around him as he started down the ladder. Holding the torch made the task difficult, but it was not his first time climbing one-handed.

Rung by rung, he made his way down into the depths of the earth. With the flames shining in his eyes, he could no longer make out Erika's light, while those who came after him blacked out the surface. Soon there was only the darkness, only stone walls pressing in, the cold steel beneath his fingers. It seemed the shaft must go on and on, all the way down to the source of the world.

Until finally, it ended.

The sound of his boot striking stone seemed impossibly loud in the darkness. Romaine grunted, surprised to find solid earth rather than another rung. Holding the torch away from himself, he checked to see whether he had truly reached the bottom.

Firelight illuminated a wide chamber, its walls, ceilings and floor all carved from the same plain grey stone of the shaft. There was something abnormal about that stone, an unnatural smoothness and lack of patterns within the rock, as though it had been formed by magic rather than ordinary forces.

His light also illuminated three tunnels leading from the chamber. A heavy layer of dust covered the ground, revealing the footprints of those who had passed before. There were dozens, though all had taken the same tunnel, and returned from the same direction. It seemed the Tangata had known where they were going.

The Archivist had vanished, though the faintest glow revealed she'd followed the same path as the creatures. Did she realise the Tangata had left, or was she simply insane? Either way, Romaine was done with the woman's games. She had endangered everyone by coming down here.

Romaine should never have contemplated this plan. He should have ignored her pleas and bound her in chains, carried her all the way to the Illmoor, if necessary. Anything but this mad plan.

Scuffling noises came from above and Romaine stepped away from the shaft as the others dropped into the chamber —first Dale, then Lukys and Cara, with Groner bringing up the rear. They had tied their spears to their packs with strips of rope, and quickly set about freeing them. Drawing his axe again, Romaine moved into the mouth of the main tunnel to see what waited for them.

Shadows danced in the flickering light. This was no place for living things. Abandoned by the Gods and the ancient humans who had once worked alongside them; now it was home only to the dead.

Or so Romaine prayed.

They started down the strange tunnel, surrounded by those smooth walls, following the footprints of the creatures who sought to kill them. Romaine tried to count their numbers, but the prints crisscrossed and overlaid one another. Though he did notice those leading back towards the entrance were less defined, the strides longer. Had the creatures left in a rush?

A million other questions leapt at him, but there were no answers. They could not return without the Archivist. Romaine had no plans to be labelled a mutineer

Ahead the tunnel split in two, but again the footprints only led in one direction. The glow of the Archivists light still shone, brighter now. They were closing the distance. Axe still held in hand, Romaine picked up the pace.

This new tunnel was lined with doorways, seemingly cut from the strange stone itself, though inside most were plain and empty. These the Tangata had ignored, their attention seemingly fixed on some distant goal.

A few, though, the creatures had entered. In these chambers, Romaine was surprised to find the remains of ancient devices scattered about the room, objects of metal and precious glass and other unidentifiable materials, all smashed to pieces against the unforgiving floor.

"What The Fall?" Lukys whispered, stepping up beside him.

Romaine shook his head. "Let's find the Archivist," he said. "Nothing about this place make sense."

They continued. The deeper they ventured, the more stale the air became, the harder to breathe. There was a dryness to it, a faint sweetness too, though amongst the other scents it seemed foul, like a field of flowers gone rotten. The light ahead continued to grow, vanishing at times as the Archivist disappeared into different chambers. Romaine did not call out. He was sure the Tangata must have departed now…

…so why did he still feel they were not alone?

He did not have long to wait for the answer. As they passed around a bend in the tunnel, a terrible smell touched their nostrils. They didn't encounter the source until several doorways further down the tunnel. Within the chamber, Romaine could see liquid and broken glass covering the floor—and something else. White flesh reflected the light of the torch. The stench was so strong Romaine would have done anything not to enter. But he had to know.

Taking a cloth from his pocket, he held it to his nose and stepped inside. Lukys and Cara followed, while the others remained without. Holding the torch high, Romaine suppressed a shudder.

Three naked bodies lay on the floor, human in form, though so far gone as to be almost unrecognisable. Their flesh was like wax, twisted, melted, and strange lumps grew from their arms and legs and backs.

Glass crunched beneath his boots as he moved closer, heart pounding in his ears. Three circular platforms of solid steel stood in the centre of the chamber, just an inch from the ground. Jagged pieces of glass still stuck out from the edges.

"They were…preserved," Lukys said quietly. "The glass must have formed cylinders, with the liquid and bodies inside, some chymical…" he hesitated. "Why would the Tangata break them?"

"Death," Cara whispered, eyes wide, face pale.

Lukys looked at her sharply, as though she had said something profound. Ignoring them, Romaine held his breath and knelt beside one of the bodies. Carefully, he lifted its eyelids. Even in its decomposing state, he could see the iris had been grey.

"Tangata," he croaked, rising and backing away.

"The original traitors," Dale's voice came from the doorway.

"Then why are they still here?" Lukys asked.

Romaine shook his head. "I don't care." He retreated to the doorway. "Let's find the Archivist, *now.*"

"What did the Tangata come here for?" Lukys whispered as they started down the corridor again. Erika's light had drawn further away while they'd been stopped.

"We…should leave this place," Cara said, voice so low Romaine hardly heard her.

He glanced at her. "What about Erika?"

Her lip trembled as she stared back. For a moment he thought she was going to bolt, but instead she nodded, resolve returning to her eyes.

They passed more chambers, most—thankfully—empty. In a few, they found other broken things, and in one, two empty cylinders of glass. Romaine paused in the doorway of this one, shocked at their size. Not even the crafters in

New Nihelm, once famed for their glassblowing, could have managed anything half as large.

Finally the light ahead grew still. It seemed the Archivist had reached the end of the tunnel. They picked up their pace once more, eager to find the woman and begone from that terrible place.

Crash.

Romaine flinched as the sound of something breaking carried down the tunnel. He glanced at the others, then they were running, racing towards the soft glow ahead. The light quickly grew brighter, until it lit the hallway ahead of them, seemingly too bright for the Archivist's gauntlet. Looking ahead, Romaine saw the source: a brilliant white emerging from one of chambers.

He staggered to a stop in the entrance, axe thrust out ahead of him, torch clutched tight, though it was no longer needed. The light was blinding, and he squinted into the chamber, trying to see what waited. Slowly the room took shape.

Erika stood a few feet away, head bowed and arms limp at her side. No light came from her gauntlet—instead, it emerged from a dozen crystals lining the wall. Romaine shuddered at the magic, but the other contents of the chamber were far more pressing. He stepped up beside the Archivist, scanning the bodies that lay nearby for signs of life.

Unlike before, these were no ancient, persevered things. Men and women in plain-spun clothes lay scattered about the floor, throats torn out, limbs separated from bodies. Blood pooled around them and eyes stared sightlessly into the brilliant light of the crystals.

Grey eyes.

A shudder ran down Romaine's spine as he looked on

the dead Tangata. Five of them. Impossible. What could possibly have done this to *five* Tangata?

His eyes were drawn to the rear of the room. Two more of those strange massive cylinders had stood there, and these too had been shattered by the Tangata. Except here, *light* shone from crystals set into the steel bases, the same as those on the wall.

Somehow, the magic of the Gods remained in this room, indifferent to the countless passage of centuries.

Light glinted from the liquid spilled across the stone, but Romaine's heart lurched in his chest as he realised something was missing.

The bodies. Where are the bodies from the broken cylinders?

"We need to *go*," came Cara's voice from the doorway, high-pitched, panicked. Ready to flee.

Romaine nodded, reaching for the Archivist.

"They were looking for them," Erika whispered, still staring at the dead Tangata. "How did they know they were here?"

"Archivist—" Romaine cut off as a scream came from the corridor.

Lukys, Cara and Dale scrambled into the chamber, then spun to face the doorway, spears raised. Groner followed them—then crumpled to the ground, blood seeping from a terrible wound in the back of his skull.

An unfamiliar stepped into the light. Fluid dripped from the things naked body as it moved into the chamber. Another followed, making a pair, one male, the other female.

Grey eyes swept the room, terrifying, mad, intelligent.

Tangata.

Or something else?

Romaine hefted his axe and stepped towards the creatures. Shards of glass crunched beneath his boots as he sought the rage that had saved him so many times, that had given him the strength to defeat so many of these creatures. For once it did not come.

He glanced at the bodies on the floor. Dead Tangata. Nothing could have killed so many, not in such brutal fashion. At least, nothing living.

Looking at the creatures in the doorway once more, he saw them for what they were. Not Tangata, but something new—or very, very old.

The originals; those ancients who had betrayed the Gods to gain their power.

Preserved here, hidden away from the world, asleep, waiting.

A terrible fear touched Romaine as he faced the beasts. They could not be allowed to leave this place. If they could so easily destroy the Tangata, nothing would stop them if they escaped into the world.

With a roar, Romaine rushed them, axe raised to slice the beasts in half—

Breath exploded between Romaine's teeth as a fist struck him like a club to the chest. Stars flickering across his vision, he staggered backwards, folded in two, unable to breathe. He looked up to find the male of the pair standing over him. He hadn't even seen it move.

Cries came from the others as they reacted, Dale leaping back, Lukys thrusting out with his spear, Erika raising her magic gauntlet.

The female was faster than all of them. Lukys was thrown aside, spear snapped in two, and Dale crumpled, his weapon clattering to the ground. Light flashed from the Archivist's gauntlet—then the beast was upon her. A scream echoed from the walls as a blow sent the woman tumbling backwards across the chamber.

No, no, no!

Romaine strained to recover his breath; it felt as though he were inhaling through a swamp reed. Fighting through the pain, he struggled to straighten, to fall into a fighting stance, to lift his axe. The creatures moved so fast, it couldn't be possible, couldn't be…

Two pairs of grey eyes turned to watch him. He gasped as the male suddenly came face-to-face with him, then tried to swing his blade. A hand caught the shaft, halting the blow as one might bat aside a fly. Moans came from around the room as the others struggled to recover, but in that moment, Romaine saw the truth.

None of them were leaving this place alive.

The knowledge granted him a strange sense of calm. After all this time evading death, finally it had come for him. There was no fighting it this time. These creatures were a force of nature, born of the Gods themselves, beyond any mortal man to resist. He had only to open his arms and embrace his fate…

No.

Romaine tensed, pushing back against the creature's strength. If he was to die, he would take this monster with him. He could feel the creature resisting, its power unmatched, but…

Romaine relaxed, then swung out with his spare hand, aiming a blow for the creature's throat. His change of tact threw the thing off-balance, giving him an opening—

A scream tore from Romaine's throat as pain erupted from his arm. He staggered back, gaping at the blood now spurting from his wrist. His left hand was…gone. The axe slid from his still-working hand and struck the ground with a *clang*.

His hand was gone!

He stared at his foe in horror.

The monster smiled.

❧ 27 ❧

THE RECRUIT

Danger, death, death!
The words pounded on the inside of Lukys's skull like a drum, robbing him of thought, of action. He watched in sheer terror as Romaine stood alone against the Tangata, so overwhelmed he could not move, not even when the female leapt at him, splintering his spear in two.

Even to his inexperienced eye, he knew there was something different about these two. The dead Tangata lay all around, and he knew instinctively they'd been killed by the creatures now battling against Romaine. Why they would do such a thing he could not say, but he knew now why Perfugian legends warned against disturbing these ancient places.

The Gods may have departed, but their magic, their creations, remained.

And they were terrible.

Lukys gaped as his mentor staggered back from the monster, his left hand...*gone!* A groan came from Romaine as the axe slipped from his fingers and he clutched at the severed limb, all the fight gone from him. Laughter whispered from the narrow walls as the monster stepped after him.

Rage ignited in Lukys's chest. He still held his shattered spear. Tossing aside the useless end, he took a two-handed grip of what remained to him, steel tip aimed at the monster's chest.

"All of us together!" Lukys bellowed, trying to bring their broken remnants together. "Like Romaine taught us!"

A flicker of shadow, air hissing between his teeth—then pain.

Lukys belatedly crumpled in two as the female attacked, her fist slamming into his stomach. Unable to breathe, he crumpled to the stone, vision flickering. Too late he realised they'd never stood a chance, that these…things had only been toying with them.

A grin twisted the male's face as it picked up the fallen spear. Terrible silver eyes examined the weapon, then turned on Lukys. It lifted the blade…

And disappeared.

Or rather, the creature was *flung* across the room by a tempest of copper hair and grey furs.

Lukys watched in horror as Cara and the male struck the ground and rolled. Steel glinted in his friend's hands, but a dagger was no match for these things, no match for their strength—

Blood spurted across the stones as Cara leapt to her feet, her knife left behind, impaled in the male's throat. It thrashed against the floor, hands clutched desperately at the wound, but there was no stemming the gushing of blood and in seconds it grew limp, lying still amidst the broken glass and swirling liquids.

Across the room, the female stared at its mate for a long

moment, silver eyes wide, registering disbelief. Then they narrowed, and a terrible growl echoed from its throat. The pounding began again in Lukys's skull as it faced Cara, though now it seemed there were twin beats...

Death, life. Death, life. Death, life.

"Cara, run—" Lukys tried to warn her, but his words came too late.

Faster than his eyes could track, the beast charged at his friend, teeth bared, naked limbs flashing, roars echoing in the narrow chambers.

Cara leapt to meet it.

Lukys's fear gave way to shock as he watched, stunned, as the two fought their way across the room. It...wasn't possible, but Cara matched the beast blow for blow, each movement little more than a blur. No human could move so fast—not even the Tangata were as quick.

Snarls filled the chamber as the two exchanged strikes, inhuman, wild cries echoing from the ceilings. Staring at the two, Lukys tried to reconcile the woman he had known these last weeks, his friend, with the creature that stood before him now. Blood covered her face and clothing, so that she seemed more animalistic than even the beast she had fought.

Lukys winced as a blow caught Cara in the shoulder, sending her backwards, but he made no move to help her. Whatever was happening...he couldn't understand what was going on, how his friend had transformed. What they were seeing, it was not possible.

Cara straightened with a snarl, auburn hair tangled, obscuring her face. The ancient Tangata came at her again, but this time Cara was quicker, her fist colliding with the female's head, sending it whipping backwards.

Deathlife, deathlife, deathlife.

Straining to think through the chaos, Lukys's eyes swept the room. Dale was down on one knee. He still clutched a spear, but his face was pale, eyes wide as he watched the two creatures circle one another. A body slumped nearby was the Archivist, but whether she was unconscious or dead, her magic could not help them against this thing.

Then there was Romaine.

The axeman had managed to regain his feet, though he'd left the massive axe on the floor beside him. The colour had left his tanned features. Blood stained the floor around the Calafe—a lot of blood. The sight shook Lukys from his daze, and he darted to the axeman's side

"Romaine," he said, grasping the man's shoulder.

The axeman glanced at him, but his eyes showed no sign of recognition. "Can't let them leave," he was muttering beneath his breath.

Lukys cursed. At least the Calafe had retained enough sense to clutch a rag to his wound—but a glance at the severed limb told Lukys it would need more than that to stem the bleeding. Quickly, he dragged the belt from his trousers and pulled it tight around the axeman's forearm. Romaine hardly seemed to register the makeshift tourniquet. Like everyone else, his eyes were fixed on the battle.

Death, death, death.

A scream rang from the walls and Lukys spun in time to see Cara catch her foe by the arm. Blood flowed as she wrenched, sending the creature to its knees. An answering shriek echoed from the walls, but it ended in a gurgle as Cara's fingers lashed out, tearing through flesh and cartilage and bone.

The creature fell to the floor, dead beside its mate.

Silence fell like a blanket over the chamber as Lukys and the others stared at the body, watching as the blood pulsing from its wounds slowed, then ceased. As one, they turned their gaze on Cara.

The grey eyes of a Tangata stared back at them, mad, enraged. Despite everything he'd seen, Lukys flinched. It was as though Cara herself had reached into his chest and wrenched out his heart.

Death, death, death.

"You're one of them," he whispered, eyes burning.

They had been betrayed. Somehow, the Tangata had created one who could walk amongst humans without being noticed, a Tangata without their telltale eyes. One who could speak, who could pretend, who could even adapt their mannerisms. But now she had revealed herself…

"Lukys, no…" Cara whispered.

She blinked, and the animal vanished, the grey receding from her irises, replaced by the usual amber. In seconds, it was no longer a Tangata who stood before them, but the human he had known all these weeks, the sweet young woman he had met on the walls of Fogmore. She stared at him, eyes wide and filled with fear. There was no sign of the fury of just moments before.

"Yes."

Somehow Romaine had moved without Lukys's notice. The Calafe now stood near the entrance to the chamber. Shoulders drooping, face grey from lost blood, he held his axe before him like a sword. Pain shone from his eyes, and though blood still seeped from his severed hand, Lukys sensed it was the agony of betrayal he saw.

"Romaine," Cara whispered, holding out a hand. "Your hand—"

"You're one of them," the axeman repeated Lukys's earlier words. He staggered forward, though it seemed his legs could hardly hold his weight now. "You've betrayed us…why?"

Cara retreated from Romaine, shaking her head. "No, no, no," she whispered as she looked this way and that, seeking to escape. Her eyes met Lukys's, and he could almost hear her pleading.

Help me, Lukys!

Lukys was still trying to process what he'd seen. Cara had…saved them…but she was one of the Tangata…why would she help them? His eyes were drawn to the clothed bodies, those of the modern Tangata. A cold hand gripped his heart. She had avenged them, her fellow Tangata, those who had fallen earlier to these creatures.

He clenched his fists, steeling himself against pity. She had deceived them all, had tricked them, played them as fools for weeks. This was only another manipulation, a testing on their emotions, to try and recover her act. Romaine had already seen it. No, they couldn't afford mercy, not now, not after seeing the power this new Tangata held in her hands. If they could stop her…

"Dale, get up," Lukys hissed, stepping sideways to place Cara in the middle of the three of them. His foot brushed the broken spear and he swept it into his hands.

Across the room, Dale came slowly to his feet. His face registered shock rather than pain. He hadn't known Cara as they had, wouldn't feel the same depth of betrayal. Lukys and Romaine and Travis had opened themselves to her, to the monster that lurked in their midst. Spear held extended, Dale crept closer to the Tangatan traitor.

"Please," Cara murmured, swinging to Romaine again. "I never wanted to hurt anyone."

The blood covering her heavy coat said otherwise. Lukys held his broken weapon higher, though it seemed inadequate after witnessing Cara's disposal of the two creatures. He tightened his grip. It would be enough. It had to be.

"Lukys…" She tried him again. Tears shone in her amber eyes as she extended a hand. "Please, you know…"

Please, please, please.

The sight of her tears froze Lukys in place. Blood pounded in his ears as their eyes locked, and he could almost hear, could almost believe….

No, no, no.

The scraping of leather against stone gave Romaine away. Spinning, Cara leapt back from the Calafe as his axe swept down, narrowly avoiding the terrible blades. A scream echoed from the walls—not of rage, but grief.

"Romaine!" Cara cried, but the Calafe warrior was beyond listening.

Teeth bared, eyes shimmering, axe clenched in his one good hand, he advanced. Lukys watched on, unable to move. In his mind, he saw again the creatures attacking, the awful battle, the blood…

The broken spear shook in his hand as he lifted it, then lowered it once more, trapped in a cycle of indecision.

"You don't have to be afraid," Cara gasped, hands raised to Romaine. "Please, I—"

"Enough!" Romaine bellowed.

The razor tips of his axe came up, the weapon flashing for Cara's skull. Again she leapt back, and Romaine staggered. Agony contorted his face and Lukys could hardly believe the man stayed on his feet. Any normal man would have passed out from the pain, let alone loss of blood.

Please, please, please.

Lukys stifled a moan and raised a hand to his forehead. His skull ached as though someone were banging on it with a club. Another roar drew his attention back to the conflict as Dale tried a clumsy thrust with his spear. Cara evaded it easily, but…

She was standing directly before Lukys now. Back turned, she didn't seem to remember he was there…or hadn't realised her evasion had brought her so close.

He swallowed, the spear trembling in his fingers. Across the room, Romaine met his eyes. Axe raised, the Calafe started forward again, drawing Cara's attention.

Lukys stared at Cara's back, at her unprotected spine. He imagined driving the point of his spear through that soft flesh, imagined hearing his friend's final cries, the last breath rattling from her chest…

She's not your friend!

There was no doubt. He had seen her, had seen those horrible grey eyes, sensed the violence in her soul. She was one of them, one of the Tangata, living amongst them, a spy, a traitor. A dangerous new breed, a monster that must be destroyed.

So why did this seem so wrong?

Please!

Lukys's heart throbbed. He had to act now. Cara was so close, he could have reached out and touched her, though she hated that.

Why?

It seemed an odd phobia, for one of *them*.

He shook himself. There was no time for doubt. Again he met Romaine's eyes. Silently he lifted the broken spear.

And brought it down on the back of Cara's skull.

❧ 28 ☙

THE ARCHIVIST

Erika sat watching as the light slowly grew between the distant peaks. Mist formed in front of her face each time she exhaled, and the air was so cold it hurt just to breathe. Her head ached from the blow she had received in the caverns and it still hurt to walk on her left leg.

She hardly cared.

The battle was two days past now. She could remember only flashes. A contorted face. Grey eyes in the darkness. A flash of white. Agony.

Then staggering through an endless tunnel, supported by a faceless man in blue. Climbing, hand over hand, up and up, metal rungs—then rocks. Feet slipping in gravel.

Sleep.

The first she'd truly wakened was the next day, when the sun had found her exposed on the mountainside. That had been yesterday morning.

Watching the sun rise now, she lifted her hand and squeezed. Light ignited between her fingers. Just a few days ago, the sight had given her a thrill, filled her with a feeling of power. Today, it did nothing to shift her despair.

Down in that darkness, her magic had proven useless. Before the might of the Gods, she had been powerless, knocked unconscious before she'd ever had a chance to use the power.

Worse still, she had failed.

Lukys was leading them back towards Flumeer, back to the rest of their regiment and the safety of the Illmoor. But what did that matter to Erika? Once again, her expedition had proven fruitless. The queen had warned of the consequences if she returned empty-handed…

If only she had reached the tunnels before the Tangata. Who knew what priceless artefacts the creatures had destroyed in their rage? No, that had not been rage, but a methodical destruction. Her Archivist's mind wanted to know why. But apparently not even the Tangata had expected to find those ancient monsters…

Erika shuddered, her mind recoiling from that memory. It was a relief when the images faded back into darkness, though the fuzziness of her thoughts could not hide the truth from her. She was ruined, betrayed yet again.

Her eyes were drawn to where the treacherous spy lay. She was bound hand and foot by heavy rope, her mouth gagged in case she tried to call for help. Dale also sat nearby for good measure, their one good spear at the ready. Erika still wasn't sure why they'd kept her alive. Lukys had apparently struck her hard in the head with the blunt end of his spear, then stopped Romaine from slaying her where she lay.

He thought they needed to know how the Tangata had learned to speak, and whether there were others.

Erika didn't care.

Movement came from the shadow of a nearby boulder, but it was only Romaine. He blinked as the brightness of the rising sun touched his face, then rolled over to present his back to the light.

Erika shivered as she glimpsed his stump. It was swathed in cloth, but she'd seen the ruin the creature had left of it the night before, when Lukys had changed the bandages. They'd used the burning torch to cauterise it, down there in the darkness. It had stopped the bleeding and saved the man's life.

Not that the warrior seemed interested in living any longer. Whether it was the loss of his hand, or the girl's betrayal, Romaine had hardly spoken a word since leaving the caverns. His depression made Erika seem joyful by comparison; it was as though his entire world had ended down there in the darkness.

Soon the others began to stir, first Lukys, then Dale, and finally Cara. The woman—no, the beast—had obeyed their every instruction since awakening, though Erika often glimpsed tears in the thing's eyes as they walked. If Cara thought her act would soften their hearts, she was sorely mistaken.

Romaine was last to rise. They had lost many of their possessions in the caverns, including most of their food. They had eaten the last of their supplies the night before. The Calafe started off without saying a word, leaving the rest of them standing there in silence.

"He'll be okay," Lukys said finally, glancing at the others. Erika and Dale said nothing, and after a moment, Lukys held his hand out to the other recruit. "Pass the spear," he murmured, "I'll guard her through the morning."

They started off, though the going was slow with Cara between them. The rope tying her legs was long enough that she could walk in short steps, though if she tried to run it would quickly become entangled. On the uneven rocks, it caught frequently anyway, sending her stumbling forward until she recovered or fell. With her arms bound behind her back, she often ended up on her face.

Even so, she did not struggle or say a word as the day progressed. Lukys followed behind her, spear held ready to run her through if she tried to escape. Exhaustion hung over them like a shroud, but at least the snow had held off, and soon they were back amongst the trees. The only hope that kept them going was the thought of reaching the Illmoor, of the hot food and safety that awaited them on the other side.

Erika paid little attention to her surroundings as they marched. Despite her hunger, despite her haste in the day's past, she cared little for whether they reached the camp or not. What did it matter whether she died out here, or by the queen's hand back in the capital? That day in the throne room seemed an age ago now; even that last night in Fogmore, spent enraged at the general's deceit, was a distant memory.

Anger touched her again. Could this venture have ended differently had she been accompanied by *true* soldiers? If she'd delayed, waiting for orders from the queen for Curtis to provide her with better men?

Such folly.

Maybe if Lukys and Dale—the only ones lucid after the attack—had allowed them to linger in the caverns, Erika might have found something that had survived the Tangata's methodical destruction. But by the time she'd recovered her wits, they'd already been far away.

They reached the abandoned village as the sun was setting, though walking at the rear of the group, Erika didn't realise until she saw the first of the cottages. The sight came as a relief—at least they might be able to risk a fire, even if there was nothing left to eat. And it meant there was less than a day's walk to the Illmoor.

Then she saw the bodies.

A fiery rope looped its way around her stomach. She staggered, seeing first one, then another, then…more. Choking, she stumbled on, igniting the light of her gauntlet, ready to strike. A shadow shifted in the darkness and she cried out, lifting her fist. The light illuminated Lukys's face and she sagged, the fight fleeing her in a rush.

"Lukys!" she gasped. "What happened here?"

"The Tangata," Lukys said, his voice cold, face registering no emotion. These had been his friends, but the past two days had taken something from all of them, robbed them of their innocence. "Come, this way."

Erika did as she was bid, too tired to resist, to ask questions. Bodies lay scattered in the path and alleyways between the buildings. In the growing dark, Erika could see no sign of their wounds. They might have been sleeping, had it not been for the awful stillness that lay over the place.

Lukys led her through the village to one of the cottages —the one she'd slept in, Erika recalled. Within they found Romaine slumped against the wall, Dale standing alongside him. Cara had been banished to the corner, her bonds tightened so she could not so much as stand. Erika clenched her fist at the sight of the woman, struggling to contain her rage.

"What happened here?" she asked again.

The Calafe said nothing, only sat staring at the floor. Shivering, Erika turned to the Perfugians.

"The Tangata caught them," Dale whispered. His eyes were haunted, the tip of his spear trembling.

Lukys paced the cottage, glancing from Dale to Romaine. "They're not all here," he muttered. "There's only…a dozen. I can't find Travis. Tomorrow, we'll search for tracks."

"They're gone," Romaine croaked, though he did not look up. Blood showed on his bandages but no one had moved to change them yet.

"We don't know that," Lukys said resolutely, crouching alongside the axeman.

"*They're gone!*" Romaine screamed. He lurched to his feet and Lukys flinched away. But Romaine ignored the recruit and staggered towards Cara. "You killed them all!"

The woman, the creature, Cara, did not move. She lay staring up at Romaine, helpless before his rage. Slowly she shook her head.

"It wasn't me, Romaine," she croaked, voice breaking. "Please, you have to belie—"

Her plea was cut short as Romaine slammed a boot into her stomach. Crying out, she curled into a ball, though with her arms bound behind her back, she had no way of protecting herself. The warrior drew back, preparing to throw another kick, but Lukys stepped between the axeman and the prisoner.

"*Romaine,*" he hissed, hands extended, "that's enough."

Erika raised an eyebrow at the recruit's gall. Despite his lost hand, Romaine stood head and shoulders above the Perfugian. In a moment of passion, he might have struck Lukys down, but instead the Calafe hesitated, staring at the man before him. Lukys looked back, open grief—and anger—shining from his eyes.

"My friends are *not* gone, Romaine," he hissed, though even to Erika it seemed a plea. "Travis, the others, they're alive. They're out there somewhere, either taken or on the run. I will *not* give up on them."

Silence answered the recruit's words, until finally Romaine shook his head. "Perhaps if they fled towards the river…" He trailed off, eyes distant, as though his mind was someplace else. "But even if they made the Illmoor…will the general send a ship? With so many Tangata in the area, they would risk being ambushed, overrun."

"You're saying we may be trapped here," Erika whispered.

Silence fell over the group as each contemplated their likely fate. Erika's thoughts turned once again to her failure. She couldn't understand how the Tangata had even known the site was there. It had lain undiscovered for hundreds of years; yet the beasts had reached it just a day ahead of them. Surely that could not be coincidence.

Her eyes were drawn to where Cara lay. The beast had seen the map, had known the location of the site. But Cara had been with them night and day. Could she possess some other way of communicating with the other Tangata?

Slowly Erika rose to her feet. It was past time their prisoner answered some questions.

"You betrayed us," she said, stepping towards the inert creature. "Somehow, you alerted your brethren to our destination."

Cara didn't respond, only lay looking up at her, amber eyes shining in the light of her gauntlet…

…Erika paused, glancing at her hand. The magic had ignited once more, unbidden. Her eyes were drawn back to the prisoner. Rage throbbed in her skull, mixing with the pain of her injuries. She didn't know how, but she *knew* the beast had betrayed the location of the site to the Tangata. How she longed to hear the treacherous creature scream.

A growl built in Erika's throat and before the others could react, she lifted the gauntleted fist and opened her hand. Light flashed as the magic responded. A scream tore from the traitor as light spilt from Erika's fingers, though a second later it was silenced. Mouth still stretched wide, Cara arced against the ground, unable to breathe, to so much as cry out as the power of the Gods claimed her. Erika may have found herself useless in the caverns beneath the earth, but she could at least still do this, could still take her revenge.

Other than the unnatural light, there was no visible sign that the gauntlet did anything. But its effect on the traitor was clear. Veins stood out on Cara's neck as she strained against her bindings, but even she apparently had her limits —or perhaps the magic stole away her strength.

The tiniest of squeaks came from the girl as Erika stepped closer, bathing Cara in the light of her gauntlet, determined to see her pain, to drink upon her agony. Blood began to run from the girl's nose and her eyes bulged. Romaine stood nearby, but the axeman made no move to stop Erika, only watched on, eyes dark even in the light of the gauntlet.

Then a hand grabbed Erika by the arm and pulled her back. The light from her gauntlet went out. She spun, snarling as she found Lukys standing behind her. A sob came from the corner as Cara collapsed against the dirt.

"Why did you stop me?" Erika snarled, raising her fist. She kept it clenched, the power controlled, though it would be so easy…

"I will *not* see her tortured," Lukys said, eyes shining.

"She betrayed us, doomed us all!" Erika shot back. "She deserves it."

"Maybe," Lukys said. His shoulders slumped and for a

second, he seemed to hesitate. Then he shook his head. "No, I won't become like them."

"We should kill her," Romaine murmured.

Erika glanced at the warrior, surprised by the suggestion. The man stood over Cara, staring down at her. A knife had appeared in his hand.

"Romaine, don't…" Lukys murmured.

The Calafe warrior glanced at the recruit, then back at Cara. "She's dangerous."

"She may be our only bargaining chip," the recruit replied. "If we cannot evade the Tangata. And she has information. We need to know more about…what she is."

For a long moment, it seemed the Calafe wouldn't listen. But finally he nodded. Retreating to the side of the cottage, he slumped to the ground and leaned against the wall. Silence fell once more between them, though soft sobs still came from the corner. Erika clenched and unclenched her fist, still feeling the need to unleash her anger, her rage. But she found no support in the eyes of Dale or Romaine; it seemed Lukys had won the argument for now. Slowly she relaxed, and a wave of exhaustion swept over her.

"Why do you hate them so much?"

Erika started as Cara's voice whispered through the cottage. The four of them turned to stare at the captive, but Cara had eyes only for Romaine. At first, it seemed the warrior had not heard her words, but finally his head lifted, blue eyes glinting as they fixed on the creature who had betrayed them.

"You took everything from me," Romaine whispered.

Erika glanced at the others, but no one moved to silence the traitor, and voice breaking, Cara spoke again:

"I'm sorry they took Calafe from you."

"Calafe?" Romaine asked, his voice growing bitter.

"What do I care for *Calafe*? Our kingdoms are a falsehood, a lie created to unite us against one another, so the people will not question their rulers. No, I hated you long before our king fell in the south."

Erika flinched at the mention of that first, terrible battle ten years before. How long had it been…?

"Then *why*?" Cara interrupted her thoughts.

The room was silent now, all eyes fixed on the Calafe. Erika found herself holding her breath as she watched the broken man, and it seemed the room grew a little darker, as though the moon itself hid from his pain.

"I had a cottage like this once," Romaine murmured. His eyes had a distant look; he didn't seem to be talking to anyone now. "In the southern forests. Small, far from the city, safe. A peaceful place built by my wife and I, to raise our son." His eyes flickered, focusing on Cara. "Until you took them from me."

The moment stretched out as they watched the man that had carried them so far. Then Lukys stepped forward and crouched beside him. "I never knew," the recruit murmured, placing a hand on the warrior's shoulder. "Romaine, I'm so sorry."

"Now you understand," the Calafe whispered, eyes flickering back to where Cara lay. "What is a kingdom, beside family, beside friends, beside the people we love?" He trailed off, his Adam's apple bobbing. "When the Tangata broke the truce, when they first invaded southern Calafe…" His eyes closed, the lines on his face growing deeper. "They took everything, left me with nothing but a hole, a void in my soul that I can never fill."

Erika shivered. His story sounded all too familiar, though for her…it had been her father the Tangata had slain. Left with nothing, her mother had fled back to her homeland, before the true war came.

Romaine's voice broke as he continued: "I would do anything for another day with them—one more hour," he continued, "but that can never be, not until the end comes." His eyes passed around the room, and Erika shivered as his gaze touched her. "And so I fight, seeking death." He lifted his ruined hand. "But still it evades me."

"You can't die." To Erika's surprise, it was Cara who spoke.

Romaine's eyes showed no emotion as he looked at her. "Why not?" he whispered, voice bitter. "Your kind have left me with nothing else."

"All life is precious," Cara whispered.

The axeman stared at her until she lowered her gaze, then shook his head. "Wise words, from a traitor." He turned towards Lukys. "In the morning, you will leave me here. I have nothing left to give this world."

"No," Lukys replied, still crouched beside the axeman. He held up a finger when the Calafe looked set to argue. "We're not leaving anyone behind, end of story." He hesitated. "And you still have us, Romaine. You saved me, helped me when no one else would. Let me do the same for you."

The warrior stared at the Perfugian for a long while, but finally he nodded. A tear streaked down his bearded cheek but otherwise he said nothing. Drawing in a breath, Lukys rose and faced the rest of the room.

"Anyone else have something to add?" he murmured. No one spoke, and after a moment he nodded. "Then tomorrow we march for the Illmoor. And pray to the Gods that we find Travis and the Gods already there."

𝕾ℓ 29 𝕾ℓ

THE RECRUIT

Lukys sat in the middle of the abandoned town, staring into the distance, remembering his first night in this haunted land. Just a few short days ago, and yet everything had changed. Back then, his biggest concern had been ensuring there wasn't a mutiny amongst the other recruits.

Now those recruits were dead or gone, his mentor broken, and his friend...a traitor.

Cara.

A cold breeze blew through the empty window frames and he shuddered. How many nights now since they'd last had a fire, since he'd been warm? The night they'd slept in this abandoned place? They didn't dare light one now, not with the Tangata likely close. Besides, he didn't want to see what the fire would reveal—the faces of the dead, still lying where they had fallen.

They're not all gone.

Travis and the others were still out there, they *had* to be, surely...but there was no way to know, no time to search for them. The Tangata were close, he could *feel* it. They could not remain on this side of the Illmoor much longer without being detected.

Then there was Cara. Dale had volunteered to take the first shift guarding her, saying he wouldn't sleep anyway. Lukys was little different. Would any of them ever have a full night's sleep again, after what they'd seen down in the darkness. Just the memory of those…things sent shivers down his spine.

And Cara had fought them, killed them. Had she truly done so only to save herself, to avenge the Tangata the monsters had killed, or…

To save her friends?

No, no, no.

Lukys shook his head, banishing the thought. He had seen the grey eyes, seen the terrible, animalistic rage. There was no questioning it—Cara was one of them.

The enemy.

He shivered, remembering how she'd looked as the Archivist unleashed her magic, hearing again her scream. Despite her betrayal, he could not bear to see such pain in the eyes of someone who'd been his friend.

Lukys cursed. Sleep wasn't going to come. Letting out a sigh, he rose. Picking up the spear he'd taken from one of the fallen recruits, he moved outside. The night was clear, the moon nearly full now. Using its silver light, he made his way through the village, averting his gaze from the bodies still lying in the streets. He'd wanted to move them, to do something to honour his fallen comrades, but doing so would give them away should the Tangata return to this place. And they were still a full day's march from the Illmoor.

Finally he found himself approaching the building they'd placed Cara in for the night. It was the smallest of the cottages, little larger than a woodshed, but with only one entrance and no windows, it made an adequate prison.

Movement came from the doorway and Lukys nodded a greeting as Dale stepped into the moonlight.

"Lukys," his former rival said, then glanced at the sky and frowned. "It's not your shift yet."

Lukys shrugged. "Can't sleep either." He leaned against the wall of the building.

Dale watched him for a moment, but soon resumed his post in the doorway. They stood like that for a while, their breaths misting in the darkness, listening to the wind as it whistled through the broken roofs.

"Why?" Lukys said suddenly, stepping back into the street and facing Dale.

"Why what?" Dale asked quietly.

"Why did we fight, Dale?" he replied after a time, struggling to focus on just a single mystery in his life. "I never did anything to you."

For a long while, Dale said nothing, only stood staring at the moon. "It seems like an age ago now, doesn't it?" he said finally. "The games of children." Then he shook his head. "You never had to do anything but be who you are."

"What?"

"You're a better man than me, Lukys," came the reply. When Lukys only frowned, Dale chuckled. "You don't know what it's like, to be the son of someone important. I was *expected* to be great, to become a knight, or a politician."

"What has that got to do with me?"

"Because I failed," Dale said, as though that explained everything. "I thought the frontier would be the making of me." He snorted. "What a lie that turned out to be. And then, in the moment of our greatest shame, it was *you* who stepped up. *You*, the son of a peasant, a nobody, who proved we might yet make something of ourselves."

Lukys started, then snorted. "You mean during that first attack? I didn't prove anything. I was so terrified I could barely hold my spear straight."

"You led us, Lukys," Dale murmured. "Just as you've been leading us ever since we crossed the Illmoor."

"I…" Lukys trailed off, frowning.

Had he truly become their leader? He'd tried to be brave, to stand strong as Romaine had told him. But…it had only been an act, hadn't it? Surely Dale and the others had seen through his charade?

"It's okay," Dale said, a wry grin twisting his lips. "I've accepted my place. If not for you, I think we would have all died down in those caverns. I'm glad to call you my officer, Lukys."

Lukys opened his mouth, then closed it, struggling to swallow the emotion that welled in his throat.

"Thank you," he managed at last. "And for what it's worth, you're not a failure, Dale. You saved my life, that night in the mountains. And you did not flee when those… creatures attacked."

Dale laughed. "Maybe you're rubbing off on me."

Lukys smiled, but his joy was fleeting. Dale was but one of many concerns. His eyes were drawn to the darkness beyond the doorway. "I need to talk to her."

Glancing inside, Dale shuddered. "I know." He looked back at Lukys. "She saved us. Why?"

"It's time I asked her."

Dale watched him for a long moment, as though judging whether Lukys was ready for that confrontation. Finally, he nodded. "Then I'll stretch my legs." He walked away without looking back, leaving the entrance to Cara's prison unguarded.

Letting out a breath Lukys hadn't realised he'd been holding, he stepped inside before his nerves betrayed him. The floor of this cottage was dirt, but hard and dry beneath his boots. At first, he could see nothing in the dark, but as his eyes resolved, he found a pair of amber globes staring back at him. Cara took shape as she awkwardly pushed herself up off the ground, putting her back to the wall. They had stoppered her mouth again, but her eyes said everything.

Friend…

Her amber gaze bore into Lukys's soul, until finally he strode forward and pulled down the strip of cloth they'd used to silence her.

"The creatures you killed," he said, stepping back. "Why did you do it? To avenge your brethren?"

"No," Cara whispered, her voice hoarse.

"Then why?"

"To save you," she replied, "to save my friends."

Lukys choked, a lump lodging in his throat. He struggled on.

"How can we be friends?" he hissed. "You lied to us!"

"I never lied."

"I saw your eyes. They changed. You were…*are* a monster."

Cara flinched at the word. "Is that what you see me as now?" she asked, and he could hear the pain in her voice. "A monster?"

"You're one of them."

"Maybe the Tangata are not the monsters you think."

"Why do you still insist you're not one of them?" Lukys asked.

"Because I'm not," Cara whispered.

Truth, lies. Truth, lies.

Lukys shook his head, struggling to think. "It doesn't matter what you say." He looked away. "We saw the truth. No human could do what you did." Letting out a breath, he faced her once more. "They're going to kill you, if we ever reach Flumeer. But not before they make you talk."

"Yes, I know what…your people are capable of." She shuddered, not meeting Lukys's eyes. "I thought…I thought you were better than them."

"Than who?"

"Please, Lukys," Cara whispered, ignoring his question. Her amber eyes caught his. "I never wanted to hurt anyone. Please, you have to help me…"

"I wish I could," he murmured, surprised to find he meant it.

Help, help, help.

Pain shone from Cara's eyes as he rose, but she said not a word. Nor did she turn away, and he forced his eyes closed, unable to look into those terrible depths any longer. Silently he hardened his heart.

"But I can't." Stepping forward, he shoved the gag back into place. "You are my enemy."

With that, he turned and walked away.

❦ 30 ❦

THE ARCHIVIST

S tanding on the banks of the Illmoor, Erika wondered if she had ever experienced such a bittersweet moment. Somehow, they had made it. Despite signs of the Tangata all through the forest, despite Romaine's injuries and their treacherous prisoner in tow, they had reached the border of Flumeer.

There had been no sign of the other Perfugians on the way but…Erika had little hope any still survived.

No, all that left to be seen now was whether the cursed general would send the ship.

Lukys stood alongside her, a red flag hanging from his spear tip, waving in what she presumed was some predetermined signal for the watchers on the other side. They weren't at the rendezvous point and were a day late, but with forts placed at regular intervals along the Illmoor and regular patrols on the opposite banks, surely someone would spot them.

Thankfully the day was clear, and though the light was fading fast, Erika could just make out the distant shapes on the opposite banks. So close, even a simple rowboat would have been enough to carry them safely across. But all such vessels had been taken or destroyed long ago, when northern Calafe had been evacuated.

So far, there'd been no visible response. She flashed a nervous glance at the trees. In the forest, she'd at least felt protected, concealed by the dense vegetation. It didn't feel safe, standing out here on the riverbanks, exposed. She wondered if that was the Calafe in her.

No, Erika had left that part of herself behind long ago. This past week had proven it. These endless forests, the jagged mountains—they were no longer her home. Perhaps they never had been, though many times as an adolescent, she'd longed to return.

Facing the waters once more, another realisation struck her. Despite its vast wealth and luxuries, despite all her work to climb the echelons of its society, Flumeer was not her home either.

So where did that leave her?

"What was that?" Lukys gasped beside her.

Blinking, Erika looked from him then back to the distant banks. Light flashed, once, twice, three times. From such a distance, it was difficult to identify the source, but she thought there might be something...

"Three means yes!" Lukys exclaimed, dragging her into a hug in his excitement. After his sombre mood of the last few days, she was surprised to see his sudden levity. "We're almost saved!"

Erika swallowed, wishing she could share in his joy. So close to salvation, and yet Flumeer offered her no true freedom. The queen's words rang in her mind, their threat, and Erika suppressed a shudder.

For the first time in weeks, she thought again of the

stranger that had accosted her camp, to the offer from the King of Gemaho. She still had the map. There were other sites that had not yet been explored, even...even that remote site in the Mountains of the Gods.

But could she trust the Gemaho, after what they'd done?

Did she have a choice?

Movement came from the shadows as Lukys waved to the others. Cara appeared first, struggling to walk with her bindings, followed by Dale, then Romaine bringing up the rear. The axeman seemed to have stirred from his grief now, though he still walked with his head down, bandaged arm clutched to his chest. No doubt it would take time for him to come to terms with the injury.

So few.

A shiver ran down Erika's spine at the thought, and guilt twisted at her heart. So many souls lost, all because of her ambition.

No, because of her! She thought, glaring at Cara.

Her anger flared, though it was short-lived. Treachery might have brought about the failure of her expedition, but it had always been madness to come here. The Perfugians deserved better than what the general had given them, than where she'd led them.

"They're out there, Archivist," Lukys said beside her, as though reading her mind. His eyes were on the trees.

"We'll find out soon enough," Erika whispered.

She started as a bugle cry carried across the Illmoor. Hairs stood up on the back of her neck and she swung back towards the water, wondering why the Flumeerens would sound a horn. If there were any Tangata in the area, it was bound to draw their attention.

Her heart lurched in sudden understanding, and she spun to face the trees. Shapes darted amongst the shadows, then the Tangata emerged, one by one, until five stood at the edge of the forest. They did not move to attack immediately, though the grey eyes watched the humans with terrifying intensity.

No, they're not watching us! Erika realised, following their gaze to where Cara stood bound.

Romaine and Dale were already pushing the girl to the ground and fastening her bindings. Then they strode forward to join them, though the Calafe would surely struggle to wield his axe with one hand. And that was if he could ignore the pain from his severed hand.

Catching movement from the corner of her eye, she swung back as one of the beasts suddenly rushed them. Instinctively, Erika's arm came up, the magic spilling from her palm, lighting the growing darkness. The Tangata staggered as the light fell upon it, its headward rush faltering. A scream echoed in the twilight as it collapsed, thrashing against the damp ground.

"Kill it!" Erika screamed as another leapt towards her, forcing her to divert the magic.

Too late, Lukys and Dale responded. Lifting shields and spears, they charged the fallen creature. Snarling, the beast clambered to its feet and leapt away, carrying it out of range of Erika's magic. The second had only made a feint, coming close enough to draw her attention, but not enough to suffer from her power.

Erika cursed beneath her breath. Even after all these weeks, she didn't know enough about the gauntlet—how far its magic stretched, how long it took to kill. She should have tested it long ago, despite its potentially fatal effects.

Lukys and Dale joined shields and extended their spears, then moved between Erika and the Tangata. It was a brave gesture, though futile—without her magic, they couldn't hope to resist the creature's strength. Heart pounding, she stepped forward so she stood beside them. Romaine joined on their other side a moment later.

"I'll do my best to keep them back," she whispered, "if you can kill the ones that drop…"

The Tangata watched them from across the clearing. Erika's magic seemed to give them doubt, though that could not hold them back long. If they attacked all at once, she and the two recruits would be overwhelmed. Maybe if…

Screaming their rage, the Tangata rushed them. They moved with a deadly grace, seeming to slide across the earth rather than run, though even amidst her terror, Erika noted they were far slower than the creatures they had awakened beneath the earth. What about the passage of time had so weakened them, made them more…human?

Then the beasts were upon them, and there was no more time to think. Raising her gauntlet, Erika drew on its power and swung her hand in an arc. A brief touch would not be enough to seriously harm any one of them, but she hoped to at least slow them for the soldiers to fight.

Her hunch was proven correct, as each of the beasts reeled beneath the magic light, momentarily stunned. Seeing their opening, Lukys and Dale roared and leapt forward as one, targeting the beast at the centre of the Tangata line. Their spears flashed out, catching their foe in the chest and throat just as it recovered.

Shock showed on the beast's face, and snarling, it reached for the spears that had impaled it. But Lukys and Dale were already retreating, dragging back their weapons and presenting their shields to the enemy. The injured Tangata made to follow, but only managed a step before blood loss dragged it down. The remaining four retreated out of range of Erika's magic, their movements cautious now.

"If we could do that four more times…" Lukys said lightly, though he did not smile and his eyes did not leave the remaining creatures.

"Time to trade Cara for our lives, you think?" Dale asked.

"No," Lukys said.

Erika might have argued, but at that moment the Tangata attacked again. This time two angled directly for her, moving with terrifying speed. She had only enough time to direct her magic against one of the beasts. It collapsed with a scream of agony, while the other kept on, eyes locked on Erika, fingers raised to tear out her throat…

Dale and Lukys leapt between her and the beast, and a sharp *thunk* followed as it struck their raised shields. A groan came from Lukys as he staggered back, but Dale remained standing, and with a thrust of his shield he threw the beast back. Straightening, Lukys lanced out with his spear, catching the Tangata a blow to the hip.

Howling, the beast retreated, blood running down its side. Screams came from its companion, still pinned by Erika's magic, but Dale silenced them with a thrust of his spear.

A cry from their left reminded Erika of the remaining Tangata. Gasping, she swung the gauntlet towards the sound. Fatigue struck her as she summoned the magic once more, and she staggered, but thankfully the threat had passed for the moment.

Romaine crouched nearby, shoulders heaving, great axe buried in the chest of a dead Tangata. The second was retreating with its fellow, a knife embedded in its shoulder. Shocked, Erika stood gaping at the Calafe warrior, unable to believe her eyes. Injured and alone, he had fought off *two* of the Tangata?

Then she saw the blood seeping through his shirt, and knew the skirmish had not been without cost.

A *thunk* came from nearby as something hard struck the ground. Lukys still stood beside Dale, eyes on the remaining Tangata, but he had let his shield fall. She saw with shock it had been split in two by the last attack. Ignoring the loss, Lukys took a two-handed grip on his spear, then shared a glance with Dale. The second recruit tossed aside his spear and gripping his shield, stepped up beside Lukys.

"Romaine, get back to the shore," Lukys hissed as the recruits moved to put themselves between the axeman and the remaining Tangata.

Erika followed them, though her vision swam with the movement. Her eyes were drawn to the gauntlet, and she saw now how its glow had dimmed. She'd used too much of its magic, too quickly. Again she cursed her lack of experience. Would it kill her, drain all her strength, if she continued using it?

Coming to a stop alongside the axeman, Erika fought to clear her mind, to bring back the magic. The gauntlet brightened somewhat. She prayed it would be enough. Beside her, she could hear the rattling of the axeman's breath. She didn't need to look beneath his shirt to know the injury was bad.

"Can you walk, Calafe?" she hissed, eyes still on the Tangata.

A groan whispered from the axeman, then movement came from alongside her as he staggered to his feet. Somehow he had managed to drag his axe from the Tangata corpse, though he didn't seem to be strong enough to lift it any higher. Blood dripped from the steel tips.

"Must…fight," he rasped.

"Get to the riverbank, soldier," Erika snapped, flashing him a glare.

Romaine grunted. "Don't take…orders…from you."

"By The Fall, you're stubborn," Erika gasped. She grabbed him by the arm and shook him. "But by the blood of my father, *your Gods-cursed king*, you will obey!"

"Your…father?" the warrior mumbled. His eyes were bloodshot, face growing pale. He swayed on his feet, managing to look confused. "That's…what?"

"Let's discuss it over tea sometime, shall we?" she snapped. "*Go!*"

Finally, miraculously, he obeyed. Erika watched him as he staggered away, and couldn't help but think how like her father the man was—or perhaps it was all Calafe men. Stubborn, proud to a fault. Determined to stand their ground no matter the cost. Maybe if her father hadn't been so foolish, he might have survived, might have returned from that disastrous southern campaign…

She shook herself, returning attention to the Tangata pair. What did it matter to her? Erika's mother had only ever been the man's courtesan. They would have been sent away eventually, regardless. His death had only hastened their fall from grace.

"You okay, Archivist?" Lukys said, glancing over his shoulder. "Don't think we can defeat these two without your magic."

"Thought you were superstitious, soldier?" she snapped.

Regardless, she looked again at the gauntlet. Its light had died again, and silently she ignited its glow, then stepped up on Dale's other side. Somehow, he would have to protect them both with his broken shield. A low growl sounded from across the clearing as the Tangata approached again, slowly now, testing their own resolve. They flinched as she raised her gauntlet, eyes drawn to the device, but they did not stop.

Then their foes split apart, one sliding to their left, the other two the right. Erika shared a glance with the two recruits.

"You take the one to the left," she whispered.

Lukys and Dale nodded and she turned away, attention focused on her enemy, the female of the pair. She clenched her fist and was satisfied to see the light grow brighter. A smile touched her face. It seemed at least some of her energy was returning. Lengthening her stance, she beckoned the creature forward.

Smiling back, it raised a fist.

Too late, Erika noticed the rock it held. Snarling, it hurled the projectile at her head. Instinctively, Erika raised her spare hand. A sharp *crack* followed as the rock struck her wrist and a scream tore from her lips. Red flashed across her vision and the magic died. She staggered back, and for a moment, pain washed away all thought, all reason.

Her senses returned.

Fighting through the pain, Erika forced her eyes open, just in time to see the Tangata leap. Adrenaline swept through her as she raised the gauntlet. Light burned in the gloom and a bloodcurdling scream rent the air as her magic struck the beast.

But the Tangata was already airborne, and though her power drained it of reason, she could not avoid the blow it struck as they collided. The weight of its impact drove the breath from her lungs and toppled them both into the mud.

The magic flickered out again.

Howls came from alongside Erika as the Tangata thrashed, free of her magic's grasp but momentarily disorientated. Its fingers reached for her, trying to stop Erika from summoning the power again.

Gasping, yet unable to inhale more than a whisper, Erika scrambled away. Her vision spun and pain seared up her broken arm, threatening to steal away her consciousness. Cries seemed to come from all around her, but she could no longer tell which direction was the forest, which was the river.

Air brushed against her neck and instinctively Erika threw herself to the side. A boot slammed into the mud where she had lain and she clambered backwards, staring up at the Tangata. Red streaked its eyes and its face twisted as it started towards her again, yellowed teeth bared.

Erika screamed and opened her fist, directing everything she had left at the beast. Its shriek mirrored her own as the power struck. The Tangata staggered back, clutching its ears, shaking its head in violent convolutions, as though something horrible were trying to drill through its skull.

Erika did not relent. Pushing herself to her knees, she kept the gauntlet poised, bathing her foe in its ghostly light, until finally the Tangata collapsed and lay still.

Gasping for breath, she sat back on her haunches and looked around, expecting to see the final Tangata approaching. Instead, she was shocked to find Lukys and Dale still standing, though the beast they faced had retreated once more, apparently deciding it could not face the three of them.

"The ship!"

A cry came from Romaine behind them, and Erika spun to see the white sails of a ship rearing overhead. A *thud* came from the riverbank as a plank slammed into the earth. Soldiers stood at the railings, shields and spears at the ready. Her heart soared to see them.

But they did not advance.

Erika frowned as she realised they were not coming to their aid. The soldiers were only going to defend the vessel. If those on the shore wanted rescuing, they would need to reach the ship themselves.

Following her orders, Romaine was already staggering towards the ship, Cara somehow swung over one shoulder. But the ship had landed some thirty yards downriver. They needed time, needed to ensure that the last Tangata did not pick them off as they retreated.

Heart pounding, Erika came to her feet and faced the beast. Dale and Lukys still stood strong, but the two were little more than boys. They wouldn't even be here, fighting for their lives, if not for her.

Light ignited in the palm of her hand.

"Get to the ship," she said softly. "I'll hold it off."

❦ 31 ❦

THE RECRUIT

Blood pounded in Lukys's skull as he watched the last Tangata. He still couldn't believe they were alive, that they had managed to defeat *four* of the things. Sure, the Archivist's magic had helped, but still…

He risked a glance over his shoulder. Romaine was staggering towards the ship, but his injuries and Cara's struggling hampered him. Lukys glimpsed the desperation in her eyes as she looked at the last Tangata. He shook his head—how had he ever thought of her as a friend?

"Get to the ship," the Archivist said suddenly, striding past them. "I'll hold it off."

"What?" Lukys asked, swinging on her. "Not a chance, Erika. We stand against it together."

"Together," Dale agreed, joining them.

Death, death, death.

The Tangata's eyes narrowed as it looked past them to where Romaine was nearing the ship. Lukys could see the longing in its eyes. For whatever reason, these creatures wanted Cara back. Well, they couldn't have her. She would answer for her crimes against humanity.

A growl came from their foe as it started towards them. Lukys realised it was trying to put the two recruits between itself and the Archivist's magic. He stepped sideward to join with Dale, while Erika shifted to the right so that they stood apart. Whether the Tangata attacked Dale and Lukys, or the Archivist, it would be exposing its back to someone.

Lukys didn't allow it the chance.

"Now!" he hissed.

Dale responded immediately, and they surged forward together. Lukys aimed his spear for the creature's chest, hoping to run it through. The Tangata were hardy and such a wound might not prove fatal, but it would at least slow the beast long enough for them to escape.

A rumble came from the Tangata as it leapt to meet them. Apparently, it had no misgivings about tackling two humans —it was the Archivist's magic it feared. Its hands snatched for the spear and almost caught it, forcing Lukys to retreat half a step. Snarling, it chased after him, but Dale blocked its path, thrusting out with the steel brim of his shield.

The blow connected with the Tangata's forehead, staggering it for a brief second, and Lukys attacked again, this time aiming for its throat. At the last second it twisted, avoiding the blow, though the spear tip still scored a mark on its arm.

Its hand swept down again, and this time it managed to catch the haft of Lukys's spear. Before he could react, the Tangata pushed back, driving the butt of the spear hard into his chest. Breath exploded between his teeth and Lukys felt something go *crack*. He stumbled, struggling to keep his feet, even as the spear slipped from his fingers.

Looking up, he saw the Tangata leap—then Dale was there, shield slamming into the creature and hurling it aside.

Death, death, death.

Dale leapt back as the beast swung on him. A smile spread across its lips as it saw he was unarmed. Snarling, it started towards him.

Pain radiating from his chest, Lukys wanted nothing more than to lie down and surrender to the release of oblivion. But the *thunk* of flesh striking wood drew him back to his feet. Dale was retreating from the beast's fury, his shield now splintered and broken, useless. A sound like laughter came from the Tangata as it advanced.

Seeing his spear lying nearby, Lukys swept it up and followed them. But the pain from his chest slowed him and he couldn't keep a moan from escaping his lips. The creature swung at the noise, eyes widening to see him back on his feet. Then the smile returned and it drew itself up, preparing to spring...

...and collapsed to the ground as the Archivist finally managed to unleash her magic.

Face gaunt, glowing hand extended towards the creature, she advanced past Dale. A tremor shook her, then a second. Realising she was close to collapse, Lukys staggered forward and drove his spear through the creature's chest.

Silence.

Unable to believe they had truly won, Lukys stood gasping for breath, spear still clutched tight. Staring at the dead thing at his feet, he found himself unable to look away. With its eyes closed, the thing could have been human, might have been a young man little older than Lukys.

If he had not been cursed by the Gods.

Finally Lukys tore himself away. Dale had slumped to the ground nearby, face pale as he sucked in great lungfuls of air, though he seemed unharmed. The Archivist met his gaze and offered a nod, her face grim. They had won—but what did it matter, when so many others had been lost?

Stop, stop, stop.

Silence had fallen over the riverbank, and looking back at the Illmoor, he saw that Romaine had made it onboard with Cara. Despite their victory, his heart sank. They had succeeded, but he still could not shake his sadness. They would have to hand Cara over to the general. It just didn't seem…right.

"*Lukys!*"

His gaze was drawn back to the ship as a voice carried to them on the breeze. He frowned. Why…were the soldiers pulling up the gangplank? The danger had passed, hadn't it?

Spinning towards the forest, Lukys watched in horror as more Tangata emerged from the trees. Dozens at least—more even, as he glimpsed movement further into the shadows. The hope that had swelled his chest evaporated. An army. Too many to fight, even with the soldiers on the ship.

The creatures advanced in a line, and now he could see the fury in their eyes as they watched the escaping vessel. Aboard the ship, Romaine stood at the railings, his face contorted with grief. Tightening his grip on the spear, Lukys offered the axeman a final nod.

Then he turned to face the Tangata.

Movement came from nearby as Dale and Erika joined him. The Perfugian had reclaimed his spear, but without a shield between them, and exhausted as they were, they stood no chance.

Not that they ever had, against what marched towards them.

Only the Gods could save them now.

❦ 32 ❦

THE WARRIOR

Romaine staggered up the gangway, forcing Cara before him, his breath coming in painful gasps. The Tangata had struck him hard enough to break bones and he could taste blood in his mouth. Liquid burned in his chest, dragging at his strength, adding to the agony of his arm. He continued on, though he could not have said why.

Hadn't he wanted to die?

Reaching the deck of the ship, he stepped from the gangplank and almost crashed to the floor. As it was, he fell to one knee, desperately straining for a breath he could not quite find. Men shifted around him, Flumeeren soldiers taking up positions along the railings. The vessel bobbed against the river currents, shifting in its berth…

Groaning, Romaine forced himself to his feet. Somehow he made it to the railing, but it was already too late. The ship was pulling away from the shore, though three figures still stood in the clearing, their shoulders slumped in exhaustion.

"What are you doing?" Romaine tried to shout, but the

words came out more as a croak. He swung on the nearest soldier and grabbed desperately at his coat. "We can't leave them."

The man shook him off. "We don't have a choice, Calafe," he said. There was no anger in his voice. He only pointed back at the shore.

Still struggling to regain the breath he'd lost from speaking, Romaine followed the gesture. Despair wrapped its icy hands around his stomach as he saw the reason for the soldiers' fear.

Tangata. More than had been seen in months. Several raced towards the ship, but when it became clear they would not catch it, they turned back, leaving the three lonely figures surrounded.

"No," Romaine whispered.

Something died inside him as Lukys met his gaze from across the waters. The recruit gave a simple nod, then turned away, spear raised to the hoard.

No, no, no, not again!

Helpless, Romaine could hardly bear to watch as the Tangata closed on his stranded companions. But neither could he turn away. He owed them that much. Abandoned and left behind, the least he and the other soldiers could do was witness their final stand, to tell the world of their courage.

"*No!*" a voice screamed from amongst the ranks of soldiers.

Romaine spun at the sound, recognising Cara's voice. Had she gotten free? His vision blurred at his sudden movement, but he forced himself to search the deck, determined she would not escape. Not after everything they'd been through to bring her to justice.

Two of the soldiers were trying to get a handle on his

former friend, but even bound, Cara was proving to be a handful. Thrashing on the deck, she had somehow managed to dislodge her gag. Another scream tore from her throat as she kicked out with both feet, catching one of the soldiers in the chest and hurling him across the ship. Shouts came from others as they were struck by the falling man.

Agony wrapped its thorny tendrils around Romaine's heart as he watched the woman struggle. Lukys had made them spare her, had said they would trade the traitor's life for their own if it came to it. Instead, Lukys had sacrificed his own life to save this creature.

A tremor shook him as the familiar rage ignited in his chest. Reaching up with his good hand, he drew his axe. Despite the pain and exhaustion, the weapon felt right in his hand. He stepped towards where Cara still lay struggling. Another kick sent a second soldier flying. Someone should have done this long ago.

She froze when she saw him approaching, axe in hand, and her eyes widened.

"Are you going to kill me?" she whispered.

Romaine swallowed. Those eyes, that voice. Somehow, this young woman had found a place in his heart he'd thought long dead. Steeling himself, he clenched his fist tighter around the haft of his axe. Nausea wrapped around his stomach at the thought of what he must do, of plunging his terrible blade through her chest…

"No," he croaked, opening his eyes. The axe slipped from his fingers, the twin points striking the deck and lodging in the timbers. He shook his head. "I can't."

"Then free me!" Cara shrieked, struggling to sit up. "I can save them!"

Romaine frowned at her words, unable to understand. "Save them?" he murmured.

"Please!" Cara gasped again, still struggling at her bonds. There was something about the way she lay that seemed wrong, the way her arms pressed against her back as she fought to free herself. "Oh please, quick, Romaine, if you ever cared for me at all, *let me go!*"

"Why?" Romaine whispered. Taking hold of the shaft of his axe, he dragged it from the timbers and stepped towards her. "What are you going to do?"

Amber eyes met his. "Trust me."

For some reason, he did.

Falling to his knees, he turned her so she was facedown and carefully sliced the cords that bound her arms, then her legs. Dropping the axe, he stepped away, the last of his strength gone. Even as he watched her come to her feet, Romaine sensed he had made the wrong decision, doomed them all with his foolishness. Cara was Tangata. She would slaughter them all.

But what did he care?

Cara rose slowly, fists clenched, a growl building at the back of her throat. Around the ship, several soldiers retreated a step, though they did not know what it was they faced. Only Romaine knew the doom he had unleashed.

He did not flinch as the grey eyes met his. The terrible rage of the Tangata stood amongst them, but he was past caring. Let her slaughter them all—

Cara winked.

What?

Before he could react, she was sprinting towards him. Powerful legs sent her bounding across the deck, past soldiers and sailors, over the twisted ropes and canvas that had tripped her just a few short months before, when he'd first brought her to Flumeer. Romaine flinched, yet Cara's eyes were fixed not on him but the distant shore. Tearing the heavy winter coat from her shoulders, she bounded onto the railing, and leapt…

…*and flew!*

Romaine froze where he stood, unable to believe what he was seeing. Out across the waters, great wings spread from Cara's back, auburn feathers sweeping down, sending her soaring…*upwards!* It wasn't possible, couldn't be…

Suddenly everything clicked into place.

Cara had spoken the truth—she wasn't Tangata.

She was a *God!*

Falling to his knees, Romaine watched the winged woman race through the sky. Sharp intakes of breath came from others as realisation struck them, then they too were falling to the wooden boards, struck down by awe—and terror. Had they truly tried to restrain one of the Divine, set hands upon a *God?* Prayers whispered across the decks, begging for forgiveness, for salvation.

Romaine could not tear his eyes away from his friend. The wings that had hidden beneath her coat for so long beat down again, stretching wide across the waters, ten, twenty, thirty feet. Each stroke sent her soaring upwards, higher and higher above the swirling waters, towards the distant riverbanks.

Romaine's fear came rushing back as his eyes fell upon the shore, where Lukys and the others still stood surrounded. Thankfully, the Tangata had frozen at Cara's appearance. There was a hunger in their eyes as they watched her approach, and Romaine remembered then how she had drawn the others' attention. What did the Tangata want with one of the Gods?

Several of the creatures seemed to realise she was coming for the humans in their midst. Crying their fury, they rushed at Lukys and the others. Several went down as the Archivist's gauntlet flashed, but there were too many even for her magic. She threw herself aside as a Tangata leapt, avoiding its outstretched fingers, then disappeared into the throng.

Lukys thrust out with his spear, trying to bring a creature down, but it batted aside the blow and swung on him. Romaine's heart palpitated in his chest as the beasts closed on his friends. Without shields or room to manoeuvre, they didn't stand a chance. His eyes returned to Cara, but not even the sight of her auburn wings slicing the sky could bring him hope. Even if she had the power to face so many Tangata, his friends would be slaughtered before she could reach them.

Cries came from the shore and he watched as first Dale, then Lukys, had the spears torn from their grasp. Before they could retreat, the Tangata were upon them. Romaine held his breath, waiting for the slaughter, but instead the beasts only caught the men and held them fast.

Nearby, a cluster of the creatures had gathered around where Erika had fallen, but now they suddenly leapt back. The Archivist struggled to her feet, light pulsing from her gauntlet as she directed it at any Tangata that grew close. Step by step, she retreated towards the river. The rattling laughter of the Tangata carried across the waters as they followed her. The creatures were toying with their prey.

Then with a scream and a flash of red and gold, Cara arrived. Descending from the heavens, she struck the Tangata with the fury of a storm. With fist and boot and wing, she hurled the creatures from their feet. The breath caught in Romaine's throat as she fought her way towards his friends.

But few of those that Cara struck stayed down. With so many aligned against her, the Goddess had no time to strike mortal blows, and growling, the Tangata clambered back to their feet. As the fallen returned to the battle, their greater numbers pressed her back. Cries came from Cara as they grasped at her wings, tearing at the auburn feathers.

Ice formed in Romaine's stomach as he realised why the Tangata had spared Lukys and the others. With the humans dead, Cara would have retreated, but so long as they lived...

Chaos descended upon the shores of the Illmoor as the Tangata besieged Cara, seeking to use their numbers to bring her down, to overwhelm her. But the Goddess refused to be caught. She moved through the beasts like a whirlwind, a wing sweeping out to strike one aside, a fist taking another in the chest, boot striking yet a third in the face as she bounded clear of the rest.

But there was no safe ground upon which to land. As she hovered, another of the Tangata leapt, colliding with her back and knocking the Goddess from the air. The breath caught in Romaine's stomach as the Tangata converged on where she had fallen, but a second later Cara was back on her feet. Blood now streamed from a cut above her eye, and snarling, she tossed the creature that had downed her at her nearest foe, sending both crashing to the mud.

Despite himself, Romaine was impressed with how she fought. In the caverns, against those unspeakable creatures, she had been a wild animal, all untamed fury. Now, Cara fought with precision and control. That was all that kept her alive against the hordes.

Even so, it was clear the Goddess could not prevail alone, not against so many. She was already beginning to slow, her divine strength worn down by weight of numbers. Just like the soldiers of Flumeer, the Tangata worked together against her, attacking whenever her back was turned, launching themselves at her wings, her legs, seeking to drag her down.

Romaine's heart beat faster as he realised the pattern of their attacks—they weren't trying to kill her; they were trying to take her captive.

Why?

As he watched, Cara caught a blow to the chest. It sent her staggering back, and losing her footing, she sank to one knee. The Tangata were on her in a second, rushing in a group to attack together. But the wings she had hidden all this time snapped open, striking two hard enough to knock them from their feet. Cara surged into the gap, catching the third of her assailants by the throat. Before the others could come upon her, she hurled the beast face-first into the ground. This time the Tangata did not get back up.

But the others would not allow Cara to catch her breath. They pressed closer, robbing her of space to manoeuvre, to evade their blows. She staggered as more attacks caught her, but there was nowhere left to retreat.

Then a voice carried to Romaine's ears from across the waters, a distant, feeble cry of desperation. A familiar voice.

"Cara, *run!*"

Romaine's insides froze over as he found Lukys amidst the mob, still held fast by the Tangata. He still fought, struggling to break the creature's hold, but there was no escaping the Tangata. His mouth opened wide as he cried out again.

"*Please, save yourself!*"

"No!"

Screaming, Cara laid into the creatures around her. They leapt back from her fury, apparently happy for the Goddess to expend her energy. In frustration, Cara charged them, trying to break through to the others, but she was flagging now. Hands grabbed at her wings, her arms, her legs. She fought them off, but still more came on. Step by step, she was forced back from the captives.

A shriek tore from Cara's throat, and Romaine heard the despair in her cry. The Tangata retreated, expecting another assault, but with a whirl of feathers, Cara spun and hurled herself into the air. A beat of her wings carried her over the heads of the nearest Tangata, to where a diminutive figure lay forgotten. Before those nearby could react, Cara had the Archivist over her shoulder.

Too late the Tangata realised what was happening. They raced at her, howling their fury, but with a giant beat of her auburn wings, Cara hurtled skywards.

Kneeling on the deck of the ship, Romaine watched her come, his heart in a vice, the hope of a few moments before crumbling to ruin. He looked again at the riverbanks. The Tangata dragged Lukys and Dale forward and held them there, taunting the humans floating offshore, daring them to return. But there would be no rescue now.

There was a heavy *thunk* as Cara landed on the ship, followed by a cry as Erika staggered away from her. Face pale, the Archivist crumpled to the ground and began to sob. Romaine and the other soldiers ignored her. Aboard that ship, not a soul had eyes for anyone but the Goddess standing in their midst. Just a few minutes before, they had tried to restrain this creature. Would she now take her retribution?

Cara did not even look at them. The auburn wings drooped, then folded behind her back as she tucked them away. A shudder shook her and amber eyes searched the deck, finally settling on Romaine. He swallowed at the grief there, a mirror of his own. She took a step towards him, lip quivering, a single tear upon her cheek.

"Romaine," she croaked. "I'm so sorry."

❧ 33 ❧

THE ARCHIVIST

Erika sat at the bow of the ship. Her entire body shook as she watched the shore grow closer, the lights of Fogmore a lantern in the darkness. She dared not look back to where the Goddess sat in the aft. It felt as though her entire foundation had shifted, as though every part of her world had changed in the last few hours.

The Gods were real!

A God had saved her!

This changed everything. Though she had always *believed*, she had never…known.

Her eyes fixed on the approaching shore and she tried to focus her mind. In the chaos of battle, she had forgotten about her other troubles, but now they came rushing back. General Curtis would want answers. Erika had found nothing but death in the caverns, and they still did not know what had become of the other recruits. It seemed certain they were dead, though…where then were the rest of the bodies?

And what if there were more of those terrible creatures

that the Tangata had woken? Was that why the Tangata had been seeking them? Did they think of those ancient monsters as *their* Gods? Would they seek out more of them, now that the secret had been uncovered?

Despite herself, Erika's gaze was drawn to the aft of the ship once more, to where Cara crouched alone on a crate. Not even Romaine, not even her magic, could stand against those monsters. The Gods alone could defeat them. Humanity needed their aid, to discover the source of their power. Could an emissary be sent into the Mountains of the Gods to seek them out?

Excitement touched her at the thought, before reality dragged her back down. Regardless of Cara's revelation, Erika had failed. The queen would have no more use of her now, other than prying the magic gauntlet from her corpse.

Erika could not allow it.

Her mind worked quickly, another possibility opening itself to her. Gemaho bordered the Mountains of the Gods. Solaris wasn't far from the hidden site on her map, as the bird flew. And travelling from east of the mountains, they wouldn't have the Tangata to contend with.

The only difficulty would be smuggling Cara out from under the noses of Queen Amina and her general. They would not allow her to leave Flumeer, and certainly not to go to their eastern rival. Nor would Cara leave without the Calafe warrior.

Romaine himself had lost consciousness shortly after they had begun the journey downriver. Erika was surprised that he'd been able to resist the pain of his wounds as long as he had. She swore, at times the Calafe did not seem entirely human himself. The ship's medic was tending to him, but it was obvious the warrior would not be leaving Fogmore for some time.

Erika did not have the luxury of time on her hands. She could not wait for him…

She shook herself, irritated to realise she'd grown to like the man's company. But just because he knew of her heritage now, didn't mean she could trust him. After all, his people had already betrayed Erika and her mother once, hounding them out of the kingdom after her father's death. No, it was time she left the last traces of her past behind.

Looking out across the deck, she clenched her fist, but did not summon the power of the gauntlet. Her entire body ached as though she'd been riding for days and she dared not waste what remained of her strength.

Stones crunched and the ship shook beneath her. Erika's head jerked up as she realised they'd already reached Fogmore. The voyage had passed unnoticed while she'd dreamed. Her doom was already at hand.

No. She forced her mind into action. *The general cannot touch you; it's the queen you must fear. There is still time yet.*

Exhaling, she rose unsteadily to her feet and turned to where the gangplank was being lowered. She started to find Cara standing directly behind her. The young Goddess's eyes had returned to their usual amber. They were wide, anxious. The Tangata had torn strips in her tunic and she sported a black eye where a blow had caught her unaware, but otherwise she appeared unharmed from the battle.

"Are…are you okay, Erika?" Cara whispered.

As she spoke, her wings lifted a little from her back, giving Erika another glimpse of the auburn feathers. The sight summoned memories of their flight across the river, the water flashing past far below, the screams of the Tangata still ringing in her ears.

Erika banished the image and focused on Cara's words.

"I'm okay," she replied, bowing her head in respect. "Thank you for rescuing me, Oh Great One."

Red crept into Cara's cheeks at the words and she quickly looked away. "Please don't call me that," she croaked. "I'm…not what you think."

Erika hesitated, before offering another nod. Whatever the girl asked, it would be difficult to think of her as anything but Divine now. Though…it was clear Cara also was not immortal. Her arm *had* been broken the first time they'd met. She could be hurt—by the Tangata, and by Erika's gauntlet. Why was that?

Questions for another time. For now, she pushed aside her confusion, bit back the pain of her broken arm, and forced herself to smile. A plan was coming to her, though she would not survive for long without the Goddess on her side.

"Very well," she said, trying to keep her voice even. "Well, would you accompany me to shore? I am still some-what…weak from the magic."

Cara licked her lips, eyes flickering to the distant shores of the Illmoor. Though darkness had fallen, Erika had the distinct feeling the Goddess could see the other side perfectly.

"Poor Lukys," Cara whispered.

"You did everything you could," Erika murmured, placing a hand on the young woman's shoulders.

Cara did not react—confirming at least one of Erika's suspicions. The Goddess had never been afraid of touch— only of someone feeling the wings beneath her heavy cloak.

Gently, Erika led Cara towards the gangplank. It felt strange, offering comfort to this creature, to a literal God. But…there was something distinctly human about Cara's pain, about her grief. And perhaps it created an opportunity.

Most of the soldiers had already disembarked. Word would have already reached the city of the God they had brought back from the south. Fogmore would be abuzz with rumour. Dozens had already appeared on the shores, ignoring the obvious danger of the Tangata that they had left behind on the other shore. Whispers rose from the crowd as Erika stepped onto the plank, but it was not the Archivist they had come to see.

Gasps spread through the gathering as Cara followed. Her wings lifted at the sound, half-unfurling. An involuntary reflex, Erika guessed, after the way the Goddess had tried to go unnoticed for so long. The crowd drew back as they reached the shore. And who could blame them? The Gods were remembered not just with deference, but fear. After all, they were responsible for The Fall.

"My lord...Goddess...Saviour!"

The whispers grew louder as they stood there, and Cara pressed close to the Archivist. She shuddered as a feather brushed her arm, and had to suppress a scream. There was something unnatural about those wings. They reminded her far too much of the Tangata.

That...will take some getting used to.

"Soldiers, at your stations!" The hairs on the back of Erika's neck stood on end as a voice bellowed from the top of the slope. General Curtis came marching through the ranks of men and women, his face a carefully controlled mask. "Get these civilians back into the city—there are Tangata about this night."

He came to a stop before Erika and the Goddess while around them the soldiers leapt to obey. Erika drew herself up as he stood regarding her, resisting the urge to shrink before the rage that glinted in his eyes.

"General," she said, offering a polite nod.

"The Perfugian recruits?" he asked curtly.

Guilt stoppered Erika's lips, but finally she managed to blurt out a single word: "Gone."

"And the magic of the Gods?"

"Lost."

He gave a curt nod. "As expected." His eyes flickered to Cara, taking in the auburn wings. His jaw clenched, though to his credit, he showed no other reaction. "Great One," he murmured, bowing. "The gates of Fogmore lie open to you."

Cara's cheeks brightened and she lowered her eyes. Seeing her opportunity, Erika spoke into the silence. "The Great One is somewhat…unaccustomed to human scrutiny. She will accompany me to my quarters."

The general's eyes flickered in her direction. "My orders were to take you into custody, should your endeavour prove fruitless." Erika's heart lurched, but the general drew in a breath and continued: "But…I am certain the queen would not wish to go against Her Divinity." He faced Cara once more. "I hope that you might break your fast with us come the morning, Great One."

Cara flicked an uncertain glance at Erika before offering a nod. Suppressing a smile, Erika linked arms with the Goddess and led her up the slope.

"What about Romaine?" Cara whispered as they walked.

"I'm sure his wounds are already being tended to," Erika reassured her. The Calafe had been one of the first off the ship, carried on a stretcher. "We can visit him in the morning."

That seemed to reassure the Goddess, and they continued up the path. The gates opened before them and Erika strode through without looking back. Let the general worry about the Tangata; she had other concerns now. She led the Goddess through the streets, steadfastly ignoring the stares of the crowd as they passed.

She was pleased to find her quarters still empty. Hastily constructed from timber boards, it wasn't much better than the abandoned cottages back in Calafe. But at least it was private, and would give her the chance to question the Goddess, to figure out her next move.

Pulling open the door, she held it for Cara. "Come on in. You'll be safe from the stares here. At least until morning."

Cara hesitated on the threshold, eyes wide, cheeks a bright red, but finally she stepped inside. Erika swung the door closed behind them, plunging the room into darkness. Throwing the latch to keep out unwanted visitors, she hesitated, then decided she had strength enough to summon the magic. The soft light of her gauntlet lit the room.

"So, you survived."

Erika almost leapt out of her boots as a voice spoke from the shadows. Beside her, Cara gave a shrill cry and leapt sideways, wings snapping open. Something went *crash* in the gloom—the potted plant beside her window. Heart racing, Erika raised her fist, and a brilliant light cast back the darkness.

The stranger from Gemaho sat at her table, one leg crossed over the other, fingers drumming against the table. A sheathed sword lay beside the woman, as though to say she was not there to fight, though Erika was sure she would have other weapons at her disposal.

Still struggling to catch her breath, Erika lowered her

fist. "I am," she said softly, then paused, before adding: "No thanks to the queen."

A smile tugged at the woman's lips. "So I heard." She uncrossed her legs and stood. "So your quest failed?"

Erika hesitated, heart thudding painfully in her chest. She found herself holding her breath, unsure how to proceed. Glancing to the side, she saw that Cara was watching her, wings spread wide, ready to flee.

Forcing a smile, Erika raised her hand. "It's okay, Cara," she said softly, seeking to reassure the Goddess. "She's with me."

The girl said nothing, though her wings retracted an inch. Releasing her breath, Erika faced the Gemaho spy once more.

"Not entirely," she said in answer to the question. She gestured at Cara. "As you can see, other discoveries were made."

"My king knew you were resourceful," her visitor said with a smile. "And what of our offer?"

"I accept," Erika said at once. "I will go with you to Gemaho."

"Excellent." The stranger's eyes flickered to Cara. "And your…friend?"

"Gemaho?" Cara whispered, looking to Erika. "But they're your…enemies, aren't they?"

"Not anymore," Erika said soothingly.

"But Romaine," the woman continued, frowning. "We can't leave him, not after…" Tears formed in her eyes as she trailed off.

"My king will require a demonstration of your goodwill, Archivist," the woman said softly.

Erika sighed. This wasn't how it was meant to go. But nor could she ignore the general's words on the shore of the

Illmoor. The queen had already condemned her. She might have fooled them for now, with her claim of friendship to the Goddess, but that could not last. One way or another, the queen would find a way of disposing of Erika, and taking the magic for herself.

She could not go to Gemaho empty handed. That left only one option.

Sucking in a breath, Erika spun and brought up her gauntlet. Realisation showed in Cara's eyes and she opened her mouth to cry out, but Erika didn't give her the chance. The magic struck and the scream died in Cara's throat. With a flash of light, she fell to the ground, and knew no more.

❧ 34 ❧

THE RECRUIT

Lukys watched with a mixture of relief and despair as the winged Goddess that was Cara threw the Archivist over one shoulder and took to the sky. His heart soared, glad at least someone had escaped. The joy was short lived as the remaining Tangata turned towards them. Terror rose to take its place.

The others had escaped.

But their nightmare had only just begun.

Rage burned in the eyes of the Tangata. He realised now it had been Cara the creatures had wanted all along. But there was no time to consider what significance the Gods had to the monsters.

Fight, live, kill.

Drums sounded in Lukys's mind as the creatures crowded them. Beside him, Dale still fought to break free of his captor, but Lukys stood frozen, overwhelmed by the horde of grey eyes watching him.

Suddenly the Tangata released them. Lukys staggered as the hands holding him vanished, swaying on his feet. Before he could look around, a fist struck him in the stomach, driving the breath from his lungs. He doubled over, gasping, even as he heard the *thump* of Dale striking the ground alongside him. Eyes watering, he tried to straighten, but a second blow slammed into his back.

He screamed as the ground rose to meet him, the broken bones grinding in his chest. Pain wrapped itself around his body as a boot struck him in the side, hurling him sideways. From somewhere nearby, another voice cried out, but Dale was lost amidst a forest of flashing limbs.

Fight, kill. Fight, kill!

Another boot caught Lukys in the side of the head and stars flashed across his vision. He tried to roll away, but the creatures were all around. Falling on his back, he cried out, begging for mercy, but another blow slammed into his stomach, stealing away the last of his breath.

He collapsed to the ground, vision growing dark. Overhead, a sea of faces spun, mouths twisted in anger, yellowed teeth bared, murder in grey eyes.

Kill, kill, kill!

Lukys opened his mouth to cry out, but all he could manage was a whisper. The Tangata retreated slightly, and for a second he thought they were showing mercy. Then one amongst them stepped forward. Sunlight flashed and even through his fading vision, Lukys glimpsed the spearpoint in its hands.

Desperately, he tried to scramble away, but now iron hands grasped him by the arms and legs, pinning him down. A cry came from nearby as others did the same with Dale. Then all Lukys could do was watch as the beast raised the spear overhead.

Death, death, death…

NO!

Lukys wasn't sure whether he screamed the word or thought it. Only thought it, surely, for he still had not recovered his breath. Yet the creatures around him reared back as though they'd been stung, as if he had suddenly turned into something foreign, something dangerous.

Grey eyes stared down at him, and though their mouths did not move, suddenly it was as though there were a hundred voices screaming in Lukys's mind, so many he could not make out a single word—though he sensed their rage, their confusion.

All at once the voices cut off. Movement came from amongst the crowd as a new creature appeared, a female. It moved to stand over him, eyes narrowed. The silence in Lukys's head was practically deafening as the female knelt. He flinched as a hand reached out, expecting death to follow, but the Tangata only traced a finger across his face, touching his nose, his cheeks, his lips. He lay there in terror, hardly daring to even breathe as she inspected him.

Finally she sat back, though her eyes never left him. He realised then how strange her eyes were—still the grey of the Tangata, but somehow deeper, as though this creature carried a great weight on its shoulders. She inspected him for a moment longer. Then a voice spoke in his mind.

Who are you?

———

Here ends Warbringer, book one of Descendants of the Fall.
Continue the adventure with:
Wrath of the Forgotten

———

Hey folks, just a quick note to say thank you for reading this far! I hope you enjoyed the journey. Either way, it would really mean a lot to me you could stop by Amazon and leave your honest review—even if it's just a few words. Reviews are such an important part of marketing our books to the world and without them I literally would not be able to continue writing these stories! Thank you in advance and read on! - Aaron

NOTE FROM THE AUTHOR

Well that was fun! I forgot how refreshing it could be to step into a new world, even though it is A LOT harder than I remember to create one! Although that's not to say I haven't written similar works. My Evolution Gene trilogy also features superhuman creatures, but is set in the dystopian Western Allied States. Or if you're interested in my fantasy works, there's no better place to start than my The Sword of Light Trilogy - the first series I ever wrote! And you can get the first books in each of these series absolutely free by signing up to join to my newsletter. You'll also be the first to hear about my upcoming works, specials, and what I'm up to each week. If you fantasy you can't go wrong:

www.aaronhodges.co.nz/newsletter-signup/

THE SWORD OF LIGHT TRILOGY

If you've enjoyed this book, you might want to check out my
very first fantasy series!

A town burns and flames light the night sky. Hunted and
alone, seventeen year old Eric flees through the wreckage.
The mob grows closer, baying for the blood of their
tormentor. Guilt weighs on his soul, but he cannot stop,
cannot turn back. **If he stops, they die.**

THE EVOLUTION GENE

If you've enjoyed this book, you might want to check out my dystopian sci-fi series!

In 2051, the Western Allies States have risen as the new power in North America. But a terrifying plague is sweeping through the nation. Its victims do not die—they change. People call them the *Chead*, and where they walk, destruction follows.

ALSO BY AARON HODGES

Descendants of the Fall

Book 1: Warbringer

Book 2: Wrath of the Forgotten

Book 3: Age of Gods

The Evolution Gene

Book 1: The Genome Project

Book 2: The Pursuit of Truth

Book 3: The Way the World Ends

The Sword of Light

Book 1: Stormwielder

Book 2: Firestorm

Book 3: Soul Blade

The Legend of the Gods

Book 1: Oathbreaker

Book 2: Shield of Winter

Book 3: Dawn of War

The Knights of Alana

Book 1: Daughter of Fate

Book 2: Queen of Vengeance

Book 3: Crown of Chaos

Printed in Great Britain
by Amazon

66761076R20194